Dead Dog Lying
& Other Stories

Dead Dog Lying
& Other Stories

NORMAN GERMAN

2015
University of Louisiana at Lafayette Press

ISBN 13 (paper): 978-1-935754-63-3

http://ulpress.org
University of Louisiana at Lafayette Press
P.O. Box 40831
Lafayette, LA 70504-0831

Printed on acid-free paper in South Korea.

Front cover designed by Pattie Steib.
Rear cover illusration by Harriet Burbeck.

Library of Congress Cataloging-in-Publication Data:

German, Norman, 1955-
[Short stories Selections]
Dead dog lying & other stories / Norman German.
pages ; cm
ISBN 978-1-935754-63-3 (alk. paper)
I. Title. II. Title: Dead dog lying and other stories.
PS3557.E678A6 2015
813'.54--dc23

for Raejean,
always

Contents

Dead Dog Lying 1
Merger Talks 23
Deerboy 45
Ditchboy 55
Dogboy 75
Sportfishing with Cameron 97
The Threshold of Plenty 115
Snake Summer 133
Is 143
Second Wave 149
Suburban High Tide 153
Controlled Burn 173
Call Forwarding 189
The Girl and the Green Gas Can 201
The Arrow That Never Came Down . 217
Always On My Mind 231

Bibliography 239
About the Author .240

{1}

Dead Dog Lying

Carlee thinks she smells something dead in her oven, but she knows this is impossible because she keeps her kitchen as clean as her life.

A former Ponchatoula High Strawberry Queen, Carlee Tantillo is married to an electrical engineer and has 2.7 children. She is choir director at the First Methodist Church and has just become president of the Junior League. She can solve any domestic problem.

Right now she is cooking breakfast in her newly remodeled kitchen with Corian countertops. As she smiles over a pan of scrambling eggs, Randall, eight, pulls at her apron, Nathan, five, is singing "I'm a Little Teapot," and Donna, seven-tenths, is hanging from a sling on Carlee's shoulder, taking her breakfast from a modestly exposed breast.

The last course Carlee slides onto the boys' plates is pan-fried tomato slices. As she sips Earl Grey tea and watches her children eat, she thinks of their futures, thinks of everything she has, which is everything she has ever wanted and planned for. Her mind drifts back to high school, then takes a reflective turn.

Even without a college degree, this is still the land of opportunity. Like Victor. He opened a photography studio. Carl got a Texaco franchise, and Alice Ann sold Mary Kay.

1

"What is that smell?" Carlee thinks. *"Odor,"* her mind corrects.

*There is simply no excuse for not going out and getting what you want. I dated Blain in tenth, eleventh, and part of twelfth grade, but he wasn't going anywhere. Blain was a star athlete and **very** good looking, but not the caliber I wanted for a mate. So I set my sights on Cameron. Cameron was well-liked and smart as a whip and knew even then he was meant for higher things than chasing a football down the field and getting injuries he'd pay for for the rest of his life.*

The commotion of the boys putting up their dishes rouses Carlee from her reverie.

"What would y'all like for lunch, boys?"

Nathan screams, "Fried tuna fish!"

Randall, with a sore throat, croaks out, "No! Hamburgers!"

Nathan, as if it's a contest, yells, "No, Roman Numerals!"

Randall pushes Nathan so hard his neck whiplashes. "You're such a dork."

"Randall, I've told you not to push your brother. And use kind words to each other. Right? Look at me. Now what does he mean by Roman Numerals?"

"You know," Randall pouts, "those noodles you boil. Roman noodles."

Carlee laughs. "Those are *Ramen* noodles, Randall. So you didn't get it right, either, and you're in third grade. And it sounds like you've got a frog in your throat this morning."

Wide-eyed with wonder, Nathan stares at his brother. "A *fro*-og?"

His mother laughs. "It's just an expression. It means he has a sore throat and sounds croaky, like a frog. Probably because of the cold nights and hot days of this false spring."

Carlee turns to the stove. "That reminds me. What *is* that odor?"

Randall suddenly remembers and rushes to the oven door. He and his mother open it together. It is an expensive oven. The rack slides out when the door opens and presents the family dog as if it were a soggy, unplucked Thanksgiving turkey.

"Oh, my God," Carlee says. In a flash her mind remembers what she has taught her boys. "Oh, my goodness, oh, my goodness," she repeats as she swings around looking for something to pick up the dog with. She is not used to confusion. She turns the oven off and pivots to Randall.

"What is the meaning of this? Have you lost your mind, young man?"

"No, ma'am," Randall says. He feels like he is about to cry. He looks at his bare feet and thinks about how to get out of this. He points to Nathan with dead seriousness. "*He* lost it."

Nathan's eyes widen at the false accusation. He thrusts his spiky, crewcut head forward. "I did not! I did not! I did *not*!" His face crumples, he takes a deep breath, and he is about to let go with everything his little body has when his mother picks him up and rescues him.

"That's okay, honey. I know you didn't lose anything. It's just an expression." After she calms Nathan down, she sets him on a dinette chair and turns to Randall. "I ought to spank you good for this."

"Maybe you ought to, but you won't," Randall taunts, "because you don't believe in spanking."

Carlee inhales to begin a lecture, then stops. She closes her eyes and counts to ten.

Randall swivels to Nathan, who is still pouting. Randall flips his eyelids inside out and peels them back until they stay. Then he crosses his eyes and twirls his index fingers around his temples. "Yes, I have lost my mind, young man." Nathan wants to laugh but he is still mad at his brother. He looks away, then back, and it's so funny that he starts to cry to let Randall know he's still mad, but when Randall hangs his tongue out the left side of his mouth and wiggles it, Nathan starts bawling and laughing uncontrollably.

"Stop it! And I mean stop it right now, little boy, or I'll whip your behind till you can't sit down."

The boys have never seen their mother this mad. In pure self-defense, they both break into a genuine gale of squalling.

- Randall's Story -

Smokey was barking and barking next door at the Prudhommes'.

Then Dad said—he was watching bass-fishing on TV—"That dog wouldn't bark so much if somebody'd give him a little antifreeze."

Smokey, he was trying to tell somebody he was cold. Mocha is our dog. He don't bark too much. Daddy trained him not to. So he don't know how to tell us he's cold. He's an Australian shepherd. So Nathan and I got a lawn chair, then we got the blue ice chest, then we put Daddy's tackle box on top of those, so then we could get to the antifreeze on the top shelf.

It was green and shiny in Mocha's bowl. He drank it right away, so we knew he wouldn't be cold in the night.

The next morning he was curled up against the door sleeping. He must have been pretty cold, even with the antifreeze, because we couldn't wake him up even though he tried to move a little. So I got him by the back legs—he ain't got no tail—and dragged him in the house.

In school we learned water boils at two-twelve so I knew that was too hot so I turned the oven on to one-fifty. I figured ten minutes would be long enough to get him going again, so I looked at the clock on the wall. Then we ate breakfast. We forgot about Mocha but Mom smelled him. I think he was overdone when she took him out because he wasn't just sleepy anymore. He looked real tired, with his tongue hanging out like it does on hot days, only it was black instead of pink. If Mocha could talk like Daddy when he comes home from work, I know just what he would say. He'd say "I'm exhausted" 'cause he sure looked it.

- The Trip -

Carlee holds her hands up and tries to regain her composure. "Okay, all right, it's okay. We just have to deal with it. These things happen. It's sad, but they do. Why don't we just bury him in the backyard, how does that sound?"

Nathan says, "Mocha's dead?"

Carlee goes to him, still standing on the chair. "Oh, honey, I'm sorry. We can get you another dog." Nathan doesn't feel sad, but his mother's tenderness affects him and he starts to cry softly.

"It's okay," Nathan says. "I just never saw a dead dog. Birds and things, but never dogs."

"Have, too," Randall injects. He holds his sore throat. "On the road to Granny's. We see dead dogs all the time."

Nathan glares at Randall. "I mean real dogs, you stupid."

"Oh, like those aren't real."

"All right, boys, let's take Mocha out back and we'll have a nice funeral for him, with flowers and everything."

Carlee thinks for a moment, then opens one of her new cabinets and pulls down the crystal platter Cameron gave her on their third anniversary. With oven mitts, she lifts Mocha from the rack and places him on the crystal. Nathan watches his mother moving around. His face has been worrying itself to the boiling point about something uncertain and when it comes to him he screeches like a teapot.

"No! If we bury him here, we won't be able to take him with us when we move to the trophy room."

Now Randall is furious. "Mama, he is so stupid! I hate him!"

"Randall, what have I told you about that? He's only five. What does he mean by the trophy room?"

"You know. The trophy house you're always talking about. When we move into the trophy house, we'll have to leave Mocha behind all by himself."

Carlee laughs and reminds herself to put that down in Nathan's diary. Then she sets herself to solving the childhood crisis.

"What about Granny's, then? Would y'all like to drive out to Granny's and put him under the old pecan tree?"

Carlee sets Mocha in the back of the Ford Expedition, which cost more than her parents' house, then washes her hands and straps Donna into the child restraint seat. The boys have already buckled themselves in the backseat when Carlee says, "Randall, have you taken your medication this morning? Run inside and take it real quick like a good boy." Randall opens his door. "And take some Robitussin for that throat."

While Randall runs inside, Carlee adjusts her seatbelt and turns on the air conditioner she hasn't used in a week. From the clock on the visor she notices it's 10:00 a.m. but the humidity is already building like it's midsummer.

When Randall entered first grade, he just wouldn't mind Carlee, so she decided he had Attention Deficit Hyperactive Disorder. Dr. Dave confirmed her diagnosis and put him on Ritalin. On their trip to Disney World last summer, when they had forgotten his medication, he played a Game Boy for four straight hours and Carlee wondered if her diagnosis had been right.

Carlee drives expertly through the neighborhood, left, right, around Dr. Monsour's RV, left, right, around Dr. Wu's sailboat, then rolls to the four-way stop at the end of her gated community. She notices a doorless jeep rushing to the stop sign on her left and eases into the intersection. Sailing through the stop sign, the driver of the Barbie-pink Tracker jammed with teenagers sweeps around her on screeching tires.

Stopped in the middle of the intersection, Carlee looks at them quickly disappearing, laughing and yelling at her. A young girl makes a vulgar motion with both hands, and Carlee finds it so sad the girl would even know such things at her age that she feels like crying. She checks on Donna, then looks in the rearview mirror.

"Nathan, Randall, y'all okay?"

Randall unbuckles and looks over the back of his seat.

"We're fine, but it looks like Mocha done slid off the plate."

"Yeah," Nathan adds, holding his nose, "and he stinks! Pee-you. Pee-you-ZEE!"

"All right, buckle back up. We'll fix him when we stop at the Eazy-Tote for ice cream, how does that sound?"

Carlee clicks the fan up a notch, then opens all the windows to flush the car with fresh air. She turns onto Highway 51 and heads north. The first billboard always makes her laugh: "If You Love Your Kids, Belt 'Em." It's part of a campaign to increase seatbelt use, which she agrees with, but she dislikes the implied violence of the message.

As Carlee settles into the drive, she thinks of the kids in the jeep, labels them privileged brats. She remembers working her way through college in three years, how it taught her to value what she now has.

Carlee had paid her dues by teaching second grade for two years while Cameron finished graduate school, then waited another year while he established himself at Conoco before starting her family. They had worked and planned together for the life they wanted. That's why she was able to stay home after Nathan was born and give her children all the attention they needed.

A drop of sweat trickling down her temple breaks her reverie. Carlee rolls the windows up and turns the fan up another notch. Her nose tests the air for any lingering odor and she settles back into her drive. At the caution light in front of North Oaks Hospital, she hears a small pop under the hood and wonders if she has hit something.

Five minutes later, just as the Eazy-Tote comes into view, Carlee sees wisps of smoke escaping near her right windshield wiper and notices how hot she is. She checks the baby. Donna, asleep but sweating, is wearing a puckered frown.

Carlee is relieved when she remembers that her ninth-grade boyfriend owns the Texaco station attached to the Eazy-Tote. She glides under the awning and stops by a gas pump. When Carl walks up, they laugh.

"Carl!"

"Carlee!"

It is the same greeting they've been exchanging for almost twenty years. When they met in Mrs. Mullin's algebra class, they thought because of their matching names that they were destined for each other. Carlee told Alicia that Carl must be deep because he didn't say much, but as the months rolled by she realized he was just boring. In tenth grade Carl took to Alicia, married her the summer after graduation, and worked hard for five years to buy the Texaco franchise.

"Looks like someone planted a smoke bomb under your hood. Better pop the latch."

"Yeah," Carlee says, "I think my A/C just died."

Carl lifts the hood and waves his hands to clear the smoke. After a minute, he walks around to Carlee's window.

"Whew," he says, waving his hands again. "Smells like something died *inside*, too."

"Oh, I'm so embarrassed. I can't even smell it anymore."

Then, under her breath, "The boys' dog died this morning, and we're taking it to their grandmother's to bury it."

"Yeah," Nathan pipes up. "We gave him some antifreeze last night but he was so cold this morning my brother put him in the oven and overdid him."

Carl looks at this possum hanging over Carlee's shoulder. "Well, at least you know he didn't freeze to death." Then, to Carlee, "It'll take a few minutes to check things out. Why don't you go into the Eazy-Tote and get out of this heat, maybe get the boys a Freezee?"

The boys yell and tumble out of the SUV while Carlee works the baby loose.

"How do you stand working in this heat day in and day out?"

"Well, it's not always hot. This morning it was cold. The weather tends to lie this time of year."

Standing and holding the baby, Carlee says with real concern, "Aren't you afraid, Carl? I mean, with all the insta-lube places and Walmart and such, it's got to be hard to compete these days."

Carl looks at her with the slightly smiling eyes she remembered from their teenage years. The look came, she realizes now, from a calm confidence she mistook as dullness years ago.

"Nah," Carl says. "We do the work right and earn their respect. Customer loyalty ain't free. After a few years, they're like family. They speak sharp, you can even snap back and they know you don't mean nothing by it. Nothing permanent, anyways."

Donna starts to fret, and Carlee jostles her. She looks at Carl and smiles, and something from long ago comes back to them both. Carl laughs, then steps back and shoos Carlee away by waving the red rag in his hand.

Carlee approaches the convenience store and reads the

sign in the window: No Shoes, No Shirt—No Service. As she opens the door, a young teen rushes out in front of her and stops. Shirtless, he has countless silver studs and rings in his eyebrows, nose, ears, and lips. A black spider-in-a-web tattoo spans his chest, and his forehead is stigmatized by a red skull with blue words on either side: Eat Death.

Carlee is not afraid of the boy, but she feels sadness and revulsion mix in her stomach like a bad drink.

"What're *you* looking at, Mama?"

Carlee clutches Donna tighter and sidles by the boy. "Nothing, I'm sorry, excuse me."

Inside, the boys run up to their mother waving things in their hands.

"Can I have this, Mom, I just gotta have it, can I?"

"Me, too, I want this, it's so awesome!"

"Whoa, whoa, what is this y'all just can't live without? One at a time."

Randall screens Nathan out and holds up a magic-marker in a clear plastic bubble attached to a sheet of cardboard. Beautiful children with colorful tattoos on their faces and arms suggest that all happiness is wrapped in this package.

"Absolutely not, young man. Next thing I know, you'll be wanting real tattoos. And what do you have, Nathan, some Play-Doh?"

Instinctively, Nathan tries the shy approach. Without a word, he holds his treasure up to his mother, who reads the label.

"Tub o' Gum." On the package is a bug-eyed cartoon boy blowing a pink bubble bigger than his head. Carlee imagines the canister holds a plug of gum big enough to choke five children.

"Out of the question." She shifts Donna to her other hip and digs in her purse. "Here. Here's a dollar apiece. Why don't y'all get some ice cream to eat on the way to Granny's?"

Carlee threads the aisles a couple of times, then calls to the boys from the door. "I have to talk to Mr. Carl about the car. Y'all make your selections and meet me outside in five minutes, hear? Randall, you see that clock over the register? Five minutes. And I don't mean six, seven, or eight."

At the cash register inside the station, Carlee has to wait for Carl to finish with a customer. She looks around and notices maps, belts and hoses, and boxed parts neatly hung and stacked and racked. A movement outside catches her eye and she looks up in time to see the boy with the facial hardware take a yellow quart of oil off a dolly.

She spins toward Carl, who is waiting on an elderly man signing a credit card receipt. Carl subtly shakes his head "no" to Carlee so his customer won't be interrupted.

When the room is empty, Carl chuckles.

"What's so funny about that, Carl? You just lost money because of that kid."

Carl opens the middle drawer of a metal filing cabinet and pulls out a folder.

"I'll add it to his father's tab and tell him about it. 'Course, he probably won't do anything but pay. That's why he's got such a confused kid. Won't give him any direction."

Carl writes in the folder and refiles it.

"I couldn't tell anything from a quick look under your hood, Carlee. It's something electrical and that's always tricky in these big SUVs. You'll have to bring it by tomorrow when I'm not so backed up."

A mild dread comes over Carlee at the thought of driving without air conditioning. She looks out the door that opens onto the two work bays. Two men are working under hoisted cars, and a boy is fixing a flat. Carlee attempts the desperate baby talk that worked on Carl almost twenty years ago.

"Oh, Carl, can't you wook at an old girlfriend's boken down car? Pitty-*pitty* please?"

Carl laughs and looks out the window away from his old girlfriend. He scratches the back of his head, then looks back at her. "Now, you know I can't do that, Carlee. It wouldn't be fair to my other customers."

Carlee pulls out of the Texaco station a little hurt, a little angry at making herself look like a foolish schoolgirl, and a little sad because for the second time she feels like she is leaving behind something worthwhile. It takes her almost a minute to adjust her mood.

"Hot!" she finally says, enthusiastic as a cheerleader. She swivels the rearview mirror around to look at her boys licking their dripping ice cream, Nathan with an orange Push-Up, Randall with a waffle cone. "When life gives you lemons, boys, you just have to make . . . ?" She glances back and forth from the road to her sons as they stare at her blankly. "You have to make what, boys?"

They frown hard for a while and look outside the window as if the answer might be there. Randall whispers in Nathan's ear and his eyes brighten.

"Lemon pie!" Nathan shouts.

"No, no," Carlee says with exasperation. "Lemonade. When life gives you lemons, you just have to make lemonade."

Randall says, "Well, if somebody gave *me* lemons, I'd make a lemon pie."

"It's just an expression," Carlee says, feeling a twinge of irritation she quickly suppresses. "It means if something bad happens, you can turn it into something good. Like now. Our air conditioner is broken, but we can make it fun by opening the sunroof." She lowers the four windows a bit, then hits the sunroof button.

As the sunroof slides open, Randall unhitches his seatbelt and drops his cone onto the seat. Knowing the routine, he takes a tissue from the Kleenex box in the center console and swipes at the mess, leaving sticky shreds of fiber on the leather seat.

Although she wouldn't ordinarily let her boys do such a thing, this one time, to make lemonade, Carlee allows Randall and Nathan to stand up and put their heads through the open sunroof. She enjoys hearing their playful screams and recalls her father letting her hold a carnival pinwheel out the window of their two-door compact. Happy she has made something good out of a bad situation, Carlee thinks of her childhood while driving and leaves the boys to their play.

Ten minutes from her mother's house, she sees a single rain cloud up ahead. She flicks her headlights on, then makes a quick mirror-check in the backseat. Randall's head is above the roof, but she sees black markings on his arms. She swivels her head to look at Nathan. Unbuckled, he is sitting quietly chewing a huge wad of gum while holding his stomach in obvious pain.

Carlee processes this in a fraction of a second. The boys could only have bought ice cream with the money she gave them, so they must have stolen the marker and gum.

She brakes and jerks the car onto the gravel shoulder of the blacktop. Randall tumbles down onto the console between the front seats.

"What," Carlee says, grabbing Randall's arm, "is *this*?"

"Stop it, you're hurting me," he whines, "you're hurting my arm."

She looks closely at the arm. A black snake drawn with the tattoo marker winds from his wrist and disappears up his shirt sleeve. Carlee grabs Randall's chin and turns his face toward her to talk to him, but she almost loses control when she sees his fake black eye and a black smiley face on his forehead. She pushes him carefully into the backseat and rests her head on the steering wheel. Sadness displaces her anger as she realizes her sons have stolen from a good man. Have stolen, period. Are thieves.

She is thinking how to approach this subject in a way that won't damage her sons' self-esteem when a gurgling sound interrupts her. She looks at Donna, properly strapped into the child restraint facing the back-rest of the passenger seat. As if on cue, Donna spits up foamy white milk that slides down into the crevice of the seat.

Instinctively, Carlee grabs for the Kleenex box and returns with nothing. She reaches into the backseat and snatches a clump of sticky tissues and does the best she can with that.

She knows this will take a while and thinks of the wet-wipes in her purse. As she hits the button for the emergency flashers, a noise like a sick-cat meow comes from the dash and the entire instrumentation panel goes dark. She feels now like she is about to cry.

She has one wet-wipe left and a small tissue with a perfect red imprint of her lips, and when they are saturated with the baby's sour spittle, a light rain begins. She punches at the array of buttons to roll up the windows and close the sunroof, but not one of them works. Then she hears a car pulling up behind her and thinks with relief that help has finally arrived, maybe one of those roving mechanics in a car-garage on wheels. Just as she checks the rearview mirror, the officer turns on his flashing blue lights. Now, she cries.

But only briefly. She has time, as she watches the officer put a plastic sheathing on his hat, to pat her running mascara. When he walks up with his ticket book and says, "Ma'am," she is all sunshine and birdsong.

"Oh, officer, I'm so glad you're here, everything you can imagine is wrong with my car, you're an absolute knight in shining armor." Carlee looks up and takes a surprised breath as she recognizes him. He is The One. This is what she calls him to herself and to no one else, not even to her best gossip friend and bridge partner. He is The One she gave up because he lacked ambition.

When she looks at him—the yellow-green eyes, the beautiful, angular cheekbones—it feels like he squeezes a small, harmless creature living inside her throat. She had forgotten it hibernated there because Cameron had never roused it and so could never hurt it.

"Carlee," he says flatly as she reads his tag: Sgt. B. Stoddard.

Blain had been captain of the football team when Carlee was head cheerleader. He was tall and wore number 88. Carlee has only one memory from the playoff for the district championship. She looks at the field to see why the fans have exploded. Blain has already broken away from his defender, and she sees him in a fluid, open stride, his white shoes flashing in the stadium lights. With effortless speed, he is sliding along the sideline, the ball spiraling down to meet him. Just when she thinks he is going to miss it, he looks up as if the ball would be right there, and it was, and because she has never seen this combination of precision and grace and speed, she will always remember it like a vivid dream.

"Carlee, I know you know better than to let your boys put their heads through a sunroof." He tilts his head to look in at the boys.

"Oh, I know, Blain, I know. But first the air conditioner went out and then something with the electrical system—."

"Carlee."

They look at each other in the light rain and she sees a firm but kind resolve on his face.

"It's wrong because it's dangerous. The roads are wet." He puts his pen to the ticket book. "I don't have to tell you the rest."

Carlee picks up her large red-and-white striped umbrella and steps out of the car.

"No sense in your getting wet over this." She stands close to him and holds the umbrella over them both. "How's Marcie, Blain? Are y'all attending the fifteen-year reunion?"

Sergeant Stoddard continues to write. "Marcie's fine. We won't have time to go to the reunion."

"Blain, do you have to do this? Can't you just let it slide?" With her free hand she squeezes his arm. "For old times?"

"Sorry, Carlee, but the law's the law. I'm just trying to protect your children."

"I haven't seen you in years. How many children do *y'all* have?"

"I have two by Marcie." He looks at her. "And right now I'm trying to keep my third one in one piece."

Shocking herself, Carlee slaps him, hard, on his beautiful cheek.

Carlee made one mistake, almost ten years ago, when Conoco sent her husband, early in his career, on a six-month assignment to Dubai. The math was so close that even Carlee has never been sure which man is Randall's father. Several times she has gone through an entire year without thinking of it, and then a sudden reminder would make her nauseous with the possibility.

Blain stops writing and firmly tells Carlee she has just committed a felony.

Randall sticks his head out the window. "You leave my mother alone!"

"Randall! You get back in that car." Turning to the officer, she says, "Surely. Blain. Surely you wouldn't arrest me."

Blain looks at her with his clear green eyes. "The law applies to everyone, Carlee. Even you."

When the officer finishes the ticket, he looks into the car. He smells first the baby puke, then something dead, and then he sees his son tattooed like a Borneo native.

"How're you doing, tiger?"

Not sure what to say, Randall gives him a mad frown, then croaks out, "It's raining in our car."

The officer turns to Carlee. "Sounds like you need to take care of that boy's cold." Then he looks at Nathan bent over holding his stomach. "Hey, little podna, what you got there?"

Nathan moans.

"Huh, what's the problem, little buddy?"

Squinting one eye, Nathan turns to him and says, with a mouthful of juicy gum, "I got a squib in my stomach."

"A squib? What's a squib?"

Nathan doesn't know how to explain, so he bends over and starts to cough out little sobs.

"Randall," his mother says, "what does he mean by a squib?"

After some hesitation, guilty, Randall explains. "At Joey's we watched *Alien* and the monster that comes out of that man's stomach scared him so we told him it was just a squid, that everybody has them and if you ate too many sweets it would grow real big and break out."

"Randall, I told you not to watch those kinds of movies, especially not with Nathan."

Randall sinks below sight into his seat.

Blain looks at Carlee, then steps into the rain. He moves with a slight limp to the back of the vehicle and peers into the cargo area at the dog.

When he returns, he shakes his head, then speaks in a low voice.

"Carlee, you listen to me. And look at me." She looks up. "If I thought you were doing any real harm to that boy, I'd set it up to take care of him myself."

Carlee has never thought of his claim on Randall, and a seizure of fear grips her entire body.

"You understand?"

She nods. "I didn't think you even knew."

"Carlee, in five more years, only an idiot won't see the resemblance. You might consider that, if Cameron asks you what you think about a transfer." He tears the ticket from the book. "Now. I need your license. When you pay the fine, they'll return it by mail."

Carlee leans through the window and reaches for her purse.

The officer takes Carlee's ID, then looks at her. "Let's just let a dead dog lie, why don't we?"

- *Inside Nathan* -

Carlee pulls onto the blacktop in a steady rain, thinking nothing. She stares ahead and drives out of the thunderstorm and doesn't hear the wipers chattering on the dry windshield. Despite the open sunroof, the car is now a leather-padded box of sweltering heat.

Randall pulls a bottle of red Robitussin out of his baggy shorts and takes a swallow. Nathan chews his gum sullenly, then his eyes close, his body leans forward, and his head drops. The shoulder harness holds him up as he chews slowly in his sleep. Then he stops chewing. He partially awakens, rights himself and, heavy-lidded, looks around. Then he resumes chewing. When he falls asleep again, he stops chewing but his mouth stays open. His chin drops and a pink stream of saliva slips from his bottom lip to his chest. He tilts to his left, then slowly, in stages, settles onto the wet seat with a groan. His stomach hurts.

The squid in his stomach has a single, large eye, like the alien octopus on *The Simpsons*. The eye is purple, like Marge's hair. The squid grows and tightens in his stomach until it has no more room. One gray, suction-cupped tentacle snakes out of Nathan's mouth, then another and another, and he can't breathe. He grabs a tentacle and pulls hard. He wants the squid out of his stomach. Now he has a tentacle in each hand and he wrestles with the others as they spiral around his arms, but the squid has grown too big and can't come out. Nathan barely manages a whimper.

Randall, heat-dazed, looks over at his struggling brother and takes another swig of Robitussin. Cheesy bands of gum form a network stretching from Nathan's mouth to both of his hands. With lives of their own, his hands keep returning to his mouth and pulling the gum, band after band of it, sticking it to the shoulder harness, his thighs, and the car seat.

Randall looks at the back of his mother's head, then again at his little brother and he chuckles. He suddenly feels very hungry and takes another pull at the Robitussin. He looks at the bottle while working his numb tongue over his lips and he decides to take another hit.

Carlee turns off the highway onto the horseshoe-shaped shell drive of her parents' house, then eases onto the lawn. When she switches off the ignition, the wipers stop in the middle of the windshield. Without looking in the backseat, she says, "Okay, boys, we're here." She opens her door and steps onto the running board, then slowly to the ground. "Okay, boys, y'all step down and let's bury"—she forgets Mocha's name—"the dog."

She walks to the back of the Expedition and pops the lift gate up. She stares blankly at the dog.

"Randall, come on, son. Let's do this."

Randall grumbles something and shoves his door open. He misses the running board and falls onto the grass. He is startled at first, but when he sees he is not hurt he rolls over and looks at the sky, one arm flinging out to his side, the empty bottle of Robitussin rolling free. He turns over and laughs and tries to right himself on all fours but he tilts over and laughs again.

"Randall! Quit playing and get back here."

He finally stands and guides himself to his mother by sliding his hand along the groove of the side panel. When he reaches the bumper, he leans heavily on the car.

Still inside herself, Carlee looks at the pecan tree a hundred yards away in her father's pasture.

"You grab one side of the platter, baby, and we'll carry it out to the pecan tree."

Randall looks at the dog. Its head is lolled off the platter upside down. Slowly, Randall turns his eyes toward the pecan tree. It looks very small and as far away as his next birthday. A loose, clown-like smile grows on his tattooed face. In a raspy voice, he pronounces the words carefully, one at a time, so they don't go out of control.

"I don't give a shit if we throw the damn dog in a ditch, I'm hungry!"

Carlee comes awake like someone ugly has stripped naked in front of her.

"What did you say?" Her blanched face is a picture of emptiness. Too many unbelievable things have happened to her today for her to believe this one.

Randall looks at his mother and is reminded of a stalking man from a Stephen King movie. In horror, he takes a step back and away from the car and his mother.

Carlee's fist pounds the syllables onto the carpeted cargo bed: "Ran-dall."

A low, growling moan comes out of the car. Randall and his mother turn to the cargo area. Mocha, glaring at them with one waking eye, is trying hard to bare his teeth.

Carlee turns back to her son.

"It's just an esspression, Mom. Like you say." He tries to laugh. "Chill out, Mom. It's just an esspression."

She approaches him slowly, like you would a skittish pony who has gotten loose in an unfenced pasture.

"Randall." It is almost a question.

"What?" He is almost crying.

"Honor. Do you hear me? Honor your mother."

Randall turns and looks at the tree in the pasture, then back at his mother just as she lunges for him.

"Make me," he says, stumbling out of range as her hand brushes his shirt.

Carlee reaches for Randall again and he almost slips from her grasp, but she catches him by the right ear and it probably hurts him, but for now it is the only purchase she has on her son's life so she does not let go, but chases him in a small circle while he flails his arms to escape.

Finding her rhythm, Carlee swats his legs at every other step, commanding him to be good, and he croaks out the words as he runs in the circle described by his mother, promising, promising.

{2}

Merger Talks

- Grant -

It's garbage day and I'm washing dishes when I look out the window and see my new neighbor step out of her house, walk to the curb, and plant a see-through trash bag next to her mailbox. She turns and saunters back inside, looking athletic but feminine in her tattered bluejean shorts, white tank top, and bare feet—looking, that is, nothing like the way she looks at the end of her shift in her nurse's uniform.

I stare at the see-through trash bag, wondering what details of her private life I could read with a good pair of binoculars. I'm almost done stacking bachelor dishes in the drain rack (buttertub bowls, jelly-glass tumblers) when her garage door lifts and a red sports car glides out and stops midway down the drive. The taillights wink off, and her left leg comes from the Miata like it will never end. She begins the mechanics of washing her car.

After a minute of watching, I know I've got to get closer, so I tear off a black garbage bag and run through the house like a kid on a scavenger hunt, stuffing it with anything I can live without until I have something that looks like a sincere offering.

I walk down my driveway, swinging the bag to catch her

eye. I'm almost to the curb with no luck when the air goes completely out of my balloon as she turns away to spray a wheel. Then, even though it's happened a dozen times, I'm startled when I set the bag down and a cat stuck halfway in the one already there blasts off in a hissing fit like that Tasmanian devil in the cartoon. I holler. That's when she looks up, letting off on the nozzle to hear better. The cat is now on her side of the street, standing dead still looking over its shoulder, one foot poised in the air like some beautiful, wild animal you want to stop with a camera or a gun.

Apparently, she thinks I've yelled hello to her, so she stands up, the nozzle raised waist-high like we're about to have a shootout. I wave at her feebly and point to her mailbox.

"Cat," I say. She looks over the car roof, but the cat is blocked by her see-through trash bag. I'm trying to figure out how to exit gracefully so I can go inside and kill myself when she aims her pistol at the mailbox and says, "No, that's a giraffe."

A smile grows on my face. "Nice to meet you," I say. As she nods with her pistol, I see Jenny coming up the sidewalk pushing a baby buggy with a frilly pink canopy.

"Hey, Mr. Grant." She waves like I'm a mile away.

In my peripheral vision, I notice my new neighbor watching us, and I think, here's my chance to redeem myself, so I talk extra loud and clear, like you do to children anyway.

"Hey, Jen-Jen, watcha got there, a new baby?" I look in the pram but all I can see is a blanket moving around like something from a horror film. "Is that your mom's new baby?"

"Nope, it's mine." She points proudly at her chest. I raise my eyebrows and look at the nurse.

"You don't say. What's her name?"

"Rattles," she says matter-of-factly, and I laugh.

"That's a funny name for a baby. Where'd you get her, at

the hospital?"

"Nope. Darnell gave her to me." While I'm pondering the several possible meanings of Darnell, the only black kid on the block, in any way giving Jennifer a baby, a fuzzy black snake crawls from under the blanket, wavering nervously about. With motherly concern, Jennifer hurries to the front of the buggy and tucks the tail back under the cover.

"You be good now, Rattles," she says. Then she reaches in and lowers the blanket to reveal the black and white face of a cat flat on its back. It's not frightened, but it looks as if it's had all it can stand of this kind of fun.

I turn to see the nurse's reaction to the cute little scene when the garbage cat hisses and arches its back. Rattles gives one of those yeowling screams as she fights her way out of the blanket and spills onto the pavement, angry black fur exploding out of a tight-fitting doll dress. The two cats bolt at each other, meet in a mid-air ballet of razor-clawing swats, and land in a hissing standoff.

Thinking I should do something, I run to Rattles and pick her up. Instantly, my mind tells me it was the wrong thing to do, but it's too late. Things kick into fast motion as she turns around and scales my arm, her thorny claws ripping flesh until she reaches the top of my head and staples herself to my scalp. I grab her and my mind tells me, rightly again, not to move—don't pull and don't take your hands off. Stay like this forever.

But the garbage cat still wants Rattles and poises itself to climb my body like a tree when another cat noise hisses and whisks the garbage cat down the street. Still frozen, I realize it's the nurse saving my sorry ass with her spray pistol.

My eyes rotate in time to see her aim the nozzle at my cat-hat. Then she thinks better of it and without a word walks to her car. She opens the door and reaches in—the nurse unruffled by emergencies, though a mite testy at having to deal with someone's stupidity on her day off. She calmly walks up to the man standing in the center of a suburban street with a furry doll stuck on his head and says, redundantly, "Hold still." She pries open a bobby pin, then with meticulous care threads it around the first of twenty hook-like claws and gently extracts it.

I feel a drop of blood trickle down my forehead and spread into my left eyebrow.

"Please don't hurt Rattles," Jennifer says in a cracking voice.

"Don't you worry, Jenny. We'll have her free in no time."

Faintly from the nurse's car radio comes the day's financial news: *The NASDAQ jumped three-and-a-half percent Monday as investors hunted for bargains among semiconductors, while the DOW slipped thirty points.*

- Bryce -

I was working as an intern during my senior year at Mc-Neese State the first time I smelled rotting flesh. As soon as I opened the door of the unpainted shotgun house, I knew she was dead. Bertha was an obese diabetic living on a welfare check. She had her gallbladder removed the month before. The incision wasn't healing, so my assignment was to change the dressing every two days.

"Miss Bertha?" I called from the front door, holding my hand over my nose.

My stomach clenched like a fist when she replied, "Me chère, is dat you, petite Bryce?" because now I couldn't imagine what smelled so foul, but I knew I'd have to clean it up.

When I walked into her room, a fly buzzed out of a rip in the window screen by Bertha's four-poster bed. She was propped up on a bean bag watching a talk show on a six-inch

TV at her side.

"You go right ahead and change dat gauze," Bertha said. "Me, I don't like the looksa dem stitches, no." Then, "Want one-a these here fortune cookies? Chère, dem tings is good, yeah!"

"No thanks, Miss Bertha, I need to hurry and get done here so I can tend to Mrs. Courville."

"Whoo, girl, I wouldn't be dat woman for all the tea in China. Fed through a hole in my side? Not me. . . ." As she continued to talk, I opened my canvas bag on the bed and took out tape, scissors, and gauze. The tape on one side of her dressing had curled up from the clammy rolls of her stomach. Lifting the old bandage, I exposed a writhing colony of maggots working in the wound.

The next thing I remember was Bertha leaning over and flicking iced tea in my face.

That was almost eight years ago, and I've seen worse several times since. But I've never *smelled* worse until right now, and it's coming from under the hood of my car. I just returned from my sister's in New Orleans, and the heat of the engine is baking whatever's dead under there.

When I lift the hood, a cloud of flies rushes around me. I step back to let my gag effect subside, then hold my breath and try to get a look by waving my hands through the swarming flies. Something with a hairless tail, a possum maybe, is wedged head-down in a tangle of wires and hoses. When I come up for air, my head turns away from the smell and toward Grant's house.

Mrs. Snipes gave me the rundown on him. Divorce, his ex got the house, now he's renovating a fixer-upper. He seems like a nice guy, but he tries too hard. Strange. I told Kevin before I left him just the opposite, that he didn't try hard enough. Why can't we ever hit it just right? That's what Ellen was saying not an hour ago.

When I reach Grant's door, I hear a lot of pounding inside, so I wait till it stops, then knock. As if in answer, the pounding resumes. At the next silence, I knock louder. After a pause, two tentative thuds answer me. Half amused, half impatient, I knock eight or ten times and step back.

Grant opens the door. When he sees me, he recoils like he's been hit with a wrecking ball.

"Hey," he says. Gripping a small sledgehammer, he's covered head to boots in white dust. He's breathing hard and stumbling through an apology about how he looks, and I barely hear him because this is the best-looking I've seen him in three months. They just don't get it, do they?

I'm trying to regain control of my thoughts when he flips his goggles up on his head. Those big deer-eyes look out of a raccoon mask and something flutters in my stomach.

". . . can I do for you?" is all I catch.

Mouth open, I point towards my car, but nothing comes out.

"Something dead," I finally manage. "In my car."

His dusty eyebrows lift, and I resist the urge to reach up and brush them off.

"Something dead's in your car?"

I realize by his confusion I haven't made myself clear, and I'm angry at myself for sounding like a foolish girl.

"Under the hood," I snap. "Something's dead under the hood of my car." His face goes slack with disappointment, and I feel like I've just struck an innocent child. I reach across the threshold and touch the bare arm holding the hammer. "Could you please come over and take a look?"

He glances at my hand. As I pull it away, he lifts the hammer like a tomahawk, and I see the bands of his forearm's flexor and extensor muscles. From the radio on his kitchen counter comes a staticky market report: *The DOW was up 42 points in heavy trading, and the dollar slipped against the yen, while the NASDAQ plunged 250 in some profit-taking.*

He looks at the radio spewing gibberish, then back at me. "I'll be there in just a sec."

- Grant -

Through the heat waves radiating off the cement, I can see she's holding a see-through trash bag in front of her car's raised hood. My heart sputters arrhythmically and I cough to get it back on track, but when I reach her the rotten smell is overwhelming and I forget all about romance.

"Whoa, you didn't tell me it was a dead hippopotamus." The roiling heat has released the putrid essence from the dead animal, and the humidity has suspended it in the stagnant air.

"Thank you so much for coming over." She greets me with a worried smile. "I think you'd better put on one of these gloves before reaching in. I'll keep the bag open for you." She holds out a pair of latex gloves.

Only half joking, I say, "Wait a second. You deal with this kind of stuff every day. Why don't *you* grab, and I'll bag?"

"This is not the same," she pleads. "Injuries I can handle. Decayed flesh is another matter."

I hold my breath and look under the hood. I can't make out what's covered by the black mass of agitated flies and shake my head. Under my breath I say, "This better be worth it."

"What?"

I step back and take a few breaths. "I said 'Let's get it over with.'"

I wiggle into the left glove and snap it on my wrist like a surgeon.

"All right," I say. "Hold the bag open." She stretches the

mouth between her hands. "Wide. Hold it open wide so we can get it all in at the same time without lapping it over the side."

She works her left elbow into the bag and creates a triangular opening.

"Okay," I say. "Ready?" I inhale deeply, then hold my breath and peer into the shade under the hood. Stuck between the engine and firewall, I see the bony tail and back legs of a cat. Its fur has either burned or rotted off. I gather the legs and tail in my gloved hand and pull slowly, thinking the thing'll come out like a newborn and I can dump it into the bag in one piece.

No such luck. As the legs and tail tear away from the body, I hear a mucky suction, like a rubber boot pulling out of deep mud. I stop. I've skinned rabbits before, and I can imagine a length of intestine following me like a chain of link sausages all the way to the bag.

"Okay," I say. "Here it comes. Better close your eyes." I take two breaths and hold the third. With my eyes closed, I lift my hand high so the entrails won't slide across the newly-waxed Miata, then pivot away from the car and finally have to look so I can find the bag. It ain't pretty, but I'm relieved I'm holding just the tail and legs, no trailer, and I quickly deposit my treasure.

I make the mistake of breathing and discover that all the demons from stinking hell were loosed when the cat's swollen body burst at the hips. I gag and stagger away from the car.

"Better drop the bag and take a breather," I say. Bryce is standing next to me in no time. My left hand is sticking out from my body as far as I can get it. I'm swallowing bile, my eyes are watering, and tears are streaming down my face. I swipe my right eye with my right shoulder, then Bryce reaches up with a square of gauze and swabs my left.

"Thanks" is all I can manage. I shake my head to clear it. "Whew," I say, trying to lighten the moment. "We should do this more often." She laughs and our heads swivel back to the car. Dark globules of cat are dropping onto the pavement.

I think for a long time about my next approach, my gloved hand still extended like I'm a one-armed scarecrow. Finally, I say, "I think this is a two-glove job."

When Bryce hands me the glove, we realize I can't put it on by myself. We work it out awkwardly, like young teenagers trying to fit together for their first slow dance. When she stretches and wiggles the glove over my fingers, it reminds me of something else, which embarrasses me because she's *got* to know what I'm thinking, so I look at the car and see the bag limp on the grass like a used condom and that doesn't help at all. Then, like an angel of mercy, she says, "All right, we got the back third of a cat at the end of its ninth life. Let's get the other two-thirds."

She walks briskly to the bag and positions her arms carefully to maximize the opening.

I brace my legs against her car and reach down to feel between the engine and firewall. The engine is still hot and the cat is just mush, no definable organs at all. Everything has melded together to form a single mass the consistency of liver Jell-O. I don't know what else to do but gouge a big scoop with both hands and transfer it to the bag. In the second and third scoops I feel bones. When I dive in the fourth time, my fingers feel something hard stuck to the engine. As I try to grip it, I discern the ridged roof of a cat's mouth, the pink part you see when they stretch and yawn. I pull the half-skull free and deposit it in the bag, saying, "Hallelujah."

Breathless, Bryce says, "The gloves, the gloves." I peel them off and drop them into the bag. Bryce leaves the bag right there, and we run across the entire yard, the smell is that bad.

We reach her neighbor's driveway, turn back to the car, and unexpectedly burst out laughing. Then we just stand in the shimmering sun and recover for a long time, emitting explosive sounds of relief, a faint, faint breeze reminding us that better times are just ahead.

When she's got her courage back up, Bryce says, "Okay, the cat's in the bag. Time to clean up." She walks around the side of her house and reappears, gripping the green spray pistol.

"Here," she says. "I'll back the car out and you hose down the drive, okay?"

I start spraying before she's halfway in the street. A piece of the cat, one of those clay blobs that plopped onto the cement, turns over in the wash. As I scoot it off the driveway, it comes clean and I see it's a fetal kitten. By the time Bryce reaches me, I've sprayed off another and another, then four, five, and six. "Look at this," I say. The premature kittens are hairless and waxy. See-through.

Bryce bends down and says, "Aww," and I don't know what to say, so I look around dumbly until I spot a familiar object next to one of the naked kittens. It's an air-rifle pellet, shaped like a gray badminton birdie, and it's big: .22 caliber, not a .177. Somebody meant business, meant to kill the animal, not merely sting it and scare it off.

Bryce inspects the kittens, turning them over gently with the point of a stick. I put my shoe lightly on top of the pellet and when she's not looking flick it into the grass. Bryce asks for a shovel. Somehow I knew she wouldn't just throw them in the bag. When I return from across the street, I guess right again. She won't let me do the digging. She finishes the hole in the loamy flower bed under her picture window, then lifts each of the kittens and carefully places them on the shovel blade in two rows. After raking the soil over the kittens, she pats the mound softly with her hands. My third guess was that she would burst out crying at some point, but I guessed wrong that time.

Bryce helps herself up by gripping the shovel handle. When she is standing, she offers me the shovel and smiles sadly. "Well," she says. "That was an interesting experience."

She laughs a resigned laugh, like death is just one of those things, you know, and soon it will be our turn. Her voice reminds me of the wistful tone of Doris Day singing "Que Será, Será."

Then we're awkward teenagers again, trying to fill the empty space between dances, and, not thinking, just trying to fill that space, I say, "Hey, are you hungry? I'm starved. Why don't we go get a bite to eat? I know a great—." I look at her, and she's looking at me like "I thought I was getting to know you and liking what I saw, but I don't know you at all."

Then I say to myself, "Oh, brother." I look toward the street and see Jenny, serene in the sweltering heat, sitting on her pink Barbie bike with white tassels sprouting from the handlebar grips. She's balancing herself against the curb with one of her glossy black Mary Janes, smiling like she's plotted for months to get me and Bryce together and finally succeeded.

Then, barely audible as she shoves off from the curb, she says, "I thought I missed, but I see I got that mangy son of a bitch after all."

- Bryce and Grant -

Bryce felt terrible about hurting Grant's feelings. He had gone beyond the call of duty and done a wonderful, disgusting thing for her. She felt bad all through a very thorough shower, and while preparing her supper she couldn't get her mind off him. She wanted to apologize in a way that wouldn't lead him to expect something she was not interested in. She ate while watching a *Seinfeld* episode. Elaine brought Jerry a gingerbread man, and that gave her the idea.

The pounding inside Grant's frame house shakes the entire structure. Bryce wonders what kind of renovation could take him three months. It seemed like he was at it all the time.

Bryce waits for a break in the hammering and knocks very loud five times.

There is a brief pause, then two tentative responses from the hammer. Amused but impatient, Bryce opens the door and yells inside, "Okay, I'm not playing that game again!"

In a few moments, Grant is at the door. Swinging it open and seeing Bryce, he tries on a smile, but it doesn't fit very well and he loses it. He is covered with a flour-like sprinkling of Sheetrock dust, and Bryce quickly suppresses the wish that she had met him ten years ago.

"I brought something for you," she says, holding out the dish. It is a lime-green Bakelite plate, rectangular, with several partitions, and has anything but the feel of country kitchen warmth.

Grant looks at the offering—a slice of roast beef soaking in thin brown gravy, glazed carrots, new potatoes and English peas in a cream sauce, half a canned pear—and he thinks, "hospital food."

After a while, Bryce tries this: "It was warm when I left the house an hour ago."

Grant smiles and it fits more comfortably this time. "Thanks," he says, taking the plate from her. There is an awkward moment. Bryce tries to peer inside the house around Grant's body.

"What exactly are you doing in there, building something to destroy mankind?"

"Oh," he says nervously, "come in and take a look. It's not

finished, but you'll get the basic idea of what it'll look like in a month or so."

Bryce steps into the kitchen, and it is nothing like what she was expecting based on the peeling exterior of the old frame house. New white cabinets with gold handles are set against wallpaper embossed with field flowers. A flecked green countertop. Matching almond stove, dishwasher, sink, and refrigerator. A microwave recessed in the wall.

"Wow," she says. "Bright."

Grant allows a gentle laugh. "You were expecting a dungeon with torture instruments on the walls?" He sets the plate on the countertop. "This is nothing," he says. "Take a look in here." He is about to reach for her hand but thinks better of it. He disappears through the doorway and Bryce follows.

"Whoa," she says. "*This* is different." The house is small and she can see into every room because they are all missing a wall. The rooms are freshly painted and sparsely furnished. The surfaces are eggshell white, and she feels as if she's in a large but clean rat maze.

Grant lets her look around for a minute. She walks to a wall jutting into nowhere and touches a smooth, well-finished corner.

"What I've done is knock out all the nonbearing walls."

She glances at him. "Nonbearing?"

"Yes. If you look," he points, "you'll notice all the walls going this way are gone. Those were nonbearing. The rest run this way, perpendicular to the ceiling joists. That means they carry part of the load of the roof. You knock *them* out, and the roof'll sag and fall on your head. That means you can knock out any wall running parallel with the joists. And I've knocked out all of them."

"Yes," Bryce says, "but there's something else you've done."

She takes a step, then realizes her rudeness. "May I?"

"Sure," Grant says, leading with his hand. "I have nothing to hide. That's the point of taking the walls out. No need for privacy when there's only me."

Bryce strolls down the hall, looking into the former rooms, now part of one large interior.

"It feels so . . . open," she says. "And closed off at the same time." She looks up where the nonbearing walls once butted against the ceiling and sees no scars. The remaining walls have nothing on them. No pictures, floral swags, sconces, shelves. None of the things people cozy up a room with. She thinks Grant will decorate when he's done, flesh things out, put up curtains.

"That's it!" She wheels around. "No windows! What did you do with all the windows?"

"Look here." Grant walks to the front of the house and sweeps his palm across the area once occupied by a window. "What you do is, you nail some two-by-fours in a tic-tac-toe grid inside the frame, then cover it with Sheetrock. After that, you put a mesh tape along the seams, trowel on Sheetrock mud, let it dry, and sand it. Do that three times, then prime and paint it, and no one can tell what was there before."

Bryce runs her hand along the wall like she's touching a work of art. "Wow," she says. "Or maybe I should say, 'Why?' Why would you want to shut out the world?"

"What would I want to let in? Mosquitoes? Humidity? Barking dogs and ranting blue jays?"

"And leaf blowers," she contributes.

"Right. How could I forget? And pounding car stereos. Those are the worst."

"Grant," she says, snapping her fingers. "You got to go with the flow."

"It's not the fury that bothers me," he says. "It's the

sound."

"Whoa, a literary man," Bryce teases. "You know what Thoreau said? He said the word *window* was originally the *wind's eye*."

They look at each other in a new light, not sure what to make of their discovery.

"You don't say?"

"I do say. And you know where I learned that? In a biology class. In nursing, we had to take biological Latin and Greek. It was taught by this guy who knew six languages, Dr. George Van Sickel. Hippopotamus means river horse. Aardvark means earth pig."

Grant looks at Bryce with raised eyebrows. He's not sure what to say. "Thanks for the lesson. Did he tell you what *Van Sickel* means?"

"Sorry. It was really interesting stuff," she says. "But so is what you've done here."

"Yes, in a different way. Look at this." Grant walks toward what used to be the hall. "Doesn't it have an airy, open feel to it? Things aren't partitioned off into mine, and hers, and theirs. It's all mine. It makes you feel different, lighter, just walking through your own house. You expand to fit the space."

Bryce surveys the area. "It's fascinating if you think about the psychology of it. Covering the windows contracted the interior, and knocking out the walls expanded it. We can't give up something without replacing it. If you give up smoking, you'd better start chewing gum. Otherwise you'll be doing a lot of eating." She looks at him. "You know, oral gratification."

Grant frowns, uneasy again. For a moment he had forgotten about the two of them as man and woman. He wonders now if she is flirting, trying too hard to make up for snapping at him.

"Here," he says, continuing down the hall. "I've turned this bedroom into a workout room." Bryce looks at a Universal gym in the middle of the floor. "And this, on the right, is under construction." He lifts a sheet of Visqueen. "I like to finish one room at a time, so while I'm knocking out the wall between the master bedroom and the bathroom, I've got it covered for dust control."

"Interesting concept." Bryce ducks under and looks around. "Renovation as unbuilding."

Grant is puzzled by her comments, like she's telling him a secret about himself that she knows he won't understand. It's a feeling he hasn't had since boyhood.

"And this, on the left," he continues, "is the computer room."

"Ah-hah," she says, "so this is where your new windows are."

Grant gives her a quizzical look.

"Windows 98? Windows 2000? Actual windows replaced by virtual windows. Click on the folder icon—new window. Click on the file—new window." She makes the motion with her finger on an imaginary mouse. "Click-click. Windows within windows for the cyber-space Peeping Tom."

Grant looks at her as if she is Cinderella changing before his eyes into the wicked stepmother. He is not sure if she is flirting with him now or mocking him.

"Excuse me," he says, "but what the hell are you talking about?"

Bryce laughs. "Oh, come on," she says, "you're not *that* naïve. It's all about voyeurism. It's locked in our genes, or at least male genes."

Grant is getting the uneasy feeling that Bryce is smart in a different way than he is smart. He thinks of her see-through trash bag and feels embarrassed, as if she has caught him in the act. She talks like she is onto something about him that even he hasn't figured out.

"Okay, tour over." He gives her a slightly chastising look. "And lecture over, Dr. Freud."

Bryce laughs and follows him to the kitchen. While he is putting the prepared dish into the microwave and pushing buttons, she looks around.

"Oh, an actual window," she says, looking over the sink and across the street to her house. "How original. You could start a movement."

"That one, I need," Grant explains. "I have to look out for the mailman, the garbage man, and my buddy Lance picking me up to go fishing."

Bryce laughs. "You actually have a friend named Lance?"

Grant shakes his head. "Let it go, girl, just let it go." He opens the refrigerator and looks around. "What's your poison? Beer, water, Coke, Diet Coke, caffeine-free Diet Coke."

"I'll take the water."

Grant hands her a small bottle of Evian, then removes the plate from the microwave and places it on a TV tray. In the den, he has a dilemma. There is only a loveseat.

"Here, sit," he says, offering the sofa to Bryce. As she sits, he positions the dinner tray in front of her and sits on the floor with his plate, then reaches up for his Coke. Instinctively, he takes the remote from the arm of the couch and turns on the television, then quickly turns it off.

"Sorry," he says. "Habit."

Bryce points at the television. "Another window."

Grant has no idea how to respond, so he ignores the comment and cuts a piece of roast beef. He is surprised. It tastes better than it looks.

"Well," Bryce says after an awkward silence. "Grant." She

says his name as if testing it out for the first time, then claps her hands. "Since we're such chummy neighbors now, tell me this. Most couples last three to five years, then become friends or enemies. How long, if you don't mind my asking, was your last marriage?"

Chewing, Grant looks up at her. He swallows, then points his fork at her. "My *only* marriage lasted three years. And yours?"

"Five. But it should have been three. And I'll bet you're friends with your ex, right?

"Yeah, you?" He stabs a couple of carrots.

Bryce sips from the bottle. "Yep. Not at first, but now we're thick as thieves. In fact, I'm going to his wedding next month." She looks at him with big eyes. "I'm his best man." She shakes her head. "The world do change, don't it?" Then, as an afterthought, "Hey, you wanna go?"

"You mean you really are going to his wedding?"

"Yes, and I mean I really am going to be his best man."

He laughs and thinks of the opportunity. "Well, then. Sure. I'm with you."

His enthusiasm makes Bryce think he has misunderstood the invitation.

"Hey, we've made it this far. Grant." She points the water bottle at him. "You got your buddy Lance. And now you got your buddy Bryce. Don't go getting any silly ideas about *us*. We wouldn't be any different, you and I." She points back and forth with her free hand. "Insane love for a year. Escalating squabbles the second. Sparring for who's going to leave who the third. I mean, why even bother? Grant." She lifts the bottle as if proposing a toast. "Why don't we just skip the tawdry middle and jump right to the friendship, shall we?" mocking him, mocking everything.

Chewing on the pear, Grant quickly comes up with two

good reasons but holds his tongue. The pear has retained the sweetness of the canned syrup and he thinks of his boyhood, eating pears right from the can after school. "Did y'all have children?" he asks.

"No, did you?"

"Nope."

"Why don't things ever work out?"

Grant works his way up, Coke in one hand, plate in the other, and starts for the kitchen. Bryce follows with the tray.

"Beats me. You're the psychologist. People try to get too close. Even when you're married, you need your space." He makes a sweeping gesture with his Coke. "As you can see." He laughs as if he has just discovered something. He wonders what he was thinking—what he would gain if Bryce stepped into his fantasy, and what he would lose. He sees that what she has said is true and laughs again in the kitchen.

"Hey," she says. "I don't like the sound of that."

He looks at her and feels like he has regained some control. "Good," he says. "Gotcha back." She gives him a puzzled look. "Here," he says, "hold this open while I scrape the plate off."

Bryce opens a black garbage bag and Grant scrapes the last bites of his meal into the opening.

"Not that I'm not grateful," he says. "But the conversation was so engrossing I lost my appetite." Grant opens a drawer and pulls out a plastic tie for the bag. "Why don't you put this on the bag while I rinse the plate?"

Bryce gathers the neck of the bag and lifts it. A number of sharp objects puncture the bag.

"Wow, what do you have in here? I can barely lift it."

Grant turns from the sink. "Oh, sorry. I forgot." He dries his hands. "That's just part of the house. Here." He takes the bag from her, lifts and spins it. "Now, you tie while I hold." She works the twistie around the neck. "It's mostly scraps of

Sheetrock, floor tile, and crown molding." He reaches for the plate. "Here, I'll get the plate, and we'll each grab a side of the bag."

Bryce opens the door onto the carport. The bag sagging between them, they waddle like penguins between Grant's car and the wall of the house.

Grant says, "Can I make a confession to you?"

"Careful. I'm a nurse, not a priest. I fix. I don't forgive." She nods her head in the direction of her yard, where she had snapped at him. "That was minor, Grant. Don't push your luck."

He walks a few steps, thinking. "Anyway," he says, "it was your see-through trash bag I was initially attracted to."

Bryce laughs as they make their way down the drive. "You see? I was right about you." She steps away from him, pulling the bag in her direction so it lifts between them in a friendly tug of war. They pull back and forth, the bag a weight that pulls them together again. At the curb, they set the bag down and Grant looks across the street at Bryce's car. He passes her the plate, and she holds it at her side like a schoolbook. They look up the street at the neighborhood in the early evening sun. Three houses over, Jenny's baby carriage is turned on its side, next to Darnell's bike.

"Grant." Bryce says it flat, like it means nothing.

"Bryce."

She hums the words to a childhood song: "First comes love, then comes marriage, then comes daddy with a ba-by carriage."

Grant looks at Bryce, then up the street. "Yeah, right."

The garbage bag between them, she gives Grant a gentle push. "Don't be so cynical. People are starting to give their friends babies. A single woman can't find the right man to marry, so she asks her guy-friend from high school to do her a favor. Right now, that sort of thing sounds bizarre. But really the only amazing thing is that it wasn't thought of a long time ago. Making a baby without a marriage, without all the romantic mumbo-jumbo. Ever think about that? Grant."

Grant's heart speeds up as he thinks of the slender body that washed the car writhing with pleasure under his. Her smooth skin. The endless legs.

He looks across the street at her car. "Sure. That's doable."

Bryce looks where he's looking. "I said without all the mumbo-jumbo, and I meant *any* of it, including the tango and the rumba."

He laughs and looks at her. "And the cha-cha-cha," making a little motion.

"Exactly." She seems to be thinking, and Grant wonders what is passing through her mind.

"It will only cause you a brief embarrassment when you donate at the sperm bank." She slaps Grant's arm, releasing a powdery white cloud.

He laughs and looks straight into her eyes, disbelieving. "You're serious, aren't you?"

For the first time, she turns her eyes from his. "Absolutely. I've got a clock."

"Damn, I thought I'd finally struck it rich. All the benefits with none of the hassle."

Well, he thinks, he has seen worse arrangements. Much worse: his own marriage to Sharla. Lance's to Beth. His mother and father's.

He snaps out of his reverie when Bryce slaps his arm again. "Think about it." As if waiting for that cue, the neighborhood comes alive. A mockingbird dives at a calico cat stalking a squirrel foraging in Mrs. Snipes's bird feeder. The cat flips in the air two feet and lands crouching, frightened at nothing, a disoriented look on its face.

Darnell runs out of his driveway onto the sidewalk. He has a rope tied around his waist and he's pulling Jenny on her skates while she squeals. Coming toward Grant and Bryce, the children seem unaware of the rabid slobbering of a vicious Rottweiler, standing six feet tall at the end of his chain, his front legs thrashing at them when they pass. Grant has to step back to let them by.

"Just go with the flow, huh?" He laughs and shakes his head doubtfully. He looks to Bryce and sees she is lost in a smiling reverie of the teeming life swirling around her, the first delicate wrinkles forming around her sparkling eyes.

Something like lost opportunity catches in Grant's throat and he finds he must swallow and look away. A few moments later, he has composed himself and sneaks a sideways glance at her again.

Realizing he's standing just the right distance from her and may never be this close again, he reaches across all the garbage of the world and crooks his rough index finger around her slender left pinkie. His chest filling with anticipation, he waits two, three, four heartbeats, then she closes the deal with a barely perceptible squeeze.

Grant's eyes wander out to the street and he recalls the time Bryce removed the cat from his head. He smiles and wills himself to be still, afraid that if he hopes too much and looks, she will slip back into that other world.

All the major indices were down on this triple-witching Friday. Philip Morris and R. J. Nabisco bucked the trend and closed slightly up in late trading as rumors of an unlikely merger circulated on the floor of the exchange.

{3}

Deerboy

At first, he was no different from most of my buddies at Arnett Junior High. He was quiet, even shy, like lots of kids in junior high not knowing what to make of certain body changes. In Westlake, a little oil town across the river from Lake Charles, it was important in 1968 to prove you weren't what we called a pantywaist. The best way to do this, short of beating up an A&W hood three or four years older than you, was to join a sport and be, if not a starter, at least second string. The blue-collar families in Westlake, depending on the season, lived for Friday night football, or midweek basketball, or summer baseball. Wearing the orange and black of the Westlake Rams made you somebody.

Donny John's sport was track. Until junior high, he was like most of us, still looking for the right event to reveal his hidden talent. Nowadays, it's not unusual for children five or six years old to run in ten-kilometer road races. Then, however, the longest distance in grade-school track meets was a half-mile, and that's where, after two seasons of fidgeting with various distances, Donny John finally landed. He was good, too, and when he got to Arnett, he was even better at the mile.

The next year, our eighth-grade year, changed the town of Westlake forever. That year Donny John sat in front of me in Mr. Hamby's homeroom and though we were never close friends I got to know him better than before. In the fall, Donny John ran his first year of cross-country while I made a half-baked attempt at football, which I gave up in November for basketball. I was still trying to find my niche. That was about the time I noticed Donny John always rubbing his temples and missing a good bit of school. Before meets, he complained of headaches. Later, after we knew the cause of the pain, we learned that his head felt better when he was running. That's one of the reasons, I suppose—and it's no wonder; you'd do the same thing—he took to running longer and longer in the afternoons, even after practice. At a time when walkers or joggers were rare sights on the road, you could see him making the big circle around Westlake: north on Sampson, east on Smith-Ferry Road, then the long route down 378, and finally cutting across to his house on Miller Avenue.

Before Christmas break, Donny John developed two strange-looking, bruised knobs on the top of each side of his head, just inside the hairline. When we returned in January, he sported what on deer are called "spikes." This would have caused a stir anywhere, but especially in a junior high, whose little scholars are about as sensitive as mud turtles. As you might imagine, he got ragged quite a bit and grew increasingly distant. In March, when he was what you'd call a two-point buck, his teachers moved him to the back of the room so he wouldn't distract his classmates. No matter what room he was in, some punk was always playing ring-toss on his antlers. In English, Larry Daudrill and Danny Lambert finger-kicked folded-paper footballs through the uprights of his spikes.

"Don't pay 'em no mind," I told him. "They're just a couple of dilberts."

"Hey, it's no big deal," Donny John said, slipping me some

skin as he made his way to the last seat on the row. "Thanks for the backup, though."

Before Donny John got bumped to the rear, I was lucky enough to see that second set of tines, which I noticed when they were no bigger than pimples, emerge from his main beams. Curiously, he didn't have what hunters call "velvet." Not even bone-like, the material of the horns had the fine-grain look of hardwood, like ash or elm, and were a shade darker than pencil wood.

Memory makes some interesting maneuvers in the long haul. Besides gym, the only course I had with Donny John was Mr. Robinson's math class. Long after I've forgotten most of my teachers' names, I remember Robinson's because he was the first black teacher I ever had. In 1968, the second year of desegregation in Westlake, nearly every student carried switchblades or brass knuckles. Another thing I connect with that time was my older brother and his friends checking their birthdays against the Vietnam lottery numbers. I bring up memory here because when I think of math, I think of the word "bifurcation," a word I heard for the first time in Robinson's class on a hot March afternoon when the weather warms but the janitors leave the boilers on because they know if they cut them off they'll have to be up at 4:00 a.m. to fire them again for the chilly morning. In south Louisiana, at least for school kids, spring is never spring. It's hell. But "bifurcation"—the reason Robinson and math and Donny John DeMoss have survived twenty years as a single intact memory is that I was inspecting the first hint of a forking in Donny John's spikes at the very moment Robinson defined bifurcation in relation to something I have now forgotten.

In January and February, the guys on the track team noticed that more than Donny John's profile had changed. Good in his seventh-grade year and during the cross-country season of the eighth grade, now he was exceptional. I want to be careful here not to make this sound more remarkable than it is and diminish what is truly extraordinary about Donny John DeMoss's story. The five-minute mile, in the '60s, was the time barrier for ninth-grade runners. At the second dual meet of the season, one of the trial meets where competition is not especially stiff, Donny John—an eighth-grader, remember—ran a 4:58. In his excitement, Coach Spurlock aspirated his gum and nearly choked to death. After recovering, he forgot to congratulate Donny John and instead ran from coach to coach asking what the record was.

The next week, Donny John ran a 4:50. Which was impossible. Nobody improves that much in a week. Yet, there it was, suddenly turned possible because it registered on four stopwatches, two of them held by Westlake High's head track coach, who had come to check out Donny John and, if he proved authentic, to borrow him for their first "real" meet of the season, the Golden Tornado Relays in Sulphur. By week's end, word had gotten around about the "deerboy" from Westlake and the stands were packed—an unprecedented event in the '60s, a full stadium at a *track* meet. The only sport less popular was tennis. Only pansies played tennis.

When the pistol fired for the mile, I was over by the long jump pit trying to pick up some techniques to catapult me out of mediocrity in my own event. Coming out of the first curve, Donny John was in the lead, looking relaxed. Leaning on the sandpit rake, I detected something peculiar about his stride. It had the faintest suggestion of a prance. His feet slapped a little harder than the other runners' feet, and in mid-stride he stayed in the air longer. When he came around the second time, I watched closer and noticed that his shoes sprayed cinder against the runner behind him, who seemed really pissed about his shins being sandblasted, since he was the Tornadoes' star runner, an Indian named something-or-other Lightfoot. At the half, he was the only person within striking distance of Donny John. Windhorse, that's his name, Windhorse Lightfoot.

On the third lap, Lightfoot labored around the first turn, while Donny John looked breezy. I mean weightless, like he didn't feel the extra burden every runner feels when lactic acid starts building in his thigh muscles. As the two came out of the bend, I clearly saw Lightfoot swipe his hand at Donny John's heel. Most runners, if they recovered at all, would come up with strawberried arms and legs. Donny John hit and rolled, one of his spikes plowing into the cinder and sparking red brick-chips, then sprang up in the second lane without a scrape. Surprised at his agility, he paused in mid-stride, his shoes two feet off the ground, waiting to hit the cinder and continue without a hitch. He remained in the second lane and, when he passed Windhorse a hundred yards later in the next curve, let his inertia sweep him into the third lane, out of harm's way. Twenty yards into the gun lap, Lightfoot pooped out. In the current slang, he was dragging a piano. Then the bear jumped on his back.

Waiting for me at the finish line was an image that will stay in my head for as long as I live. Forget that everybody was going apeshit and Spurlock was screaming 4:47 as if it were a world record instead of a pretty decent early-season time for a local prep star. What I saw was my friend Donny John, whom I'd known for ten years, transformed into something godlike. Calm, with the faintest smile, he stood absolutely rigid, head erect while runners toppled around him as they finished. He had a satisfied, almost bored look in his eyes, which seemed fixed on something beyond the track that I could not see and knew I would never see.

In early April, Donny John broke the southwest Louisiana *prep* mile record—4:31. Remember, this was 1968, and Donny John was only thirteen years old. At the finish line, he stamped his right foot a couple of times and, unlike a runner who's gone all out, closed-mouthed, he blew explosive bursts from his nostrils, which flared impressively at each breath and sounded like a porpoise spouting steam. At the Triple-A district meet, he broke the state record—4:19. Jesus, what a sight. Now and then, during the final lap, his head tossed from side to side as if he were actually a deer trying to shoo a fly from his face. When he broke the tape, he nodded his head up and down like a horse after a good workout. Then he sneezed, which I thought was pretty clever, as if he had planned it.

The May issue of *High School Athlete* featured him on the cover as the only non-prep athlete ever to appear in its pages. His antlers, now an impressive rack, looked great bracketing the magazine's title. At the regional meet, he slowed to 4:30. In the rain. On a mucky cinder track. The 1968 state meet was held at the LSU track in Baton Rouge, only an hour and a half away at the time, when the speed limit was still seventy on interstate highways and you could push it to eighty without getting stopped. I offered my brother five dollars, gasoline both ways, and two hot dogs to take me.

In homeroom and math class those last days of May, Donny John was rubbing around the base of his antlers again, like when they were first cutting through his scalp. I asked him in the hall by his locker if he was having headaches again, and while he mumbled something about soreness, I noticed his nose had turned an ashy gray. By now, he was almost pathologically shy. In the past months, too many people had asked too many questions.

The day of the state meet, the temperature hit ninety-seven. The south wall of the brown-brick stadium blocked

whatever Gulf breeze might have relieved the distance runners on the straightaways. Perfect conditions for sprinters,
though. The confined air in the stadium bowl was thick with
the smell of cut grass and Atomic Balm, an aromatic and very
hot gel that athletes rub on sore muscles or swab into jock
straps as a blistering joke.

Multicolored parachutes from dozens of high schools were
planted both in and outside the track oval. Those on the far
ends of the field billowed out and deflated in the sporadic,
fickle wind, undulating like huge, exotic jellyfish locomoting
to nowhere. I tried to be interested in the pole vault, taking
place on our side of the bleachers, but kept a secret eye on
Donny John. Between events, he'd jog on the track a little,
trying to adjust his already bounding stride to the springy
Chevron-440, the first artificial turf of its kind in Louisiana.
The distorting heatwaves squiggling off the red surface made
him look like something from Greek mythology when it was
still groping for the form of what turned out to be a centaur.

While running events were under way, Donny John, reclining beneath Westlake High's orange and white tent with
two coaches and a Westlake *Rambler* reporter, was doing
what he had taken to as a habit in the past weeks, chewing on
clover stems and sucking their juices with inhuman relish.
Finally, a disembodied voice announced the third call for the
milers. The runners lined up, jiggling their arms and kicking
their legs out. Donny John shook his head back and forth to
loosen his neck muscles, reminding me of a reindeer jingling
its bells. He broke out of the pack quickly, determined to
avoid any spills caused by over-zealous or over-jealous com-
petitors. After the first 220, he settled into his odd bouncing
style, glancing back only to see if he had staggered himself a
safe distance from the cluster of second-rate milers.

The race is not as exciting to tell about as it might have been under ordinary circumstances. Everybody knew who would win. More interesting than the race as a race was Donny John's hypnotic intentness. Going into the third lap, a light, snow-white foam had built around his mouth. It was not the thick saliva that gathers on the lips of athletes during extreme stress. If you try to spit that kind away, it recoils back on you like a cheesy band from a hot pizza wedge. This was a frothy meringue that Donny John tossed off with quick head-jerks on the backstretch. For the end of the race, I squeezed in at the rail between a fat kid and a maniacal father who almost broke my Instamatic with his elbow. Twenty yards beyond the finish line, Donny John stood as still as a tree. For the first time, I noticed his eyes close and his head drop. I would have given anything for a 35mm. With a slow shutter speed, I might have captured in a faint blur, even at that distance, the trembling of his sinewy legs. I had never seen his muscles quiver, and when his time blurted from the staticky PA system, I knew the reason.

The Sunday Westlake *Rambler* front-page headline read: DEERBOY NEARS RYUN'S PREP RECORD. At age thirteen, Donny John had run a 4:07, within ten seconds of Jim Ryun's high school mile mark. Dumb as it may sound, all I could think was, "Wait till next year, wait till next year."

After a good deal of waiting, a good deal because Donny John disappeared that summer, the next year finally arrived. In the halls, there was talk of changing the school's mascot from a ram to a stag. Our ninth-grade class was the first to be "at the high school." Junior highs were morphing into middle schools, and ninth graders suddenly transformed into "freshmen" were getting used to being banged on the noggin by senior rings. The bumpy heads almost made us believe we'd have an epidemic of antlers that year.

I would like to tell you that Donny John came to school

with a royal ten-point rack, but the fact is that his forehead had two half-dollar sized craters, as if his skull had been trephined like a paraplegic's. He had shed his antlers.

Tim Parker, one of my fishing buddies who ran cross-country, said Donny John was struggling at practice, though of course he was fleecing all his teammates. Midway into the season, he was still the man to beat, but he labored at the finish line. Donny John sat across from me in Mrs. Mullin's English class. In late November, two cowlicks appeared where the indentations had been. I didn't want to nag him with questions, so I got the lowdown from Tim. Tim said Donny John didn't care whether the spikes showed up this year or not. In fact, he was glad they were gone, and you can see why, what with the constant questions and rubbernecking. Over the summer, he'd had a hell of a time with the supermarket tabloids, whose photographers kept popping up at odd moments. Finally, the DeMosses took a long vacation. Despite these irritations, when Donny John's progress wasn't even close to the previous year's schedule, I caught him in Mullin's class several times an hour hopefully testing the cowlicks with a tentative finger. Then something interesting happened—maybe not the strangest thing possible, but probably stranger than you might be able to guess.

Nothing happened. Or, actually, something did happen. The cowlicks disappeared. And the antlers never returned. Ever.

As freshman years go, Donny John had a good year—what most people would call a damn good year. His best mile time was 4:47. His sophomore year, it was 4:35. Junior year, 4:29. Senior, 4:23. An excellent year, remarkable even. For 1972. All the state colleges and many major universities recruited him. The newspapers had nothing to report because Donny John had withdrawn more and more as the years passed, but the rumor was that he didn't care to run any more. It had gotten too painful. What was the point of running if you couldn't have fun?

Those years made up Donny John DeMoss's fifteen minutes of fame, and he had begun to ask himself toward the end whether it was worth it. So Donny John, after graduating, turned into a normal person—not a bad thing to be, considering what you see these days. Now he works as a pipefitter at the Cities Service refinery. He married Rita Vandermay, a pale Pentecostal girl with long, curly, and startlingly black hair. They have two children.

{4}

Ditchboy

The first time I saw him, he ducked his head below ground and I wasn't sure I had really seen him. Then he popped up on the other side of the street. Even from a distance he looked different, peculiar.

In our partially completed subdivision, there were open ditches before some houses and covered drainpipes before others. I reached him on my bike just in time to see him back into the culvert in front of Randall's house and disappear. Flat on my chest, I hung my head over the lip of the cement pipe, then looked and called into the blackness until I was dizzy.

That night, putting a big star by the date, I made a long entry in my diary. No matter how serious I tried to be, my brother would not believe me. In the bedroom dark before sleep, I tried again.

"Really, Karsen, I promise. Cross my heart and hope to die, stick a needle in my eye, I think it was an elf." He knew I was giving him our second-most-solemn oath.

After a long silence, he said, "Eat a crushed-up grasshopper?"

"With spinach and liver," I swore. There, I thought, now he *knows* I'm telling the truth.

55

"Don't be an idiot," he said. "If there's no such thing as Santa Claus, there can't be elves, either. Go to sleep."

———

Three days later Karsen, Randall, Darnell, and I were playing flies-and-grounders with a lopsided softball in the street. I kept score in the back of my old geography notebook. When we missed the ball, it would bounce and roll in crazy curves, and Randall's dog, a tailless Australian shepherd, would speed after it low to the ground. Off balance at a deranged hop of the ball, he would leap and snatch it in midair, then crash somersaulting onto the cement or grass and spring up running.

Mocha was a good dog, but he started having problems after Randall and his little brother tried to keep him warm one night by feeding him antifreeze. They were just about to bury him when he came alive again, but he was never his old self again. Sometimes he would growl at Randall or Nathan like he didn't know them and give the ball only to me or Karsen. Other times he'd look at the ball whiz right by him like he couldn't have cared less. If you clapped your hands close to his ears, he would fall down unconscious, so if things got boring Randall would do it on purpose and laugh and say Mocha was having an "ekpalectic" seizure, which is what the vet said Mocha was having when they took him in.

Earlier that summer, Randall had saved all his Ritalin for a week, then crushed it up and put it in Mocha's food to see what would happen. He seemed okay for most of the day, except he kept looking over his shoulder like something was after him. Right before dark he started running around in circles, like he was chasing his missing tail and biting at something that had ahold of it. Then he ran around and around a car parked in Mr. Grant's yard. Then he fell down and started quivering and foaming at the mouth with the biggest seizure he had ever had, so Randall never did that again, not even for fun.

That particular day Randall hit a long, high fly and ran around some imaginary bases yelling "And Mark McGwire cracks the ball out of the park to win the World Series in the last at-bat of the game!" Darnell, a black kid spending the summer with his grandmother, was pitching, I was behind him, and Karsen was playing deep.

Mocha was playing deepest, and the ball even went over *his* head. Crouching to spring into action, Mocha swiveled his head to track the arc of the ball. When it hit, he looked away like a kid afraid the teacher's about to call on him. The ball crazy-bounced so far down the street Mocha didn't want to have anything to do with it.

We watched it settle into the slope next to the curb and run down it like a guttered bowling ball until it slowed and dropped into the mouth of a metal drain. We all started walking to the end of the street. When Randall caught up with Mocha, he stepped toward him quickly and clapped his hands right by the dog's ear and Mocha fell over in a dead faint.

After we took turns peering into the dark drain, Randall looked back up the street. "I guess one of us could go into the pipe by old man Bickham's house and army-crawl till we reach the ball." He looked at Karsen.

"Not me," Karsen said, shaking his head.

"Darnell?"

"Not me, uh-uhn, no way, no sir, no siree, not old Darnell, he smarter than that—"

"Alright, alright, put a lid on it. Dale, what about you?"

I looked at the distance between Mr. Bickham's and the drain, trying to imagine myself crawling in the muddy dark.

"Dale?" He pushed me. "Come on, don't be such a sissy."

"No," I said. "Why don't you get it yourself? You hit it."

We started walking sullenly toward Mr. Bickham's, knowing none of us would go into the pipe. We had heard the story of the kid a few blocks over going into a drainpipe after a rabbit and getting caught in a squirming nest of water moccasins. Halfway to Bickham's, I heard a whistle behind me. Not a human whistle, but something like a coach's whistle.

When we looked back, a tiny hand snaked out of the metal drain. It held the softball up and twisted it around like someone turning a doorknob.

We all looked at each other. I pushed Karsen's arm. "Told you."

He glared at me. "It ain't a elf." I didn't look convinced. "It ain't a elf, all right? It's just a, you know, like—." He glanced up the street at the hand teasing us with the softball. "—a ditchboy. It's just a kid who hangs out in the ditch."

I shook my head, disbelieving my brother's willful ignorance. "Whatever," I said and ran toward the drain with everybody falling in behind me. As we got closer, the hand drew back through the grating. Just as we arrived, the ball spit out of the drain and bumpy-rolled towards us.

We tried to see the ditchboy through the narrow opening, then tried to lure him out to play, but he kept his silence and his distance and his secret. When Dad turned the corner coming in from work, we ran for the house. Picking up my glove and score book, I got an idea. I dashed off a quick note and left it in front of the drain: "What's your name?"

The next day, a small orange card had replaced my note. I picked it up expecting to discover the ditchboy's name. "Get Out of Jail Free!" It was the Monopoly card with the smiling man, hardly believing his luck, getting booted out of jail.

Squinting into the underground darkness and talking through the iron grate, Karsen and I tried to coax Ditchboy out of the drain. We told him we wouldn't hurt him, said he could ride our bikes, promised him candy. Finally Karsen said he was heading for Mr. Grant's to help him knock out a wall in his house.

After Karsen had gone, I whispered, "Okay, you can come out now. We'll go down to the snowball stand and I'll treat you to a big blue snow cone." I waited for a long while. "All right, here," I said, digging in my pocket, "here's a dollar to get one by yourself." I placed it under a rock near the entrance. "I'm going down to Darnell's to play in his tree house. I'll see you later."

I ran down the street slapping my bare feet extra hard, then doubled back on the sidewalk on tiptoes and squatted over the drain to wait for the tiny hand to reach for the bill. I waited and waited and waited. Then I had to pee, so I tiptoed away and didn't think about returning until late that afternoon because Darnell's grandmother had bought him a Styrofoam airplane that we launched with a rubber band again and again until one of its wings hit a highline and broke.

When I returned to the drain, there was a Payday candy bar sitting where the dollar had been. We didn't see the ditchboy for a week, but every time we returned to the drain, he had left us something. They weren't gifts exactly, because sometimes the objects weren't worth much. We put down a pink Mardi Gras doubloon one day and came back to find an old skateboard wheel. We left two acorns and a nickel, and he gave us a Jack of Diamonds. A pinecone replaced a banana. We decided the ditchboy wasn't able to talk and was telling us something in code.

A four-leaf clover was exchanged for a red-and-white fishing lure with rusty hooks. We would set down one thing, an old key, and he'd leave two or three, even though it might be just sticks. The ditchboy was trying to tell us something.

Finally, while Darnell, Randall, and I were playing Reckless in front of my house, the ditchboy ran across the street, out of one culvert into another. The object of Reckless was to keep your bike inside a street square without touching the cement with your foot. If one or two players boxed you in, you had to keep your balance until they either fell over or pedaled away. We were yelling and taunting one another when I saw the ditchboy waddle across the street three houses down.

"There he is!"

"Ha!" Darnell said. "You might fool Randall with that stuff, but you can't fool old Darnell, he way too smart for that kinda trick."

"No, really. Look!" I put my foot down and pointed, and they looked up just in time to see Ditchboy duck into the culvert in front of old lady Snipes's house. We biked down as quick as we could, then Darnell crawled a little ways into the pipe before chickening out.

Karsen came out of Mr. Grant's house to see what all the commotion was about. A fine white powder covered his clothes. Karsen liked to get dirty and talk about the *work* he and Mr. Grant were doing. "What's up guys," he asked, beating the dust from his jeans.

We all talked at once about Ditchboy running across the road. Then Darnell stepped up and challenged, "Betcha don't know *why* he crossed the road." He slapped Karsen's shirt at "why," popping a cloud of dust in his face.

Karsen looked at us, then up and down the street, trying to guess. "I give up. Why?"

Darnell laughed and pushed Karsen. "Ha, gotcha that time! To get to the other side, you dope!" Then he ran, because Karsen had a temper and you didn't want to be on the receiving end of it. That's when Karsen decided to capture the ditchboy. It might never have happened if Darnell hadn't made him feel stupid.

He went into Mr. Grant's house and came out with a five-foot strand of fishing line Mr. Grant had cut for him. "Mono-filament," Karsen announced, "twenty-pound test," like *that* right there meant the ditchboy was as good as caught. Karsen ran through the door to our kitchen, came out with a giant-sized Butterfinger tied to the line, told us to stay away, and walked straight for the drain at the end of the street.

All through the afternoon, we checked on him after returning from the park on our bikes or during skateboard races down the street. And there he sat, as patient as the little fishing-darkie statue in front of old man Bickham's goldfish pond, holding the line and watching the candy bar.

When Karsen finally hollered, we were at the dead end of the street searching for four-leaf clovers in front of Toi's house. Toi was a Japanese girl who hardly ever got to play because even in summer her parents made her take piano lessons or attend special schools. Randall and Nathan were bickering over a Game Boy while perched in a mimosa tree in Jennifer-the-rich-girl's yard.

"I got him, I got him!" Karsen yelled. We jumped on our bikes and headed that way as fast as we could, watching him struggle with Ditchboy's arm, trying to keep it outside the drain.

When we skidded to a stop, Karsen was holding a torn piece of blue cloth, the look on his face balanced somewhere between scared and amazed.

"Oh, man, you're not gonna believe this," he started, wild-eyed.

"It really *is* an elf?" Randall asked.

"No, man," Karsen said, shaking his head. "It's not a ditch-*boy*. I think it's a little old *man*, 'cause his skin's all rough and scaly."

"Ha!" Darnell said, slapping his hands together. "I bet it's one-a them lizard boys my grammaw done told me about."

"I'm telling you," I said, "it's an elf! An *old* elf."

Karsen stared at me. "I don't know what he is, but this is freaky. I mean like *Twilight Zone*, *Creepshow* freaky."

———

At supper that night, we mentioned it for the first time to our parents. They laughed, saying it was probably a boy with a skin disease like psoriasis and he was too embarrassed to play with us.

This made Karsen furious. The next morning, he stayed away from everybody and sulked up in the front-yard tallow tree, just staring at the drain at the end of the street.

That afternoon, without telling me his plan, Karsen got Randall to knock on the Bickhams' door and ask if Suzie could come out and play with Mocha. Suzie was Mrs. Bickham's little Yorkshire Terrier, and Karsen didn't like her because she always had a pink bow between her ears and a shiny tuft of hair covering her eyes. Mr. Grant called her a yip dog, and that pretty much summed it up. Anytime we were playing in the street, Suzie would stand on the sofa back and go on and on, yipping and yapping at us from the picture window.

Karsen and Randall threw sticks for Mocha and Suzie to fetch, and when they started throwing them into the drainpipes I knew what Karsen was up to. What I didn't know was whether the ditchboy saw any of this. Sometimes we wouldn't see him for days, but even then I always had the feeling he was watching us.

Then—I remember it was the Fourth of July because Karsen was trying to flush the ditchboy out by pitching firecrackers into the culverts—Ditchboy finally made a mistake. Jennifer and Toi and I (Jennifer on a soft white baby blanket) were sitting on Toi's lawn making clover-blossom necklaces. Darnell had borrowed Randall's Spyder Bike and was popping wheelies, trying to break Randall's record of three squares without losing his balance.

Suddenly I heard Mocha's toenails clicking on the cement like they do when he scrambles for a stick. I looked up to see Mocha flash past Darnell low and determined, the ditchboy disappearing into Mr. Grant's culvert just as Mocha reached him. We all ran and biked to the other end of the street. When we arrived, Mocha was growling into one end of the pipe while Karsen egged on Suzie at the other end. Suzie's pink bow was barely hanging on as she yapped.

Then Karsen called off Suzie and signaled to Randall, and Randall sent Mocha in like they had planned. Karsen was at the other end, ready to catch the ditchboy when he flushed out that side of the pipe. But Mocha emerged by himself.

We thought the long pipe in front of Mr. Grant's and old lady Snipes's house was a single pipe, but it must have led to another one. Karsen mumbled something about a maze, then Randall said maybe it crossed to the other side of the road. Just as we looked down the street, the ditchboy popped out of the pipe in front of our house and ran limping across the road to freedom. Mocha blasted off in a growling frenzy.

When the ditchboy saw that he wasn't going to make it to the next pipe before Mocha, he twirled and faced him, then grabbed a whistle hanging around his neck and blew it frantically. Running full blast, Mocha fell right at Ditchboy's feet in a tumbling splash of yellow and white fur, out cold. As we were all running, even Jennifer in her frilly white dress, I was actually hoping the ditchboy would escape, but then Suzie blocked his way to the culvert in front of Darnell's house and latched onto one of his pant legs, jerking back and forth like a demon-possessed dog trying to rattle its own brains out.

We formed a loose circle around the ditchboy, then closed in. No one wanted to touch him, he was that scary looking. Darnell pulled Suzie off Ditchboy's cuff and calmed her down. I saw her pink bow on the cement and picked it up.

Then we just stared at the ditchboy as he crouched down, making strange animal-like noises between a whimper and a growling moan. He had almond-shaped eyes like Toi and his labored breathing exposed small, widely-spaced teeth. He was almost bald, his scaly head populated by a few malnourished patches of limp gray hair.

We all felt sorry that we had cornered the ditchboy. He was not looking at us but was trying to peer around our legs. We swiveled to see Mocha lying on the cement with his tongue hanging out, sprinkled with dust and decayed leaf flakes. Karsen was the first to understand.

"Oh," he said, turning back to the ditchboy, "don't worry about him. He dies all the time."

The ditchboy slowly stood up. His nose was dented on both sides, like someone had pinched it hard and mashed it. And he was short, even shorter than Toi. We speculated as if the ditchboy wasn't there or couldn't understand us.

"See," I said, tugging on Karsen's shirt, "it's an elf."

"No, man," Randall argued, "it's a UFO alien. You know, like Yoda."

Karsen turned on Randall with utter contempt. "Are you some kinda idiot? Yoda's not even real. He's from the *movies*, you moron."

"Well," Darnell interrupted, trying to save Randall, "what *chew* think he is, smart boy?"

We all looked at Karsen, and Karsen looked at Ditchboy and squinted his eyes. After a long pause, he announced confidently, "He's a leprechaun."

Darnell raised his eyebrows. We looked carefully at the ditchboy. After a thoughtful pause, Darnell said, "How you figure that?"

"Because, look." Karsen pointed at Ditchboy's wrinkled arms without touching him. "He's got leprosy."

"No!" the ditchboy cried out. Our mouths opened and we stopped to look at this marvelous creature that could suddenly talk. "I have an old-age disease." He ducked his tiny head and folded his arms to hide them. His voice was musical but sad, and he sounded like an adult pretending to talk like a child. Or a child trying to talk like an adult.

"I'm only ten years old, but I have a disease that ages me real fast." He paused to let us think about this. "It's called progeria, and you're born with it. Some doctors say we age seven years for every year and others say eight." He held out the backs of his hands for us to inspect. "That makes me either seventy or eighty, but as you can see, it doesn't make much difference. When you're seventy or eighty, you're just old."

None of us knew what to say. After a while I took a short step forward and reached my hand out. "What's your name?"

The ditchboy gazed at me through the most unusual eyes I was ever to see—young and bright, sad and old. "My name is Hayley, what's yours?" We all blinked and stared at each other.

The ditchboy was a girl.

———

That night at supper, Karsen told Mom and Dad we had captured the ditchgirl. Everyone stopped eating. Mother, turning towards Dad, finally spoke.

"I bet that's the DeMosses' daughter, honey. I heard she had something wrong with her, but when the kids kept talking about a ditchboy, I never made the connection."

My father split open a roll with his thumbs, then buttered it while thinking.

"Maybe," he said. "They live on Live Oak. That's two streets over, though I guess the child could crawl through the drain pipes and come out here on Maple."

Dad said Hayley's father had been a world-famous track star. He had broken Jim Ryun's high-school mile record when he was only in eighth grade. He was a fast runner because he had grown antlers like a deer. After he shed the antlers and they didn't grow back, he never ran that fast again.

"That's why they're such private people now and home-school Hayley. They called Hayley's dad Deerboy. Someone was always popping out of bushes to take his picture or pull off his antlers to prove they were fake. Most people now think all that Deerboy stuff was just a hoax. But the fact is that his mile mark still stands, even though some parents made the officials put an asterisk by his records to separate them from the normal runners' times."

Karsen and I had a lot to talk about that night. I said maybe Dad was pulling our leg. I pointed out that he looked just as serious when he used to send us into the woods looking for spaghetti bushes and marshmallow trees. Karsen agreed: "If we couldn't trust Mom and Dad about Santa Claus, how can we believe them about this?"

After we had worked through the complexities of parental deception and the wonders of the natural world, I made my way to the bathroom by sliding my hand along the wall opposite the master bedroom. I stopped when I heard Mom and Dad talking in the dark.

Mother said Mr. and Mrs. DeMoss already had grown children. "Any woman over forty should know better than to get pregnant. There's too much risk of something going wrong with the baby." My father said the Ditchgirl's progeria was more likely caused by the haywire genetics that made her father sprout antlers. Mom added that, in any case, both factors were a sure formula for disaster. They didn't say anything else, but I imagined my father nodding his head in the dark.

- Act II -

We were all excited about our new friend. Now that she didn't have to hide in the ditches, she drew us a map of the pipe maze and traced her usual escape routes. Karsen and Randall called her Ditchgirl for a while, finally understanding that she was able to scurry around in the maze because of her size. Hayley explained that dwarfism was a side effect of progeria, like her pinched nose. Later, everybody just called her Hayley.

We tried to involve her in our play: biking, street baseball, skateboarding, tree climbing. Hayley never complained, but she couldn't move very fast and was easily hurt. When she told us her mother said she was as delicate as a snowflake, that settled the name issue.

To include Snowflake in our play, I wrote a skit based on Karsen's King Arthur picture book. It started simple—the first draft was only a page—and grew longer as we made up new characters and events.

Naturally, Toi and Jennifer alternated as the exotic princess, wearing clover-chain necklaces and mimosa blossoms in their hair. Randall was the bad guy and went by a number of names: the Highwayman of Death, Mordred, Bertilak. Karsen, riding his golden Spyder Bike with an old cane pole for a lance, was the knight in shining armor. And Snowflake played—who else?—a character named Snowflake, a kind old wizard with supernatural powers and a magic whistle.

Mordred would abduct Jennifer from the castle (Darnell's tree house) and tie her up near the mouth of the pipe in front of our house. Darnell and I, the evil spirits, would circle the princess on our bikes, which had playing cards clothes-pinned to the spokes to make a hellish racket. Randall had trained Mocha, the dragon, to come out of the pipe and crawl on his belly, growling and showing his teeth. Right when Mocha was about to devour the princess, Snowflake would blow her whistle and knock him out just in time for Karsen to gallop in on his golden steed and whisk Jennifer away. On some days, we killed Mocha three or four times.

It took two weeks for us to develop and get bored with that plot, so one night I stayed up late, writing by flashlight underneath my bedspread while Karsen taped together some typing paper to make a scroll. The next day, when everybody was in their places, I pretended to be the King's page reading a document to the Snowflake Wizard.

"O, Wise One, for years we have argued over a matter that greatly concerns us. Our father and his father before him back to the days of Moses and Noah"—I paused to roll down to the next lines—"have told us that when the sun shines and the sky rains at the same time, the devil is surely beating his wife, and we ask you now to solve this ponderous question." I wasn't sure what "ponderous" meant—I had gotten it from Karsen's picture book—but it sounded great.

Understanding her role, Snowflake looked a long way off, to the horizon and beyond, and finally came back to us and spoke. "Dear over-believing friends, it is always raining somewhere, and in some of those places the sun is shining while in others it is not." Snowflake paused as if consulting an unseen oracle, then delivered her measured words. "So it cannot be that the devil is both beating his wife and not beating her at the same time."

We looked at each other with open mouths, and frankly this spooked me so much that I went home that very night and started writing a new script for the next day. I decided on the scene from *The Wizard of Oz* where the Munchkins are dancing and singing because the Witch is dead.

Wearing one of his grandmother's wigs, Darnell played the Wicked Witch of the West. Suzie, Mrs. Bickham's Yorkie, was of course Toto. Toi and Nathan and I filled out the cast as the Lollipop Munchkins, and Snowflake stuffed a pillow under her shirt to mimic the Mayor of Munchkinland. With her odd voice and compact body, she played him perfectly.

Karsen cut out some cardboard wings, then spray-painted them black and attached them to Mocha so he could be a flying monkey. When Randall killed Mocha by popping a paper bag by his ear, Snowflake shifted to the Coroner Munchkin and sang,

> As Coroner, I must aver,
> I thoroughly examined her ("HIM!" we shouted.)
> And she's not only merely dead,
> But really most sincerely dead.

Once, when Mocha came back alive before Coroner Snowflake had finished her pronouncement, Randall said, "Well, he might be most sincerely dead, but if you only had a brain, you would see that he's not absolutely, truly dead." We laughed till the tears streamed down our faces.

Then Snowflake started missing practice. One day while we were waiting for her, Randall wondered aloud how old he would be if he had aged eight years every twelve months. Then we all used my notebook to figure out how old each of us would be. Since we ranged in age from nine to thirteen, we would be from seventy-two to a hundred and four.

"That's awesome," Randall said. "By the time Snowflake graduates from high school, she'll be, what? Do the math, Dale." When I came up with 144, he went on and on about

how nobody had ever been that old and we'd all be famous because we knew her and might even be on *The Tonight Show*
with her.

Another two days of Snowflake being away made me lone-
some for her, so I biked over to her house to see how she was.
It always seemed to me that Mrs. DeMoss was walking around
in slow motion, and that day was no different. She led me to a
room I had never been in and shut the door to leave me and
Hayley alone. Snowflake was immersed in a little bathtub-like
vat with bubbles swirling around her neck. She put on a smile
when I approached, but she looked tired and old, even for
Hayley. The thought ran through my head that she was melting in the warm water. She was watching a video of *The Wizard
of Oz* on a television mounted on the wall in front of her. From
that, I guessed she spent quite a bit of time in the tub. After a
while Hayley moaned, then explained that her legs hurt and
the warm water helped ease the pain, which felt like a throbbing toothache moving up and down her legs.

When Toto exposed the Wizard by pulling his green curtain
aside, Hayley paused the tape and looked at me. "Dale," she
said, "I need you to do me a favor."

She looked like she was about to fall asleep, so I stood up
and stepped toward her. "Sure. Anything. Just tell me what it
is."

She smiled slightly, then with effort said, "No, not now."
She breathed a couple of times to gather her strength. "I mean
later." I nodded yes. "You're a good writer." She looked at me
through her sleepy almond eyes. "When you grow up, I want
you to write about progeria."

I liked the way an ink pen felt moving across the page. I liked
forming the letters, the personality of each one, and stringing
them together into words, then rolling out the sentences to
make a story we could all work on. But it never crossed my

mind to write something entirely by myself for anyone outside our circle.

"But Hayley," I protested, "you can write about it when *you* grow up." She smiled a weary smile at me. "Or we can work on it together."

With the look she had perfected as the Snowflake Wizard, she gazed off at some faraway horizon, then turned slowly, painfully, to me. "Write it before you get old," she said, "okay? Promise me."

"I promise. But we can work on it together when you get well. I'll get a brand new yellow pad from Daddy's briefcase, and we'll sit under the mimosa in Jennifer's yard and write a whole book about it."

She actually managed a laugh when she looked at me. "Dale, you don't seem to understand. I'm getting old and I won't be able to move around much longer."

A lump of sadness grew in my throat. "But they're bound to find a cure soon, won't they? Maybe even next year."

"Even if they did, they could only stop the disease. They can't reverse it. You're twelve, Dale, two years older than me. Even if they cured me tomorrow, next year I'll be eighty-one. I'll never be ten again. I was ten before I was two years old."

———

I worried about Hayley on my way home, and I was still worrying when Mother called me to supper. When she noticed I was poking at my food without eating, I told her my stomach hurt and she excused me from the table. Lying in my bed, I could tell it wasn't a normal stomachache. I didn't remember what my mother had been warning me about until it happened.

There wasn't a lot of blood, but there was enough. And it scared me.

For over a year, my mother had been telling me that all women have a periodic course and to be on the lookout for my monthly friend within the next year.

I don't usually think of math in the summer, but the night it happened I did some multiplication. Even though Karsen was asleep just across the room, I felt different from him, really different, for the first time in my life, and I was anxious to ask Hayley some questions. Because if two times eight is sixteen, then her monthly friend had visited her for the first time before she was two years old.

- Act III -

It took Mrs. DeMoss a long time to answer the door. When she opened it, her eyes were puffy and her voice was hoarse. I asked if Hayley could come out and play.

"Hayley had to go to the hospital, dear."

"Oh," I said. I could feel my heart pounding. "Could you have her call me when she gets back home? I have something really important to ask her."

"Oh, Dale," Mrs. DeMoss said. She dropped slowly to her knees and reached towards me. "I'm sorry to tell you that Hayley is not coming back home." Then she covered her face with both of my hands and cried for a long while.

When she recovered, she stood and walked me back to Hayley's room. From Hayley's dresser, she lifted two rectangular boxes and handed them to me, the small one on top of the large.

"Hayley wanted you and Karsen to have these."

When I got home, I went straight to my new room. After my change the previous day, Mom and Dad moved all the equipment from their exercise room to make it my new bedroom. I sat on my bed staring at the gifts, then finally opened the small box with my name scrolled across it in Mrs. DeMoss's flowing hand. It was a pen and pencil set with a letter opener, each made of smooth, blond wood. On a slip of pink stationery in Hayley's shaky writing was a reminder: "Dale, don't forget to write about progeria."

Three days later, my mother read about it in the paper and told us at supper. The ditchboy—girl—had died the previous day, of old age. She was ten.

Or eighty.

Hayley's death has never seemed real to me, even to this day. I simply never saw her again. It never had a reality because all I kept hearing was her peculiar, musical voice ringing in my head, repeating over and over throughout the following days, "As Coroner, I must aver, I thoroughly examined her, and she's not only merely dead, but really most sincerely dead." And if Hayley was singing about her own death, why, then, she couldn't possibly be dead.

After supper, Karsen went to his room, and I went to mine. I resented that it had to be this way, so I was relieved when I saw his present on my dresser and it gave me an excuse to visit him.

First, I showed him the pen and pencil set. He picked up the letter opener and carefully tested the edge with his thumb like Mr. Grant had taught him. Then, not even smiling, he slowly peeled the white paper from his gift. We looked at the items emerge as the paper was stripped away.

Hayley had remembered that Karsen liked to help Mr. Grant work on his house and had given him a screwdriver set: three flathead and three Phillips—large, medium, and small. Karsen pulled a medium driver from the case and tested it in his hand. He turned it over several times, feeling the handle's bumps that fit between his fingers perfectly.

"They're made of the same wood as my pen and pencil set," I observed.

"No," Karsen said, "look. This isn't wood. Look at the

bumps." He handed me the screwdriver and I examined it.

"What is it?" I looked up at his astonished face.

"They're made from deer antlers."

———

I have returned to the neighborhood many times over the years. The open ditches on our dead-end street are covered now and all the drainage is underground. My father died of a heart attack sometime back, when he was much too young, and my mother is now sixty-eight, though she still doesn't look as old as Hayley the last time I saw her.

I had promised Hayley I would write about progeria before I got old, but the years have slipped away, one after another, until I looked around the other day to find I was in the middle of my life.

I have been to college, married twice, raised two children: a boy and a girl, just like me and Karsen, who has three of his own. I've had several jobs in journalism and publishing. I have made so many friends in so many cities that I can't remember all of their names. Some of them, whether they had lived their allotted time or not, died by accident or disease or their own hand. And it all happened so quickly.

In a few years, my children will marry and have children of their own. In a few years more, there will be menopause, with widowhood likely to follow, then aging—that slow decline— and then I will disappear and it will seem as if we all passed in an instant, like snowflakes falling in a warm pool.

[The real-life Hayley Okines died on April 2, 2015 at age seventeen—or, in progeria years, one hundred thirty-six.]

{5}

Dogboy

Clay Horton's legs were shaped like a dog's. When he was born, his mother cried for three days. Then she made herself strong and did not break down again until Clay was two and her husband persisted in his attempts to make her baby stand up.

Tom said his son's feet were normal so he should be able to stand, then walk. As with all toddlers, Tom argued, it was just a matter of Clay learning to balance. Carol cried, not because her husband was cruel to her son, but because her baby looked pathetic trying to perform the unnatural action, like a circus dog stutter-stepping in a tutu.

Even Clay's crawling had not been normal. His left arm and leg were slightly shorter than his right, so he listed to one side as he crawled toward his goal—a toy, a pacifier, or his mother's open arms.

By the time Tom decided to teach his son to walk, the doctors had told the couple that Clay's mental development was also "anomalous." Tom was angered by the diagnosis and offended by the euphemism. He had been mocking terms like "developmentally challenged" and "other-abled" since they had come into vogue.

Tom was encouraged when Clay finally took a few awkward steps. Carol argued that Clay could get around faster by crawling and Tom was just wasting his time because in three years Clay would have the operation to correct his legs. Then he would have to learn to walk all over again.

Whenever Tom saw his son drop forward and walk around on all fours, he would set him back up and make him walk up-right.

"What difference does it make?" Carol asked at supper one evening. "Why do you torment him like this?"

"Because he's a human being, not a dog—that's why."

During these exchanges, Tom and Carol forgot about Clay's sister.

"Well, I'm not a dog, either," she said one night, "so I wish you'd think about *me* once in a while."

Everyone stopped eating to look at Tamara. As Clay looked from face to face, he became uneasy at the tension and began moaning and fidgeting with his fingers.

"Tam-Mam," he pleaded, looking at his sister, "doan *do* dat." Tamara stared at him and he grinned nervously. "Well, I nodee dog, eeder," he said, emitting a tentative giggle. Tamara ran from the table.

When Clay was five, Carol turned from the dishes to see him bent over the dog bowl about to sample Hobo's food. The swift connection between her son's legs and the dog food made her cry out.

"Don't even *think* about it, young man!"

Startled, Clay looked up at his mother, then burst out laughing. She was always overly gentle with him, so this command, out of harmony with what he was used to hearing, struck him as funny. For the rest of the day, he crawled and four-walked around the house, chanting, "Dodee *tink*abow, yoo mah!"

For a long time, Carol thought this kind of copycatting was part of a baby-talk phase that would pass, but she finally came to see that his vocalizing was patterned on the cadence of sentences rather than on accurately pronounced words.

A speech therapist tested Clay's ability to duplicate the common sounds of English. He imitated them all, joyfully, and was still repeating them when the therapist told Carol that he had a form of echolalia that focused more on tones and rhythms than words and lexical meanings. She explained that echolalia was an ordinary part of language acquisition in infants, but it was also common among autistic children.

Carol's heart sank at yet another problem her child would have to deal with. When she told Tom, his response clarified for her their differing attitudes.

"Great," he said. "Here's another problem we'll have to deal with."

———

By the time Clay was six, Tom had given up on his program to normalize his son and allowed him to move about the house on all fours in a curious, sideways, rocking lope.

In preparation for the July operation, the doctors held several conferences with Tom and Carol, outlining the procedure, detailing physical therapy, subtly moderating their expectations. In a six-hour operation, the team of vascular, neurological, and orthopedic surgeons would break and realign Clay's femurs, shave some bone here, shorten or lengthen tendons there, graft muscle in a few places.

"Bones are nothing but levers," the orthopedist, a graying man with a handlebar mustache, explained. "They're controlled by muscles in order to move the body. All we're going to do is standardize the parts, so to speak." Dr. Keenan paused. "If I had to guess, Clay's condition is nothing more than a genetic reversion to an earlier and perhaps better form."

Tamara, now twelve, was growing tired of the fact that Clay

limited her social life. She knew her father didn't want the neighborhood children to see Clay, but she had made a new girlfriend late in the spring when her family moved and she changed schools.

"I didn't even know you *had* a brother," Dale said over the phone. Tamara was babysitting Clay that Saturday afternoon while her parents shopped for new drapes.

"Yeah, that's because he's so special Dad won't let anybody see him." Tamara hinted at Clay's physical differences until her conniving tone drove Dale over the edge.

"I'm *really* interested in those kinds of things," Dale said. "I'm even thinking about going into Special Ed when I get to college."

"Well, if you want to teach Clay, you'll have to go into super-duper Special Ed."

Unable to stand the suspense any longer, Dale squealed, "Look, I'm coming down there *right now*."

When Tamara opened the door, Dale looked in at Clay sitting sphinx-like on the living room carpet next to Hobo, the family's brown mutt. Clay was making necklaces out of colorful plastic cubes and spheres, engrossed by the sound they made as he popped them apart. Hobo, wearing several of the necklaces, one covering his left eye, sat patiently next to Clay.

"Oh, wow," Dale whispered, "he is so awesome."

"You mean the dog," Tamara said, "or the dog?"

Dale laughed and punched Tamara on the arm and went straight to Clay.

Clay had been tested by so many pleasant doctors that no one was a stranger to him. Soon after Dale kneeled beside him, they were playing like old friends.

A few minutes later, Hobo jumped up on the couch in front of the drapeless picture window and barked at something the children couldn't hear. Clay was so engrossed in his play with

Dale that he wasn't aware of the barking for a while. Then, as if snapped out of a trance, he scuttled to the couch, where he put his hands on the sill and raised up to peer out the window. In the street, a boy was throwing a Frisbee to a tan and white dog. The dog leaped high in the air and caught the disk between his teeth. Clay turned to Tamara.

"Go out'ide," he said. "Go out'ide!"

Tamara got up and looked outside. "Now, you know you can't play in the front yard."

"That's Nathan," Dale said. "He lives next door to us. I'll get him to play in your backyard so Clay can watch." She opened the door and called his name.

Nathan, a fuzzy-blond seven-year-old with a permanent look of wonder in his big brown eyes, stood in the doorway staring at Clay. Tamara asked Nathan if he and Mocha would play fetch in the backyard. She looked at her little brother. "He's got a handicap in his legs, so he can't play in the street."

Because Nathan's older brother was always calling him stupid, he didn't want to appear unknowing about oddities of this sort. While Hobo growled at Mocha, Nathan held the blue Frisbee in front of his chest and looked at Clay. "That's nothing," he finally said. "Last summer, we had a friend who died of old age and she was only ten."

After locking Hobo in the bathroom, Tamara led Nathan and Mocha through the house, out a sliding-glass door, and onto a wooden deck.

"My dog's an Australian shepherd," Nathan said. "What kind's yours?"

"He's just a Heinz 57," Tamara said. "How can a ten-year-old die of old age?"

Tamara stayed with Clay on the deck while Dale led Nathan and Mocha through the gate into the yard. Dale explained that their friend Hayley had died the previous summer of a disease called progeria, which speeds up the aging process in children.

While Dale talked, Nathan dangled his Frisbee above Clay's head. Clay leaned against the wooden rail and reached for the blue discus. When Tamara and Dale paused, Nathan waved the Frisbee in front of Mocha.

"Get it, boy!" he said and sailed the Frisbee toward the middle of the yard.

Mocha dashed across the yard and leapt up, catching the disk between his teeth.

Clay squealed with delight as Nathan threw the Frisbee again. "Get it, boy!"

Nathan moved out into the yard and flung the Frisbee to a far corner.

Clay mimed, "KEE-kee, poy!" and moved sideways along the railing to track the action.

"Get it, boy!" Nathan commanded at each toss.

"KEE-kee, poy!" Clay yelled, looking between the spindles and lurching along the rail like a chimpanzee in a cage. On the next throw, Clay catapulted over the rail and ran for the Frisbee, just beating Mocha to the catch.

"Wow!" Nathan said. "Your little brother's *fast.*"

Tamara was stunned. "He's never done *that* before!" Clay loped up to the group with the Frisbee in his mouth, leaning away to keep Mocha from taking it. "Give me that," Tamara said. "Are you crazy?" She took the Frisbee from her brother's mouth.

Nathan said, "I knew Mocha was getting old, but you still have to be pretty fast to beat a dog. Can I throw it for him again?"

Tamara shook her head and handed him the Frisbee in resignation. "Suits me. If that's what makes him happy, knock yourself out."

Mocha and Clay, bumping against each other excitedly,

looked up at the Frisbee dangling from Nathan's hand.

"KEE-kee, poy!" Clay yelled, and Nathan whipped the Frisbee as hard as he could. Mocha and Clay scurried after it. Clay, beating Mocha by two lengths, sprang and knocked the hovering disk out of reach. Mocha picked it up and ran back to Nathan, Clay right on his heels, laughing wildly.

———

"What," Mrs. Horton said, "is the meaning of *this*?" She was holding Clay's face, turning it towards Tamara. His cheeks were chafed and his lips were chapped and bleeding.

Tamara covered her mouth but couldn't stop a nervous giggle. "Mom, I *swear* we tried to stop him, but he would just cry and cry if we tried to bring him back inside."

"Stop *what*?"

"The Frisbee," she said. "He loves running after it, you just wouldn't believe it, he really, *really* loves it."

Looking up with anticipation at his mother, Clay said, "KEE-kee, poy?"

———

Once he learned how to run, there was no stopping Clay. He ran from one end of the house to the other, until his hands were red and raw with carpet burns. Then he ran a path around the perimeter of the fence in his backyard. Finally, near the end of May, against Tom's wishes, Carol let her son play in the front yard for the first time in his life.

Clay was a short-lived curiosity to the neighborhood children. They had all known Hayley, who had looked eighty years old when she died at ten, so they quickly included him in their play.

As Nathan rode his skateboard, Clay ran easily alongside

him. Because Clay's left arm and leg were shorter than his right, he moved with the motion of a child galloping sideways on a stick horse. But he always stopped before reaching the Rottweiler chained in front of the Easts' house. Nathan, used to the big dog, sailed on by him within a few feet of his gnashing teeth and slobbering tongue. When the children broke up their street baseball for passing traffic, Clay stared in fascination at the effortless, gliding speed of the cars.

Within two days Clay had raced and beat all the boys in the neighborhood, including Dale's brother, Karsen, who was fifteen. Karsen just said, "Wait till Darnell gets here."

Darnell was a black kid who spent summers with his grandmother. In the spring he had won the 100-meter dash in his age division at the parish track meet.

When Darnell arrived, Karsen counted off five street squares and told Darnell he'd buy him ten Slim Jims if he won. Tamara helped Clay slip into their mother's leather gardening gloves, which Mrs. Horton insisted he wear when running in the street.

Darnell dug the right toe of his tennis shoe into the expansion joint of the concrete. To start the race, Nathan stomped a half-pint milk carton that popped loudly. Darnell broke first and easily beat Clay to the second square, but the kids kept screaming for their underdog and by the third square he had caught Darnell. By the fourth he was moving away and continued to widen the gap until he crossed the finish line.

Hands on his knees, gasping for breath, Darnell shook his head. "Somethin' ain't right, here. Ol' Darnell's the fastest ninth-grader in the parish, but this thang beat me like I's standing still. I mean, that kid, he must be some kinda *dog*boy or somethin'. There oughta be a law against it."

By mid-June, Mrs. Horton saw the joy that running brought her son. When she told her husband there would be no operation to "fix" Clay, he stared at her over his evening newspaper, teeth clenched, for a full minute. Then, seeing there would be no changing her mind, he snapped the paper and went on with his reading.

On the day Darnell suffered his defeat, he started the conspiracy against Randall. As the kids were plotting in a huddle, Dale explained to Tamara that Nathan's parents had divorced the year before and his older brother, Randall, went to live with their father in New Orleans.

During the week before Randall's monthly visit, Clay had become the neighborhood celebrity, charming everyone he met. His favorite person was the young woman the kids called Miss Bryce, "the nurse lady." That hot afternoon, Miss Bryce had left Tamara and Dale to watch Clay splashing in a kiddy pool with her toddler, Ramona, while she went inside to make Kool-Aid.

As soon as Miss Bryce closed the front door, Tamara leaned over and whispered to Dale, "So, is the nurse lady, like, divorced or what? Why do y'all call her *Miss* Bryce?"

Dale shot a glance across the street, where Mr. Grant was oiling Nathan's bike chain while Nathan twirled the pedal. "Well," Dale said secretively, "my mother said Ramona is Mr. Grant's baby." She paused to let this sink in, and Tamara's eyes widened. "Mom calls them a *modern* couple. Miss Bryce moved across the street from Mr. Grant two years ago and had the baby," she raised one eyebrow, "last year."

The girls were barely able to stop their giggling by the time Miss Bryce reappeared, and Tamara couldn't look her in the eye when she plucked the glass of red Kool-Aid from the tray.

Clay awakened the next morning to a sound he had never heard. Randall was riding his orange and white Yamaha dirt bike up and down Maple Drive. Clay parted the curtains just in time to see Randall drop into a ditch, gun the throttle, and hop out the other side three feet off the ground. He watched in amazement as Randall popped a wheelie and rode three whole street squares, balancing on the back tire by nursing the throttle.

The sound that woke Tamara was coming from her brother. She stumbled to the picture window where Clay was saying, "Wanh, waaaa, wuh-wah, waaaaa," in imitation of Randall tickling the throttle to keep his balance.

As Tamara spread the curtain, she said, sleepily, "What are you doing, huh, little man?" She saw Randall race down the street and jump off a homemade ramp in front of the snarling Rottweiler, barking back at the dog when he passed. "Oh, brother," she said, "this looks like trouble."

"What the B-Jesus is this," Randall said when he saw Clay bounding like a lamb around the group coming up the street. "Looks like some kind of mutation from Mars."

Randall knew Darnell was up to something when he egged him on to race Clay, but he didn't see how he could lose against a cripple, so they finally got down to business and took their marks. Mocha blasted off with the pair, but as soon as Randall saw the two dusting him, his tennis shoes slapped him to a stop and he spun towards Darnell in angry embarrassment.

Everybody, Darnell included, looked at the ground as if searching for something lost. Randall walked slowly back to the starting line, arriving just as Mocha and Clay came gamboling up.

Randall thrust his face within inches of Darnell's, stared at him, then swiveled and glared at the others, challenging. He looked down at Mocha, whose tongue was working fast in the heat.

For years Mocha had been the vicarious object of Randall's anger. In the innocence of childhood, Randall had fed the dog some anti-freeze to keep him warm and almost killed him. After that, Mocha had a tendency to faint around loud noises like popping firecrackers, and Randall learned, for his amusement, to clap beside Mocha's ears to knock him out. This peculiar symptom of the dog's near-death experience lasted for a few years, then began to wane.

After Randall lost the race, he clapped his hands by Mocha's ear while the dog sat catching its breath. Mocha pulled his tongue in, stopped breathing, then cocked his head sideways at his older master.

"Stop it," Nathan said, putting an arm around his pet.

"Stupid dog," Randall accused. "Ain't good for nothing anymore."

Then Randall's eyes fell on Clay, a thin rope of drool slipping from the side of his smiling mouth.

"Hell," Randall said to the whole bunch, "he ain't nothing but a re-tard."

This meanness stopped the children cold. Uneasy, they sneaked looks at each other, uncertain about what to say or do. They all knew their friend was mentally deficient but it didn't matter to them as long as no one brought it up directly. Clay, sensing something was wrong, looked up at his friends shifting with discomfort, his eyes finally lighting on the only one looking straight at him—Randall.

Not used to this kind of direct aggression, Clay fell back on the only thing he knew intuitively would ease the tension. He echoed the tone of the last sentence spoken. Looking at Randall and laughing, he said boldly, "You ain no-tee but a *tee*-ta."

The children, knowing Randall's temper from way back, horrified by what he might do, turned to see his reaction. Randall scowled at the misshapen creature crouching by his dog.

He walked slowly to his Yamaha, flipped his right leg up and, in one motion, mounted the seat and kicked the motorcycle to life. He looked at Clay and revved the engine as if he might run him down.

Then Randall busted out laughing and challenged, "See if you can beat *this*."

Relieved, everyone cheered Clay to the starting line.

At "Go!" Clay got the jump on Randall. Then, leaning forward to keep the front wheel down, Randall tagged the throttle to the stop.

Running full bore as the bike blew past him, Clay emitted a high squeal of pure delight.

———

His wife looking over the back of his easy chair, Tom Horton read through the brochure, a skeptical look on his face. He didn't want his son running in the Special Olympics, but this year he didn't have the excuse of an expensive trip across the state to Lake Charles. In June of Clay's twelfth year, the local meet would be held at Hammond High, where Tom had met Carol in their tenth-grade biology class.

"Well," he said, "at least they call a spade a spade, and not a gardening implement." Tom read a passage from the brochure. "'Special Olympics was founded on the belief that through competition against others of similar abilities, individuals with mental retardation or a closely related developmental disability can grow physically, mentally, and spiritually through sports.' That's rare, these days," he said, "anyone using the word 'retardation.'"

"Then he can run in June?"

"Fine with me," Tom said, "but the first year you're going to have one problem and the second year another."

Suspicious, Carol asked, "What's this year's problem?"

Underlining the phrase with his thumbnail, Tom held the brochure up to Carol and chuckled. "How are they going to find 'others of similar abilities'?"

Carol was relieved. "And next year's problem?"

Tom repositioned his thumb. "After your little speedster blows away the so-called competition this year, you can bet some parent is going to cite this phrase"—he held the passage up to her—"'developmental disability' to claim that Clay should be ineligible because of his developmental *super*-ability." He laughed cynically but with some satisfaction. "And that's unfair, you know."

Encouraged and hopeful, Carol asked, "Will you come and watch?"

Her husband passed the brochure back to her over his shoulder. "I'd rather not. That ain't my kinda circus," he said, hurting her heart in a new way.

———

Clay was excited about the pageantry of the opening ceremony, the colorful parachutes set up for shade, and the minty odor of liniment in the air. Carol stayed in the stands, watching Tamara and Dale escort him around the grounds.

The heats were organized according to the runners' ability, age, and gender. A classification round determined which contestants to put in which heats. Only two other runners made it into the fastest category of the twelve- to fifteen-year-old sprints. Ronnie was blind and required a sighted assistant to help him stay in his lane. The athletic-looking Bradley had participated in Special Olympics since childhood and attended sponsored training camps several times a year. He had never lost a qualifying round.

In his first race, 50 meters, Clay was so intrigued by the blind boy being guided by the assistant that he kept pace with him to the end and finished third behind Ronnie and Bradley. At the local games, every contestant received a ribbon, but only the first-place runner was awarded a medal. Clay fretted and fussed over not winning the medal.

"Well," Tamara explained, "if you want a medal, you have to finish first. Understand?" Pointing up the track, she said, "You have to beat everybody to the finish line."

Clay Horton had only three speeds: resting, the gleeful lope of a playing lamb, and full bore. He ran the 100-meter race full bore. Halfway down the straightaway, the sighted runner, seeing Clay a hopeless fifteen yards ahead, fell to the track in a heap of inconsolable bawling.

Sitting on his haunches on the top tier of the victor's stand, Clay bowed his head to receive the medal.

Clay wore his medal to sleep that night. Around the neighborhood for the next week, holding it out and repeating, "I'm O-lympan," Clay showed it off to Karsen and Darnell, Nathan and Randall, Miss Bryce and Mr. Grant, their newborn little Jack, and anyone else who would listen, including Mocha. Finally, his mother convinced him to drape the gold medallion over his bedroom mirror before it got too dirty to brag about.

The color photograph on the front page of the Hammond *Daily Star* showed Clay on the winner's podium, balancing on his hind legs and holding the medal out to the camera. Carol held the folded paper out to her husband.

"You would have been proud of him," she accused, "if he had only been normal."

"That's not it at all," Tom argued. "Those games help the parents more than the kids, and that's fine. But for Clay it seems pointless. Clay can barely remember what happened yesterday, much less last week."

"That's not true, and you know it," Carol said. "Clay is mentally deficient, not mentally absent. And no matter how you think of him, he *is* exceptional."

———

At Special Olympics competitions, no races are timed, and no records are kept. That is not their purpose. So it was still anyone's guess as to how fast Clay Horton really was.

Darnell, now on the track team at Southeastern, told Tamara he was an official timer at a post-season all-comers meet for high schoolers preparing for the Junior Olympics.

"They're so arrogant about their talent," he said. "I'd love to see Clay smoke those guys."

And that is how Clay found himself inside Strawberry Stadium at the starting line of the 100-meter run. He watched the muscled athletes warming up: shaking their legs, jiggling their biceps, cracking their necks. What he didn't hear were the whispered comments of the meaner runners. "Man, would you look at *that* freak!" "I thought he was one of those retardo helpers." "You mean he thinks he's going to run against *us*?"

Clay, not familiar with the intense focus before real competition, scooted next to the star runner in a friendly way. Crouching much too close to him, Clay said, "I'm O-lympan." Uncomfortable around the handicapped, Rusty Banks didn't know how to react, so he said nothing and moved away toward the starting blocks.

Clay approached a runner wearing the gold-and-blue top of Sulphur High. "I'm O-lympan," he said. The boy snickered, then sang in an Elvis voice, "No, you ain't nothing but a hound dog." A couple of guys hit him in a good-natured way and told him to shut up, but he had gotten Clay's attention and sang louder to entertain him: "You ain't nothing but a *hound* dog."

As he continued to repeat the line, the rhythm and tone mesmerized Clay, and he moved his lips in sync with the boy's, whispering, "no-tee but a hown-dow." Finally, Darnell told the runners to take their marks. The echoes resounding in his head, Clay was directed to the lane next to Rusty Banks. "I'm O-lympan," he said to Rusty again. Rusty placed his fingertips on the starting line, then kicked his legs out behind him as he settled into the blocks.

On all fours, Clay sidled up next to Rusty, raised his right hand, and struck himself on the chest with a balled fist, then repeated with more emphasis, "I'm O-lympan."

Annoyed, Rusty finally blurted, "Yeah, yeah, you're a-limpin' alright. Now get down in the blocks, 'cause I'm gonna wax your ass, doglegs."

Clay felt like he had been slapped. Uneasy, he lifted his right hand off the track and wiped his mouth, looking around nervously. Trying to win Rusty over, he laughed, "O-kay! On tor mar, get tah, toom!" Clay stood momentarily on his legs and slapped his chest. "Better run fas', or I gone win." Then he dropped down on all fours and backed into the starting blocks.

Clay was always exhilarated by the speed of his body and the wind rushing past his ears. When he reached the finish line five yards ahead of the fastest prep sprinters in the region, he jumped out of sheer joy and snatched the tape in his mouth, letting it trail behind him as he slowed to a stop in his curious sideways gait.

The crowd had heard of Clay, and now they cheered and roared with laughter at his childlike jubilation. Clay's new fans chanted his name as he loped along the railing that separated the bleachers from the track, letting them pass their hands over his head. Then the announcer called out his time—10.2 seconds, a winning time for most college meets.

When Clay reached the neighborhood gang leaning over the railing, he raised up, balancing on his legs, and twisted his body back and forth, yell-singing his new song, "I ain no-tee but a *hown*-dow!"

The crowd went wild, the commotion attracting the attention of a Baton Rouge newswoman. The camera crew followed her to the cluster of fans, where she singled Clay out and split him away from the noisy crowd. She glanced at some notes on a clipboard, corralled a stray lock of hair behind her ear, then signaled to her cameraman.

To the camera: "This is Christine Josef for WBRZ live TV." Turning to Clay: "Hello, Clay." To the camera: "This is Clay Horton, the local sprinting phenom who shatters social barriers for the physically challenged every time he crosses a finish line." To Clay: "I heard you won the 100-meter dash, Clay. How does that make you feel?"

"Goo." He paused and looked up at Christine, then at the camera, not knowing what to say next. The newscaster saw that she would have to draw him out.

To the camera: "Ah, I see we have a shy one." To Clay: "And *why* does it make you feel good, Clay?" She extended the microphone towards him.

Clay thought for a second about the race and his main competitor, then yelled into the mike, "'Cause I waxi ass!"

For the next two years, Clay Horton ran in a number of open college meets. Elvis Presley's "Hound Dog" became his signature song, often playing over the sound system as he approached the starting line. Newspapers and magazines dubbed him The Four-Runner, but most of his fans and the runners themselves affectionately called him Hound Dog.

By the time he was fifteen, Clay had worked his way to the Olympic trials. A controversy brewed to the boiling point as he approached his goal. The debate hinged on whether his running style was legal. One side said quadrupedal running gave him an unfair advantage in a race implicitly meant to be run on two legs. The other side argued it was merely a new technique, like the Fosbury Flop or the spinning shot put.

Then the debate shifted, as Norman Mailer phrased it, from a question of technique to a matter of ontology, the actual "being" of the runner: "Should a person with physical differences that enhance his athletic prowess be allowed to compete against the 'merely normal' or even the merely extraordinary?"

Clay seemed oblivious to all of this. What he cared about was running, and it didn't matter to him whether he raced against dogs on Maple Drive or the world's fastest humans in a multimillion-dollar international stadium. Still, his mother was offended by the placard-carrying protesters who showed up at each meet.

Finally, a month before the Olympic Trials, the official ruling was aired: "No natural or bio-engineered anatomical defect, anomaly, or difference (including surgical alterations) that gives unfair, unusual, or exceptional advantage to any athlete in any way in any event will be allowed."

Then it was Clay's advocates' turn to protest. A nation-wide multi-media barrage did not nullify the ruling. It did, however, produce a compromise that allowed Clay to run in that year's Trials with special "Exhibition" status.

A week before the meet, the cover of *Sports Illustrated* showed Clay under his personal green-and-white striped pavilion, his nicknames "Four-Runner" and "Hound Dog" emblazoned on alternating sides. Reclining on the elbow of his short arm, Clay looked peacefully dignified, like a Greek demigod being fed grapes by his fawning worshippers.

They say—owners, trainers, and especially jockeys—they say that the great horses (Secretariat, Seabiscuit, Man o' War) *knew* they were fast. They claim they felt pride, understood competition, and hated to lose. Tom Horton would not have believed this. Because, when his wife cried over the unfairness of the ruling, Tom railed, "What's the big deal? The only people offended by the ban are Clay's advocates, and they're mad because their selfish political agenda's been shot down. As for Clay, he's not even conscious enough to care."

Carol told Clay, repeatedly, that he would run in the Olympic Trials, but Clay was unable to distinguish the event from the Special Olympics. To him it was just another race. He worked through the preliminaries with ease, but on the day of the final it rained. Clay fussed while waiting for a break in the showers. When the runners were finally called, he appeared lethargic.

The gun fired, there was a false start, and all the runners but Clay pulled up within the first twenty yards. Oblivious to the second gunshot, Clay sped past the 50-yard mark and had to be headed off by an official.

Back on his mark, his eyes looked tired. When the gun fired this time, Clay was slow out of the blocks and struggled to pull even with the pack halfway into the race. His earlier effort, added to three days of multiple races, took a toll on his endurance. As his weak left arm and leg grew heavy, his body turned even more than usual. Thirty yards from the finish line, his torso rotated twenty degrees from true north while his neck muscles strained to keep his face aimed straight ahead.

By this point, Clay was used to having open air around him as he enjoyed the last few yards—his legs thrusting his body forward, his hands extending and barely touching the track as his stomach tightened with his body stretched fully out. Then his legs caught up with his hands, which passed beneath him as he planted one foot and then the other to propel his head across the finish line.

In this race, though, he neared the finish line with a furious confusion of arms and legs whirling in his peripheral vision. Dimly, then, as if in a dream, he heard his fans clustered in the stands near the finish line stomping thunderously and rhythmically yelling the phrase that never failed to inspire him, and it grew louder as he approached the great finale of his life: "KEE-kee, poy! KEE-kee, poy! KEE-kee, poy!" Clay regained his focus, controlled his muscles for the last few yards like Darnell had taught him, straightened his body, and burst across the finish line half a length ahead of the UCLA favorite.

The crowd responded to the time immediately flashed by the on-field Seiko chronometer. Clay was still slowing down and turning to look over his shoulder when Dwight Stones announced his world record time of 9.748 seconds.

Because of his honorary status, Clay was only allowed to sit beside the winner's stand. And his record would not be permitted to stand in the books without an asterisk to indicate his unfair handicap.

———

Pushing the porch swing back and forth in unison, Grant and Bryce, now married, held hands and talked quietly as Ramona and Tamara threw the Frisbee with little Jack, now five years old. Sitting under the shade of a maple, Clay, in his sphinx position, moved his head back and forth as the laughing child ran after the disk the Four-Runner no longer chased.

After graduating from high school a year late, to everyone's surprise, including his own, Randall changed his ways and started at Southeastern, majoring in mechanical engineering. He admitted that six months of spreading blacktop in the

Louisiana sun helped teach him the merits of an indoor job. Now he rented Grant's old house across the street and drove a Honda Insight, one of the new gas-electric hybrid cars.

It was a quiet car, and no one heard it round the corner as a gust of wind caught the Frisbee and sailed it into the street. Squealing with happiness, little Jack started for the space between two cars parked in front of his house.

It was an inhuman howl that Grant and Bryce heard, a howl of not understanding mixed with the sound of excruciating pain that would not go away. So no one could blame them when they reached the accident and were relieved by the sight of their son standing unharmed and looking on in shock as Clay pulled himself to the curb on his upright arms, dragging his twisted and broken legs behind him.

"A tenth of a second, and we would have lost little Jackie." That is what Bryce told Mr. and Mrs. Horton when they reached the emergency room. "No one but Clay could have saved him." And the Hortons would not find out until later that only a nurse right at the scene could have stopped the arterial bleeding in Clay's legs.

After the initial rush of sympathizers trickled away, Carol and Tom were led to a private waiting room, where they sat in stunned silence. Carol, wondering what the doctors would say, feared the worst—that her son would never run again.

Finally, Tom said, "At least something good will come of this."

Carol looked at her husband with hope and suspicion. "What good?"

Assuming his wife had been thinking the same thing, Tom shrugged. "Now he'll be able to walk normally."

Appalled, Carol leaned away from her husband, "You think—," but she couldn't give words to the idea that her husband looked at this tragedy as a chance to repair his son. Stand-

ing, she looked down at him. "You mean to tell me you're willing to take away the only thing that makes him happy?"

"Now, Carol," he said, turning his palms up, "you know
that's an exaggeration. Clay has his family—you and me and
Tamara. The neighborhood has practically adopted him. And
the whole world adores him."

A short while later, the orthopedist with the handlebar mustache shuffled through the double doors of the operating room
in his green scrub booties. Carol was standing alone outside
the door of the small waiting room. Dr. Keenan started cheer-
fully, "It doesn't happen very often, Mrs. Horton, but sometimes great opportunities come bundled in tragic accidents."

Then he met her glaring eyes.

"Don't even *think* about it," she said. Carol paused, then
spoke again, her fierce anger softened by a faint smile. "Put his
legs back," she said. "And I mean *exactly* the way they were."

{6}

Sportfishing with Cameron

"Man, oh, man, what I wouldn't do to have one of *those* on the end of my line."

His son Randall fidgeting beside him, Cameron gazed through the thick glass of the Gulf of Mexico tank at a school of thirty-pound redfish.

Sweeping by with a push broom, the night custodian at the Aquarium of the Americas saw the man jerk his son's arm.

"Sit still and watch the fish." The boy held his arm and whimpered.

On his next pass, the janitor stopped and spoke in a low voice over the man's left shoulder.

"I might be able to he'p you with that."

Cameron turned. "Help me with what?"

"Catch one of those," he said, pointing with his chin.

Cameron turned to the fish, then back. "You some kind of a guide or something?"

"You might say that."

The small brown man was a mixture Cameron had never seen—Cajun, Creole, Mexican, and something else. Hindu. Or Mediterranean.

Cameron looked at the tag on his shirt. "Mr. Thales."

"Yep," the man said, touching his name with an index finger missing the last joint, "that's the way it's spelt, but it's pronounced THAY-leez. Like that. THAY-leez."

Cameron pulled him aside when Randall turned to watch a sawfish gliding by.

"I'll have to run my boy home first. What time should I meet you?"

"Ten-thirty," Thales said. "By that door right ch'onder." He pointed and shuffled off, trailing the push broom.

———

Cameron's wife had left him six months before. Too much drinking and too much fishing. If he had only picked one or the other, Carlee could have lived with it. But she was jealous of the neighborhood women who had lost their husbands to sailing or golf—the rolling fairways, the carpet-neat greens, the right to say "yacht club."

Carlee was the only reason Cameron lived in Hammond, so he moved back to New Orleans near his cousin Steve, a fisherman and taxidermist with a weekly television show.

Since earliest boyhood, Cameron had fished with Steve all over the toe of Louisiana: Lake Ponchartrain, Golden Meadow, Delacroix, Pointe-aux-Chenes, and dozens of little slackwater, no-name bayous. But he had never caught a thirty-pound redfish. His biggest was eighteen, and Steve barely counted that as a bull red.

Pulling his Bondo-gray Camaro onto the parking lot, Cameron realized they had not discussed money. *As soon as he opens that door,* Cameron thought, *he'll have his hand out.*

Walking to the entrance, Cameron culled out a twenty, a ten, and some ones and stashed them in his shirt pocket. "That's all I've got," he'd tell the little man when he asked for fifty or a hundred dollars.

But Thales didn't ask for a fee, didn't even speak until the two had climbed to the second-floor eye, a thick, five-foot circle of glass that watched over the marine life weaving around the barnacle-encrusted legs of the fake oil derrick below.

Cameron and Thales stood over the lens. Reef sharks, manta rays, and tarpon peacefully crisscrossed at various depths in the after-hours, blue-green glow of the tank.

Pointing, Cameron said, "How much will that gar go?"

"Oh, three, fo' hundred pounds. But that ain't why we got him. That's the oldest gah-fish on record. Been in a tank somewheres North or South for a hundred and fifty years, since right after the Silver War."

The fish swam lazily about until Thales unlocked the door to the storage room, then another that gave onto an iron-grate catwalk painted caution yellow. Hearing the sound of his brogans on the footbridge spanning the oil platform, the larger fish rushed to the surface, agitating the water.

Thales ladled cut mullet from an orange bucket, slinging the chum out over the water. Trained to the routine, the fish went about their business with a patient ferocity.

Cameron was anxious to fish. "I imagine those reds'll need at least twenty-five-pound test, huh?"

"My little rub-a-dub tub, as I call it, is twenty foot deep and holds half a million gallons of high-salinity H_2O." The shriveled man's bloodshot eyes looked at Cameron for the first time. "That's scientific talk for plain old seawater." Thales turned wearily and walked to the supply room like he had done it a thousand times too many.

In a corner by the life preservers stood two fishing rods Cameron had not seen on their first pass through. Thales grabbed the smaller rod as if he had never handled fishing tackle. "This one oughta be about right," he said, holding it out to Cameron. "For tonight, leastways."

Cameron pushed the spool-release button and let the weight spin off a few feet of line, then engaged the reel and wrapped the monofilament around his hand a couple of turns. As he pulled hard to check the drag, he watched Thales bend over the orange bucket and use his hand to chase a finger mullet around in the bloody water.

"Come on now, little friend," he chuckled, "you know it ain't no use trying to get away from old TAY-leez." A corner of Cameron's mind wondered why he had mispronounced his own name. When Thales jerked the hook through the mullet's back, Cameron thought, *I would have punched the barb through his bottom lip.*

As if reading Cameron's mind, Thales said, "Gotta take some spunk out the little rascal. He *too* lively, a tarpon liable to get him on the drop. Now, stay here while I go downstairs and give you directions."

While he was waiting, Cameron watched the larger fish moving near the surface. The reef sharks, white tipped on their dorsal and pectoral fins, moved with a slow, sinister undulation.

"Okay," Thales said. "Lower it down to the bottom." Cameron hit the release and let the line spin off the reel while keeping slight contact with his thumb. "Now, stop it there," Thales called. "Heah they come. 'Bout ten feet away and a foot off the bottom. Lift up a bit." Cameron raised the rod tip. "Right there. Now hold steady."

Cameron felt a dull thump, and the line moved slowly away. He was used to fishing in shallow marshes, so the strike was more subtle than he expected. "Now!" Thales cried. "Drive it home!" Cameron lowered the tip while turning the handle a few rounds, then grabbed the rod above the reel and set the hook hard.

It felt like he hooked a slow-moving boulder. Then the

boulder stopped, as if asking a question, surged once, twice, and headed for home, stripping line off the reel like it was a top. Cameron laughed. The redfish made a long looping arc to the far side of the tank, then ran straight for Cameron. He reeled as fast as he could to take up the slack. When it was directly below him, Cameron saw the distorted shape of the fish heading for one of the derrick's pylons. He walked in the opposite direction down the footbridge, pulling the rod to the breaking point. Under his feet, the catwalk shuddered when the redfish rammed a leg to cut loose on the barnacles.

Then the redfish turned away and the line hissed as it sliced the water. Cameron backed off the drag, knowing he could leverage the fish better when it reached the top.

In a couple of minutes the fish was wallowing on the surface toward Cameron, waggling his head as if to say "This *can't* be possible." Twenty feet away, the fish turned on its side and Cameron surfed it towards the platform. Just as it struck him that he couldn't lift the fish onto the bridge, Thales appeared with a homemade gaff, a large hook strapped to the end of a broom handle. He expertly lipped the giant fish and hoisted him onto the grating.

"Would you look at that hump on his back," Cameron said. "Looks like a Brahma bull." The bronze fish worked its mouth, then lifted its tail once in slow motion.

They admired the trophy for a while. Pointing at the black sun on its tail, Thales said, "Eclipse must be the size of a silver dollar. That eye keeps predators from knowing which way he's headed, see."

Thales pulled a large white garbage bag from his back pocket like a magician producing an endless stream of hand-kerchiefs from his fist. He held the bag while Cameron fed the redfish into the opening. He wanted it to be in perfect shape for Steve, so he squeegeed the air from the bag, then wrapped the remaining flag of material around its body.

Cameron stood, smiling. "Mr. Thales," he said, "I'm mighty glad I met you." He patted his shirt pocket. "I guess that just leaves us with your fee. How much do I owe you?"

Thales looked at him with sleepy eyes. "Whatever you think it's worth."

Cameron thought, *Well, if he's going to be that stupid.* He plucked a ten carefully from the shirt and handed it to Thales, who stuffed the bill in his back pocket without checking it. Then he turned away, almost sad, and waved a dry, leathery hand. "See you next time."

"Okay," Cameron said.

Walking to his car with the fish tucked under his arm like a huge loaf of French bread, Cameron wondered why Thales had said that, because he had no intention of returning.

———

Early the next morning Cameron kicked open the screen door to his cousin's taxidermy shop and walked in, cradling the white-bagged fish against his chest. There was always a small crowd in the shop, drinking black coffee or straight whiskey and telling about the ones that didn't get away. Cameron knew them all. Tim, a hunter with a scarred cheek from falling on a broadhead arrow, stepped aside to let him pass.

Seated behind a worktable, Steve, in a blood-spattered apron, was airbrushing a caudal eye onto a forty-inch redfish. Steve glanced over the top of his reading glasses. His practiced eyes scanned the white bag and guessed forty-four inches. "Looks like you done caught the world record boudin link."

"Ha!" Cameron said. "Boudin, my ass. Try a thirty-pound red." He set the fish on the worktable with a heavy thud.

"Where'd you catch him?"

"In the water."

Nobody laughed at the old answer.

Cameron tried to outwait them, then said, "South of Lake Pontchartrain."

One of the regulars, Larry, a lanky, bearded man with a hawk nose, said, "That narrows it down to half the earth."

Finally, thinking the crew would be amazed by his exotic adventure, Cameron said proudly, pausing at the key spot, "I caught him in the Gulf of Mexico . . . *tank* at the Aquarium of the Americas."

Steve threw his hands up like he'd heard a rattlesnake. "Are you crazy? Get that thing outta here. I could lose my license for doing that fish."

Larry eyed the fish with scorn. "Might as well be a hard-head cat for all the good it'll do you now." He spit into the clear-plastic cup he was holding. "Can't eat a redfish that size. Taste like shad."

Tim winked at Steve. "Say, I know where there's a penned-up deer you could shoot."

Dwayne, a river rat of the plaid-wearing, pot-bellied variety, threw in his two. "Hell, why go all the way to Africa for a safari when we got the Audubon Zoo right down the street? Last week, me and the kids saw a lion and a . . ."

By that point, Cameron had picked up his treasure, stomped out through the screen door, and slammed it on Dwayne's ridicule.

———

Cameron opened the door of the icebox, bent over, and squinted at the middle shelf dedicated to Busch beer. His fingers wiggled past the first two rows and grabbed a cold one.

Turning the twelve-ounce can in his hand, he inspected the label to make sure it wasn't one of the non-alcoholic brews he stocked for Randall.

He popped the top and slugged half of it back, then walked to the den and fell into the lumpy recliner covered with a dingy yellow bedspread. Staring at the blank television screen, he took a few more swallows. He pulled the TV tray closer and set his beer on it. Cameron leaned forward and retrieved a worn red photo album from the coffee table.

He flipped slowly through the pages: dove, squirrel, large-mouth bass and stripers, long stringers of bluegill, two Canada geese from his trip to Minnesota, deer, quail, redfish, limits of speckled trout, a beautiful brace of drake widgeons, woodcock, doormat-sized flounder gigged off the beaches of Grande Isle, ring-necked pheasant from his Kansas trip with Steve, an eleven-pound bass taken from Mexico's Lake Guerrero. On and on the pages went. Hundreds of pictures, thousands of stories.

Cameron closed the album and dropped it on the wobbly tray. He picked up his beer and shook it. Empty. His eyes wandered to the aquarium he and Randall had set up last summer. The thirty-gallon tank held three bass—two yearlings and a three-pounder. Their gills pumped and their fins fanned as bream of assorted sizes darted around them.

Cameron finished a second and carried a third beer outside to the patio. He had taken the redfish from the trash bag and put it in the big white Igloo ice chest to show Randall, but he was off somewhere on his bike. The lid was still open. He looked down at his trophy. The fish was already gathering flies. Cameron shooed them away and clamped the lid down. He skidded a lounge chair across the cement into the shade by the house. He sat and drank and thought about his fight with the big fish.

Walking into the house for number four, Cameron noticed how dark it was. There was only one working bulb in most of the ceiling fixtures. He reached into the icebox, retrieved a beer, and walked back to the den. The faint green glow of the aquarium drew him to the tank. The sediment was roiled from recent activity. The largest bass seemed agitated. As Cameron absently popped the top on his beer, the three-pounder lunged for a bluegill.

Cameron leaned over for a closer look. He laughed at the tail fluttering between the clamped lips of the bass. He shook his head and was about to take a swallow from the can. Smiling, he addressed the tank. "Life's a bitch at the bottom of the food chain, huh?" He lifted his beer in salute and took a slug.

The taste was so foul he wanted it out of his mouth as fast as possible. He looked quickly back at the door, decided the aquarium was closer, and spewed the non-alcoholic brew on the face of the water.

He ran to the kitchen sink and gargled with tap water, then opened a real beer, swished the fizzing liquid around in his mouth and swallowed.

Outside, the shade had receded toward the house, exposing the lounge chair to the sun. Cameron nudged it back in the shade with his shin, then sank into the white and tan rubber straps. He took a few more swallows and looked into the blue and white label on the can. He tried to imagine himself on a sunny slope of the snow-capped mountains.

He leaned forward in the lounge chair, ratcheted the headrest down, and eased back, placing the cool bottom of the can on his forehead and holding it there. He imagined hunting bighorn sheep high on the mountain. He was tracking one with the biggest rack he had ever seen. He had never hunted bighorns, but it was the biggest rack he had ever seen. Each time he put the crosshairs on him, the ram ducked behind a boulder. Cameron walked and aimed, walked and aimed, and the sun was getting hot and melting the snow off the side of the can he was hunting on. He could see himself, very small, a moving speck on the side of the can. Then he trapped the ram on the edge of a ravine. It was an easy shot and he squeezed off three rounds. His shoulder jerked three times, and the ram fell and rolled over the edge. He heard Randall calling from down in the ravine. "Dad." It was like a question. "Dad, Dad."

"Dad, wake up," Randall repeated, poking his shoulder. "Look at this, Dad."

As Cameron jolted awake, the beer slid off his forehead and hit the patio. Pouring foamy beer, the can rolled almost a full turn before Cameron reached down and rescued it.

"Dad, look at this." It was bright and hot, and Cameron realized his shade had ebbed and he had fallen asleep in the sun. Through an alcoholic haze that was almost a sound, high-pitched and buzzing like locusts in noon heat, Cameron tried to focus on the fluffy pigeon lying on its back in his son's hands. "I shot it *in the air*. I put some bread crumbs down and had a bead on him sitting on a fire hydrant and when he took off I figured what-the-heck, so I pulled the trigger and, *bam*, dropped him like a stone."

Cameron looked sleepily at the fat bird.

"Hell, that ain't nothing, boy. Take a look at this." He worked himself up from the lounge chair, staggered to the ice chest, and lifted the lid with a flourish. Randall stepped over and peered inside. A stale-plastic, warm-fish smell rose from the ice chest.

A milky film enveloped the body of the redfish. The black eyespot was gray. A single fly was parked on the dull eye.

"Wow," Randall said, "where'd you catch him?"

"Down in Eden Isles with Uncle Steve."

Randall stomped his foot. "Why didn't you take me with you?"

"I tried, but you wouldn't wake up." Cameron paused. "As usual." He knocked the lid down with a pop. "Well, maybe next time, sport." Cameron clapped his son on the back.

Randall tried again to share his own triumph. "Have *you* ever shot a flying bird with a pellet gun?"

His father looked at the pigeon. It was a splendid bird, cream-and-fuchsia with white chevrons on its wings, its dainty legs flamingo pink.

Randall looked at the bird proudly, then up at his father looking at it in disgust.

"Boy, are you crazy?" he said. "What you shoot that thang for?"

The way his father said "thing" gave Randall a sick feeling in his heart.

"You told me flying pigeons look just like dove. Remember when we saw that flock circling the mall?"

"Yes, but I didn't say shoot 'em."

"Why can't you? They're bigger than dove."

Cameron thought for a second. "Because that's just the way it is, that's all." The image of tourists feeding pigeons in Jackson Square popped into his mind. "They're scavengers," he said. "They ain't nothing but flying rats." He smiled drunkenly at the inspired thought and took a swig of the warm beer.

"But, Dad, it was such a great shot," the boy pleaded.

"A great shot on a dove and a great shot on a rat are two different things. Nobody cares about the rat. There's no sport to it."

———

Cameron told Randall to put the redfish in the white bag and throw it in the blue trash bin at the Exxon station down the street. Then he shuffled into the house to sleep off his hangover.

In the bathroom he washed and rinsed his hands, then his face. Toweling off, Cameron gave out an exhausted sound and looked in the mirror. The sun had branded a white circle on his forehead where the can had rested.

Randall tore off a strip of the white bag and wrapped his pigeon in it. He would store it in the freezer until his Uncle Steve visited, then sneak it to him as he was leaving so he could mount it for him.

He shoved aside some Mexican TV dinners, pulled out a quart of frozen fish, and gently positioned the bird so it wouldn't lose its shape.

Outside, the day was humid and yellow-hot. Randall kicked the side of the ice chest, then opened the lid. As he reached for the fish, the full force of the stench hit him.

"Gah!" he said, slamming the lid as he backed away. Randall planted his hands on his hips and stared at the ice chest. He shook his head and looked off toward the gas station.

To fortify himself against the sweltering, stinking task, he walked inside. He opened the icebox and closed his fingers around a can of non-alcoholic Busch. He looked over his shoulder at his father's bedroom down the darkened hall, then moved his hand over to a real Busch. He pulled the tab and took a small sip, swishing it around in his mouth. It reminded him of the juice from a jar of green olives. He took a larger swallow and closed his eyes against the pleasant sting, then said, "Ahh!"

Randall moved his drinking into the den. He sat on the arm of the green vinyl couch next to the aquarium and watched the fish. Half a beer later, the idea descended on him. He walked to the hall closet and moved a bass rod so he could reach his bream pole with the Zebco 33. It was already rigged with a black and red jig resembling a crawfish.

In the center of the den, he punched the reel button and payed out two feet of line. He rocked the lure back and forth to feel the rhythm, then pitched it underhand toward the aquarium.

———

Cameron awoke with a dry mouth and burning thirst. When he swung his legs over the edge of the bed and sat up, it felt like a Russian weightlifter was crushing his skull.

Walking down the hall, he heard movement in the den. He would get a drink of water, then see if Randall had dumped the redfish. The water jug was almost to his lips when he changed his mind. He replaced the jug and picked up a beer. Double-checking the label before popping the top, he turned toward the den. "Hair of the dog," he said, and raised the can to his lips. Over the top of the can, he saw Randall backpedal into view and set the hook. There was a loud splash, followed by some thrashing.

Cameron padded quickly down the hall. He turned the corner into the den just in time to see Randall reach over the rim of the tank, expertly lip the three-pound bass, and lift him out.

"Son," he said as if it were an indictment. "Have you lost your mind?"

Randall looked over his shoulder. "Just a sec. I gotta get him back in the tank." He draped the bass over his knee, then worked the hook loose.

An image of self-recognition sputtered briefly in Cameron's mind. He saw the similarity, but the difference was a great one. Less water, no sharks.

When Randall dropped the fish into the aquarium, it bounded off the glass a few times, then settled on the bottom with its nose in a back corner.

"Now," Cameron said. "Tell me. What the hell would possess you to do such a thing?"

Randall knew he was supposed to feel bad, but he didn't. He felt anger. He thought for a moment and looked at his father.

"Boredom," he said. "There's nobody my age on this crummy block, and I wanna go fishing and you won't take me. I might as well be living with Mom."

"Well, go for it and good luck. There's no telling what she'd turn *you* into. She damn near killed me with double shifts just to get her that trophy house." Cameron felt a sudden urge to pass on to Randall his hard-earned wisdom, but that part of fatherhood made him uneasy. Pointing the beer at his son, he said, "Just make sure to watch out for anyone that won't take you just as you are."

His head throbbing, Cameron took a long pull at the beer, then glanced back and forth from the bass to his son. "Boy, a three-pound bass ain't even picture-worthy." He lifted the photo album from the TV tray and tossed it onto the couch, where it bounced once and opened. "Look in that picture book. You ain't gonna find a single shot of no bass under four pounds."

A lump grew in Randall's throat. It felt uncomfortable, a blend of anger and shame about to burst into crying and he didn't want to cry, so he defended himself carefully, hoping for his father's sympathy. "It's not like I was gonna keep him. I've caught the two yearlings four or five times and the big one twice."

Cameron looked at his boy, trying to get inside his mind

and understand what would make him do something like this, but he could not penetrate that deep, so he just shook his head. "How stupid can you get."

"At least I'm smart enough to throw 'em back so I can catch 'em again." It was the beer talking now. "You, you wasted that big redfish for nothing."

In no condition to reason, Cameron spoke slowly so his son would catch the meaning of each word. "Don't fish. In the god-damned tank. Those fish are for looks, understand?"

Randall thrust his head forward. "Well, I wouldn't have to fish in the *got*-damn tank if you'd take me with you once in a while."

Cameron flicked a backhand at his son's face and stung him on the cheek with the ends of his fingers.

"And don't curse me," he said. "Ever again. You got that, you little shit?"

———

Driving to the Aquarium that night, Cameron had tarpon on his mind. Aloud, he said, "That biggest one had scales the size of pancakes. I can't wait to see the look on their faces when I haul *that* son of a bitch into the shop."

"Been expecting you," Thales said as he unlocked the door. He pointed at Cameron's forehead and chuckled. "I see you got you an eyespot. Never know when that might come in handy."

Cameron was anxious to get down to business. "How much?"

"'Pends on what you after tonight."

"Tarpon."

Thales rubbed his hands together. "Let's see if you ketch one first, then talk."

In the supply room, a single large rod leaned in the corner. It was already rigged with a silver popper. On the footbridge Cameron cast out and retrieved.

"Ever caught a tarpon before?" Thales asked.

"No," Cameron said. "No, I haven't."

Thales giggled. "Keep castin', son, keep castin'. I got to finish sweeping up."

After five minutes of casting, Cameron saw only one tarpon track the bait with half interest. He called down to Thales, "What am I doing wrong?"

Thales stopped his broom and watched Cameron chug the popper across the surface.

"Wait a minute, then try again," he called. "Don't pull it, jerk it. And work it faster, like he hurt." Thales returned to his sweeping.

A minute later, Thales heard the explosion like a wave crashing against a rock, then a holler from Cameron. He paused in his cleaning to watch the action.

The tarpon made short, frantic runs, shuddering at the hook. Several smaller tarpon excitedly trailed him, looking for other prey. Cameron's tarpon rose and broke the surface with half his length, shaking his gaping mouth. He fell back and drove down, then rushed for the surface and breached with a glorious leap, flipping over at the peak just before his body slammed the ceiling.

Stunned, the tarpon sank, angling down and away from the straining rod. The driving force of the tarpon, added to Cameron's weight, sagged the footbridge. There was a metallic bang and the panels of the bridge dropped like a trapdoor, spilling Cameron into the water.

He held onto the rod as the tarpon dragged him across the surface, shoving saltwater up his nostrils. Then the tarpon sounded, pulling Cameron under. But he would not let go.

The tarpon shot to the surface and jumped again in a series of spectacular, tail-walking leaps, then wrapped around a leg of the oil rig and broke loose.

Thales watched the rod butt hit the bottom and kick up a spurt of gray chips. Then the length of the rod settled gently against the floor as if it were falling asleep.

Cameron kicked toward the surface, struggling hard not to breathe. He felt the salt stinging a cut on his forearm. When he came clear, he dogpaddled and tried to cough out the seawater. He swiveled around to get his bearings. Twenty yards away, the broken catwalk formed two ladders leading out of the water. Cameron took the first strokes toward the bridge, then noticed a fast gray shadow gliding beneath him. He froze. Looking down, he saw blood leaking from his wound. He glanced around.

Exposed above the surface of the water, the white tip on the dorsal fin sizzled toward him. Cameron couldn't remember what to do if a shark attacked—thrash the water? sit still?

It would be a stupid way to die, he thought, to be eaten by a scavenger. Or were they predators? *I'll punch his nose. A good hit should repel him.*

But the strike was swift and violent, like a star fullback hitting a tackling dummy. Cameron felt his body tossed to the side like a ragdoll, then hit from the back.

Several streams of blood blossomed into a red cloud that suspended in the middle of the tank. In less than a minute, nothing was left. The cloud expanded in the tank, thinning to a pink fog that finally disappeared completely.

Looking on as if it were a work of art, Thales smiled and made a mental note to retrieve the rod by morning. There would be other trash to dispose of, and his friends were always hungry for live bait. Then the custodian moved on, pushing ahead of his broom the scraps of the day.

{7}

The Threshold of Plenty

This happened during the drought of 1986. I was tired of people. I shouldn't be at my age, but I had just gotten over a sour marriage like you get over a bout of influenza. You want to go off by yourself and let life creep back slowly and sometimes you feel like it doesn't matter if it returns or not.

I'd had enough of teaching, too. In Tangipahoa Parish, the dropout rate is 60 percent, over half of that from pregnant girls. If Louisiana didn't give a damn, why should I? What I needed was open spaces, time and room to heal. It's an old story that was mine for the first time.

I was living in Old Town Hammond in a repo my real estate brother gave me at a cut rate. It had been a nice neighborhood until the oil boom went to hell and pulled the tax base from under the state. Paycuts, layoffs, reduced benefits, bankruptcies, foreclosures. A political cartoon depicted Louisiana's governor holding a "We're Number One!" sign above the caption: "First in illiteracy. First in teenage pregnancies. First in pollution. First in unemployment." When I saw the cartoon, I thought, "They missed one—First in toxic waste sites." Everyone with any brains left the state. I stayed. Then, what my brother called the *nouveaux trash* moved into the suburbs. Still, the physical neighborhood had character. Live oaks draped with Spanish moss. Sidewalks cracked and buckled by ancient roots. Tall elms, old patient philosophers, inhabited by quick-thinking squirrels. So I stayed.

Then she left me. And for what? A twenty-year-old kid she met while expanding her horizons at the local college. She didn't take anything, didn't demand anything in court. Just left.

With the trash came their macho dogs: coon hounds of no discernible breed, Ridgebacks, Rottweilers, Blue Ticks, Catahoula curs, pit bulls. Incessant barkers all. The entire worldview of these people could be expressed on a bumper sticker: Oil field trash and proud of it. Don't follow me, I'm lost, too. My car may not look like much, but it's ahead of yours! GOD, GUNS, AND GUTS: They made America. Let's keep 'em. I don't brake for anything.

Weekends were a family affair. The father, fat and shirtless, washed the car or changed the oil while mom screamed at her kids on the veranda as they chased corndogs down with generic colas. To complete the chorus, the family mutt, chained to a tree, barked at the pounding stereo. This was called having a good time. Towards three o'clock, the neighborhood was abandoned for the weekly pilgrimage to Wal-Mart, which inside looked like the national white trash convention. Fifteen-year-old girls with babies on their arms. Kids with scabby heads or unclosed harelips. Parents dragging smelly brats by malnourished arms dislocated at the shoulder, shrieking without caring who heard, "Stop that bawling or I'll give you something to bawl about!" What a circus. Their solution to everything from a baby's toothache to constipation is WD-40. "Penetrates better than Ben-Gay." When they got home, dear old dad would probably spray some on the kid's shoulder.

Saturday night they all got drunk. You could hear fights a block away. Not one weekend for a whole year passed without blue and red lights flashing on my ceiling. Not one. Come Sunday morning, they were primed for church. The father stayed home, of course, but off went the mother with her brood. Many a Sunday afternoon, they told me the latest from the spiritual world. "Brother Dabney said Satan done taken over them Cabbage Patch dolls. Just over in Tickfaw t'other day one et the intrals out a grandmother." "Yeah, and I heared old Rutha May, after she divorced C-John, a big old horn growed right outen her forehead. That's *God* punishing her!"

One Friday night, my neighbors Sid and Eloise had an all-night argument. At six, I went outside to see if the newspaper had come. The air was cool and damp, the sky gray. Squirrels were moving the branches overhead. A cawing blue jay shuttled back and forth from its nest to the ground. Sid, bundled in a patchwork quilt, was camped on *my* porch in *his* rocker, an inch-long ash dangling from his Pall Mall. I nodded and headed for the paper. When I picked up the paper and turned around, Sid stood up, letting the quilt fall to his feet. He was in his underwear and Redwing work boots. He scratched his distended, hairy belly.

They can't just say hello, good morning, nice day. No, they have to start every conversation with a gem from their personal philosophy. Leaving the quilt and rocker, he clomped down the steps and walked toward his yard, untied laces trailing behind him. At his property line, he looked over to see if I was watching. He lifted his knee waist-high and drove his boot heel down hard.

"Got-damn blue jays," he said. "Ain't nothing but noise-makers." After he was inside, I checked the heel-shaped dent in the hard ground. At the bottom of the depression, looking something like the guts of a peanut butter and jelly sandwich, was a flat blue jay squab.

That did it.

The next weekend, I moved outside the city limits to Tick-faw on a thirty-acre plot a half-mile from the next house, far enough away that you couldn't with accuracy call the inhabitants my neighbors. In early March, I told Mr. Harlow, our coach-principal, that I was finished.

My new rent house wasn't much to look at. It rested on a slab, though, and I planned to store my extra furniture in the mother-in-law cottage at the back. The first week, I watched TV at night and inventoried my thirty acres during the day. There were many types of trees. And thorns, brambles, briars, nettles, stickers, thistles. Lots of weeds, too. A family of possums, three armadillos, an occasional scrawny rabbit, doves, quail, and a pair of owls. I listened to the owls exchange, in a haunting code, their hollow, fluted calls. There were also hundreds of little nondescript birds, the white trash, I suppose, of the feathered world. Soon, there would be legions of four-, six-, and eight-legged critters, above, on, and below the ground: caterpillars, butterflies, moths, ants, tadpoles, turtles, lizards, skinks, spiders, click beetles, mosquito hawks, walkingsticks. I planned to watch the cycles of their lives. I would start a collection: wasp nests, snake skins, locust husks, feathers, cocoons, eggshells, their skulls when they left them.

My real estate brother said, "Do something. You don't have to work to make money. Sell insurance." He showed me a pre-fabricated temporary building and said we could set it up off Highway 51.

In my spare time, I studied. In two weeks, I had a life and health license. In another week, home and auto.

Sure enough, just like Ray said, it wasn't long before folks from all walks of life wandered in and bet good money on dying young. I'm not talking about a steady stream of people. Maybe one per morning and a couple in the afternoons, mostly to talk about risks or tell double indemnity jokes.

In the lulls, I got to do a lot of thinking. People don't die very often. At least you don't see them. But out here, animals die all the time. Now, I thought, that's something I could really sell. Animal life insurance. I could see the sign: Ralph "Beamer" Mercer, Independent Animal Agent, Specializing in Cattle.

Forget chickens and such. Why, one minute you see them scratching around in the dirt and the next they're laid out stiff as a post. No, I'd specialize in dogs and cattle, with a death-by-car exclusion and double indemnity for snake bite. You see, cats and dogs isolate the venom in nodules and hardly ever die of snakebite.

Many people move from cities to get away from the crime only to find the country has its own brand of crime. One day, I came home for lunch and turned on a stove burner. No gas. No gas because no butane tank. A five-hundred-pound tank six feet long. One person couldn't do it. And wouldn't you know it, I had no home owner's insurance. So, for protection, I bought a German shepherd puppy, thinking to start him young and train him mean.

Some stories are too good to be true. Like the one J-Bob, my mobile home salesman cousin, told me before I bought Dusty from him. He said a couple of college girls bought a repo trailer, set up housekeeping, then bought a shepherd from him. One weekend, when the redhead was gone home, the brunette came in from a late shift at the Winn Dixie and found the dog choking. She saw something stuck down his throat but couldn't reach it with a spoon, so she called J-Bob, who was there in five minutes with a pair of fish-fry tongs.

He dug around awhile but couldn't get a grip on the slimy object. Then, as J-Bob said, "He discombobalated this *thang*."

If you're not around country people much, you might not think they use such words. What they do, though, is get one all-purpose big word and apply it to all kinds of situations, usually mispronouncing it. "He discombobalated this thang. It hit the frigerator door, stuck for a second, and slid down to the linoleum."

It was a finger. J-Bob made for his truck right quick and pulled his .30-30 from the rack. First, he hunted around under the trailer, with the girl staying close by. Then he looked in the bedrooms and bathroom. While sitting on a barstool, J-Bob found what he was searching for. On the floor by the narrow broom closet was a pool of dark, congealed blood. J-Bob aimed his rifle at the door, saying things like, "Just come on out real slow and no one'll get hurt." When no one came out real slow, J-Bob stood to the side of the door and hooked it open with his boot toe. The man wasn't dead, but he was damn near it, scrunched down in the closet passed out from loss of blood with teeth marks all over his purple and yellow arms.

I wouldn't bet on the story's veracity. You'd have to be a fool to trust someone who sells someone else's repossessed homes, some of them probably people he'd grown up with, gone to school and hunted with. I bought the dog anyway.

He was three months old when I brought him home. I fed him four times a day. When I came home for lunch, he wagged his tail hard enough to knock himself down, but only when he was really excited did something between a wheeze and a cough come from his throat.

"What's the deal with that dog," I asked J-Bob when I saw him at the Dairy Queen one day.

"Now don't get discombobalated," he said. "Truth is, when he was a pup he got into some paint stripper. I was hoping it didn't burn his voice box too bad, but looks like I was wrong."

He looked out the window for a minute. "Tell you what," he said, pulling a wadded bill from his overalls, "here's a fiver back at you for damaged merchandise."

I flattened the bill out on the table. Wanda came up and put two D-Q Dudes, a large red basket of fries, and a giant strawberry shake in front of J-Bob.

"Look at it this way," he said. He hinged open one of the sesame seed buns and farted a puddle of ketchup onto the greasy patty. "What you got is a silent killer. Hell, a barking dog ain't good for nothing but running prowlers off. Yours, now. Yours," he said, squinting and pointing the tip of the plastic ketchup bottle at me. "Burglar comes around. Gets close to the house. Shee-it, that sum-bitch won't know what's got him till he has a ass full o' teeth. Har! Har!" He bit into the burger and I pocketed the bill.

The lunch crowd thinned out. Wanda was taking a break in the back corner by the water fountain. Her baby wedged between herself and the wobbling table, Wanda shooed flies from the child's head with one hand while expressing milk from a small, uncovered breast with the other. For two weeks in high school, she had been my girlfriend. She got pregnant when she was sixteen and dropped out. She was pretty and friendly and had talked about going to LSU and studying art. Afterwards, nobody would have anything to do with her. She couldn't even get a cashier's job, so she moved outside the city to Tickfaw. She never smiles, but when she takes your order you can tell she's missing a front tooth. Her first kid must be fifteen by now. Maybe pregnant herself. Imagine that—being a grandmother before you're thirty. A few weeks back, I was buying some Twinkies at Lena's Grocery and saw Wanda paying for some Pampers with food stamps. Nobody in Tickfaw would have attracted the Wanda I had known, yet here she was with another papoose. I made a mental note of her as another instance of a world too fertile for its own good.

Despite that picture of Wanda and the baby sticking in the back of my mind, everything was sailing along like I wanted. I had plenty of time to think, read, and fish. To do nothing and not feel guilty about it. This was the life. No wife to check in or out with. No papers to grade. No deadlines to mark time by. Life could go on forever. In late spring, I spent long stretches of time watching my dumbly happy dog chase sparrows taking dust baths. That's how he got his name. Dusty.

Then my real estate brother called.

Remember that about not trusting someone who'd sell a friend's repossessed home? You'll recall the house my brother sold me in Old Town was a repo. Therefore, my brother was not to be trusted. I should have known. I hadn't had my extra things in the mother-in-law cottage a month when he calls me up and says, "Have your stuff out by the weekend. I got some suckers willing to pay three hundred a month."

———

The Fletchers showed up Saturday morning in a mid-sized Ryder van and hauled their belongings by themselves, so they couldn't have had much money. The girl played off to the side, talking away at whatever she was holding. The father was one of those straight-ahead workers. At every pass the mother made from the van to the house, she cast suspicious glances at me on my porch tossing Dusty miniature dog biscuits.

That afternoon, I heard a little knock at my door and opened it, pretty much knowing what to expect.

"Guess what?" she said. This was an auspicious beginning.

"What?"

"I lost my front tooth last week." As proof, she lifted her top lip from her teeth like a snarling dog and wiggled the tip of her tongue in the gap.

"Uh-huh, I see that."

"And guess what?" She looked like every little girl you've ever seen, except she had a lazy eye, which might have been cute, but it gave me the uneasy feeling she had her eyes on two separate things and no matter what I guessed she'd say I was wrong.

"What?"

"The tooth fairy left me a quarter."

"Uh-huh."

"And guess what?"

"What?"

"She forgot to take the tooth, so guess what?"

"What?" I saw her mother coming for her.

"I put it back under the pillow the next night, and guess what?"

"What?"

"I got another quarter." She giggled. Her mother stopped at the edge of their gravel drive.

"Wendy! I told you not to talk to strangers. Get in this house right now!" Wendy ran down the wooden porch with her arms out like an airplane and launched off the end. She hit flat with both feet and whirled around.

"Guess what?"

"I give up."

"I have another loose tooth!"

"Good deal," I said.

Monday after work, I stepped out of my car.

"Guess what grade I'm in," Wendy said.

This could get old fast, I thought. "First."

"*Fir*-erst?" she sang. "How'd you know?"

"I know everything."

"Then guess what I got for Easter."

"Eggs."

"No, you silly. Everybody gets aigs. I mean something special."

"I give up."

"An Easter bunny."

"That so? One of those chocolate jobs?"

"No, a live one, and guess what color he is."

"White with pink eyes."

"That's right!" she squealed. "And he's got a floppy ear and Mom says he's going to have some baby rabbits real soon."

"He is? I'd like to see that. What's his name?" Here came the mother hen.

"Wendy, get in your own yard right this minute and don't let me have to tell you again, little lady."

Wendy covered her mouth like she was telling a secret.

She scrunched her nose up and tittered, "Bugs Bunny."

"That's original," I said. Her mother detected my sarcasm from across the yard. Immune to her mother's shrewishness, Wendy bounded away, pleased as could be of my approval.

As soon as Bugs Bunny's cage was set up out back, Dusty went to peeing on everything in sight. Every squirt said, "This is mine. This is mine, too, stay away from it." Each day after school, Wendy took Bugs from his cage. She petted him and dressed him up in doll clothes and set him loose. The rabbit kicked his back legs up like a rodeo bull, trying to free himself from the dress.

Wendy was a child of delight. That delight escaped from her in long teapot shrieks, in flying hair and flailing arms as she windmilled after the rabbit, trying hard not to catch it. Even in the dusty yard, she played in Sunday School dresses and black Mary Janes. Her pink socks had lacy white frills at the top. She was a child of music and dance, of sunshine and joy. And I didn't like her much. She was too busy for me. She annoyed me.

The dog went nuts whenever Wendy turned the rabbit loose. Dusty stayed on his side of his marks, wearing himself out loping around, jumping in the air, and forcing ghostly barks from his parched throat. The rabbit ran from Wendy, kicking up dust and making sharp turns when she reached for him. When he tired out, he sat still and twitched his nose. Just as Wendy was about to pick him up, he'd shoot away in a dead run straight for my yard, then, without losing speed, turn ninety degrees at Dusty's invisible boundary.

Saturday morning, early, I was awakened by Wendy's high-pitched singing of my favorite songs.

"You dee-zerve a break today—at McDonald's. You dee-zerve a break today—at McDonald's." I lifted my bedroom window and peeped out. The sun icepicked my eyes. Wendy was skipping around a pine tree. "You dee-zerve a break to-day—at McDonald's." Round and round she went, tirelessly.

"This is just what I need," I said. I shut the window and turned on the attic fan to see if I could muffle the noise.

Throughout the day, as if sent by God to torment *me* personally, Wendy rehearsed the jingles of the leading brands. "Just for the fun of it, just for the taste of it, Di-et Coke!" She nearly drove me insane with one small variation, whose effect was not unlike Chinese water torture. "Just for the fun of it, just for the taste of it—Di-et Coke! Just for the fun of it, just for the taste of it—, —Di-et Coke! Just for the fun of it, just for the taste of it, Di-et Coke! Just for the fun of it, just for the taste of it—, —, —Di-et Coke!" My mind leaned in the direction of her repetitions, mesmerized by the rhythm, and then she would undercut my expectation until I thought I would scream.

That's when I decided on the fence. I thought a hurricane

fence would be amusing, one of those link affairs Dusty could get his snout through and scare the shit out of that rabbit. I knew ultimately I wouldn't build a hurricane fence, but I lay in bed a good while enjoying the fantasy. Then I decided on the basket-weave wooden fence. Just because I had to listen to Wendy didn't mean I had to see her, too.

That afternoon, I paced off my property and did some rough math on the back of a telephone book to get an idea of how many boards I would need. Monday, I put a "Gone" sign on the T-building, and drove out on 190 West to the Crapanzano Lumber Yard, where Time was rounding our old high school shot putter into shape. Even though I hadn't seen him in several years, he gave me a good deal on some cypress planks and creosote posts.

I could hardly wait until Saturday to start the project, so you can imagine my happiness when my Wendy alarm went off. "Just for the fun of it, just for the taste of it, Di-et Coke. Just for the fun of it, just for the taste of it—, —Di-et Coke." I flung the sheet off, swung my legs sideways, and said with an evil grin, "Just for the fun of it, I'd like to choke you." I was in a good mood. Today was the day I would start digging and dovetailing and nailing Wendy and her wicked-witch mother out of my sight forever. That made me think about Jake.

Where did I pick up his name? Oh yeah, Wendy called her parents by their first names. How is it these gentle men so often marry those foul-natured women? The thought of him making love to her gave me that fingernails-on-slate feeling.

I began on the side of my yard farthest from Wendy's, thinking I'd give her parents time to see what was going on so they could drag the rabbit cage away from my property line and give me room to work by the time I got there. Wendy, though, interpreted my fence-building as a social event, like a cakewalk or a barn raising. As soon as I started ramming the posthole digger into the packed earth, she snatched up Bugs for a visit.

"Whatcha doing, Mr. Beamer?" I was determined not to say a word.

"Huh? Whatcha doing, Mr. Beamer? Huh?" One eye was off a bit, but the other was dead center on me.

Dusty, now a clumsy five-month-old, jumped up to the rabbit and snuffled his fur until it was matted with slobber. Struggling with the lively rabbit, Wendy snickered the whole time, ignorant that most German shepherds would have eaten Bugs alive. If I had a watchdog, it was the kind my dad told me he had as a boy. "I owned a watchdog that watched a burglar take everything we had."

When Dusty was worn out from nuzzling the rabbit, he hiked his leg and peed on my jeans to make sure Bugs wouldn't get any proprietary ideas. This sent Wendy into a giggling fit that brought her mother out screaming. I'll say one thing for Mrs. Fletcher. She never profaned my property with so much as her little toe. I didn't think she could yell much louder, but when she saw Dusty, in the confusion that overtakes young dogs, mount my leg and give me a few thrusts, the woman sounded like a foghorn.

Without further interruption, I finished the west-side section that weekend. During the weekday evenings, I completed half the north side, and the following weekend, I finished the north side.

As the earth moved into May, the drought worsened. Lack of rain, combined with too much shade and heat, made my backyard hard as concrete. The afternoon heat postponed my work until the weekend. Early Saturday morning, when the dew was still on the dust, even before my Wendy alarm went off, I was up breaking ground. I was nearly to the cage, which Wendy's parents hadn't moved, before she blessed me with song.

With each passing hour, the curtain closed further on my neighbors. Just before noon, I reached Bugs's cage. Originally in the shade throughout the day, it was now exposed to the bare sun, as summer approached, for a few hours at midday. I saw that the rabbit's water bowl was dry and called to Wendy. She was sitting on a blanket under a tallow tree in the middle of her yard, having a picnic with some imaginary friends whom she chattered with nonstop.

She seemed really distressed as she saw the tip of the rabbit's tongue lapping in and out of his mouth. She shot open the barrel bolt of the door and poured half a glass of red Kool-Aid, ice and all, into the bowl. The rabbit went to it immediately and didn't raise up until he was through. The little red moustache and goatee pleased Wendy immensely, and she vowed to fill Bugs Bunny's bowl from then on only with Kool-Aid.

As I worked by the cage, the mild 4-H smell led me to inspect the rabbit droppings underneath. There, around the clean, corky pellets, I suppose with the help of the morning dew, grew a patch of fine hair-like grass.

My shirt had been off for over an hour. It was high time I went to my own watering hole. When I finished lunch, I filled Dusty's water pail and carried it out to his tree, and as I dodged his smelly piles, I thought, for all he was worth as a watchdog, I might as well have a rabbit.

Apparently, the Kool-Aid revived old Bugs. As I worked past his cage, he stood on his hind legs, sniffing me through the mesh. I saw his little nails hooked on the wires for support. Then he leaned on the door, which Wendy had forgotten to relatch, and tumbled onto the hard ground. He squiggled for a second, then righted himself. Braced to run, he looked around nervously with panic-stricken eyes.

Mrs. Fletcher had called Wendy in out of the heat, so it was up to me to return Bugs to his cage. I eased up on him slowly and grabbed him by the scruff of his neck. Then I cradled him while putting him in the cage, and the taut belly under the fur reminded me that he—she—was pregnant. I pulled the bolt to and dropped the hob into its catch. Even though it was only three o'clock, the heat forced me to retire for the day. By noon Sunday, I had only a small section to complete before the sun drove me inside. My private celebration at walling the Fletchers off from my world would have to wait until the next afternoon.

In the T-building Monday, I got antsy around lunch time and decided to close for the day to finish the job before the Fletchers got home. Looking down the fenceline while pulling into my drive, I found it a pleasant thought to think: on this side is my property, on that, theirs, and in a couple of hours we might as well be on opposite sides of the earth.

I ate a hurried lunch, anxious to get to it, and stepped onto my back porch with a smile that died on my face when I saw Dusty bounding around and tossing the rabbit in the air. When I ran for him, he thought I wanted to play and shook the rabbit like an old towel.

"You dumb shit," I yelled and kicked him under the ribs hard enough to send him reeling and make him release the rabbit. A sputtering whimper came from his throat as he crawled toward his tree. I rolled the rabbit over in the dust, hoping for a miracle. I couldn't have been more than a minute too late. He was still warm. His fur, muddy and matted with slobber, had only a few splashes of blood on it. The stupid dog was probably playing and didn't even mean to kill him.

On the ground where Dusty had been tossing the rabbit lay evidence of his loosening bowels. I picked Bugs up by the back of his neck. Something resembling a damp piece of clay dropped from him. I realized then that what I had taken for pellets were stillborn baby rabbits. Their furless skin was bluishly translucent and revealed their insides. I counted the wet lumps around me. Seven. I put Bugs back on the ground and squeezed her belly. Slowly from its dead mother emerged the last of the litter, faintly wriggling. I placed the little creature on top of its mother and gathered the others. Holding them in my cupped hands, I walked out to the back fence line, inspecting them along the way to see if any were alive. Dusty circled to the far side of his tree and peeked around it at me.

"You dumb shit, look what you did." I held the premature kits out to him. He lifted his head a bit and when he backed away, I tossed the bodies over the fence.

How was I going to explain to the witch what had happened? This was all Wendy's fault anyway. She probably opened the cage the day before to fill Bugs's bowl with Kool-Aid and forgot to latch the door again. I knelt by the rabbit to think. The baby rabbit moving around on the damp fur triggered the idea.

I picked up Bugs and the baby like a cushion with a rare jewel on it and brought them inside. In the bathroom, I took out a washcloth and set the baby on it. Maybe I could feed it with an eyedropper. I put Bugs in the sink and ran warm water over the dirty, clotted fur. Then I grabbed the tube of Prell from the shower and lathered her body up good. The suds and rabbit fur combined to make a pleasant odor. When I rinsed her off, I was disheartened. The wet fur had turned a dark gray, and I doubted she could be restored to her natural condition.

I started at the ears with the blow dryer. I turned it on hot and high, and as I blew against the nap and russed the fur with my fingers, her coat turned a fluffy, snowy white. Ten minutes later, I held the most beautiful pelt I had ever seen.

I nudged the baby rabbit to see if it was still alive. It didn't move. I poked it to see if it was asleep. Then I brought my head very close to see if I could detect its tiny nostrils flaring as it breathed. It smelled faintly of sour milk. And it was dead.

I looked at my watch. I had a safety margin of at least an hour before Wendy came home from school. Outside, I felt silly. A grown man holding a coiffured dead rabbit. I planted Bugs in her cage and set the baby on the bare wire next to her. It occurred to me then that I had to recover the others. For nearly half an hour, I foraged in the dry weeds and under-brush behind the fenceline. I found five of the rabbits, and had to pick ants off of those, but I couldn't chance hunting any longer and getting caught red-handed.

I was relieved to start working on the fence. Sheets of sweat poured over me immediately. I felt as if it disguised my guilt. Such is the power of sweat that a man laved by its cleans-ing influence will, while speaking, believe himself and be believed. Why did I feel guilty? I hadn't done a thing to the damn rabbit. Except give her a decent burial. Probably the cleanest rabbit alive. Or dead. By the time Wendy drove up with her mom, the fence was up and I was inside.

I had hoped the fence would insure me against ever seeing the family again, but I knew better, even as I was building it.

Someone defined purgatory as a place where you have to stay with the person you hate most until you completely un-derstand and therefore completely love him. I waited—one hour, two hours—sitting in my recliner staring at a blank TV screen. I thought, should I escape to silence, or learn to live quietly in the midst of the noise and trash? I've tried. God knows I have. It seems the only thing left for me is to dis-combobalate to Juneau, then move north, as the population closes around me, to Anchorage, Fairbanks, and at last Point Barrow, and when its cold environs are overpopulated by the last human-hating humans, jump off the edge of the world.

"Mm-mmm, good. Mm-mmm, good. That's what Campbell's soups are, Mm-mmm, good." Wendy had finished her afternoon snack. She was now playing in the backyard. "Mm-mmm, good. Mm-mmm, good. That's what Campbell's soups are, — Mm-mmm, good! Mm-mmm, good. Mm-mmm, good-good-good. That's what Campbell's soups are, —."

My chest swelled with fear. I waited. I could just about time it. I stood up. The little knock at my door made my knees go weak. I walked slowly to the door and opened it as if I expected to see the Grim Reaper making a personal call. I looked down at Wendy, who looked up at me, one eye sad, one eye full of wonder.

"Mr. Beamer," she said. "Guess what?"

"What?"

"Yesterday my rabbit died of thirst and we buried him by the fence but today when I came home he was in his cage again, all clean and white."

I opened my mouth, but nothing came out.

"Mr. Beamer?"

"What?"

"Do you believe in the Easter bunny?"

{8}

Snake Summer

I was visiting my cousin Elton, that summer of the snakes, when it happened.

Aunt Iota had grumbled about the thunderstorm all through dinner. After helping with the dishes, I stepped out onto the balcony. The rain was starting to stop. Hundreds of mosquito hawks quivered in the heat rising from the Opelousas hayfield.

Elton walked through the double doors and leaned against a column. A garter snake peeked over the rail, then slithered into a potted fern. Elton swatted it off into the rock garden below. He stared blankly at the hayfield until a hoarse, two-note moaning drew his eyes to the pond.

"That's a largemouth bullfrog calling his mate."

I looked at the pond, barely visible through a stand of pine trees, then back at the mosquito hawk wings winking sunlight.

Elton shoved me. "Let's go catch him."

I ran behind Elton until we reached the fig tree by the gate. Elton stopped and held a finger against his lips. While listening for the next fit of moaning, he reached up and plucked a ripe fig. He looked at it and passed it back to me. I ate it. He tightened his fist around a green one and yanked, showering us with rainwater.

We tiptoed through the gate and circled right. Elton motioned for me to ease down by the water. A few steps later, he froze. He looked up at me and nodded. When he threw the fig, the frog bounded three times in the shallows, stopping half-submerged in a clot of moss right at my feet. I kept my eyes on the frog's eyes and reached around behind him with my right hand.

My great fear that summer was falling asleep and forgetting to breathe. I would lie in bed listening to the ceiling-fan chain clinking against the light fixture, breathing in and out very carefully until it felt like I was falling through space. Then I would awaken, gasping for breath.

That's the feeling I had when I saw the long black snake, thicker than my arm, weaving toward the frog. I couldn't breathe. The snake stopped to consider his next move. One of the frog's eyes swiveled from me to the snake. When the frog leaned toward open water, the snake struck. Through the splashing, I saw the snake's jaw clamped on a webbed foot. The frog struggled toward deeper water, taking the snake down with it. I watched in horror as the water roiled, the tail of the snake now and again writhing above the surface. Then it was calm.

Elton's voice came to me from a distance. "Awesome! Did you see that?"

I looked at him and clutched my chest, then pounded it, and the breath came.

"He woulda fanged me for sure if I'd grabbed for your stupid frog! I'd prolly be dead by now."

Elton laughed and shoved me toward the water.

"You ignoramus! That weren't nothing but a old harmless water snake. Poisonous snake's got a head shaped like this." His forefingers and thumbs formed an arrowhead.

I ran and stood on the ramp leading to the dock. Elton

sneered.

"That old snake's long gone. Let's crawl under the dock and see if we can snatch a crawfish or a tadpole."

I shook my head.

"Well," he said, looking around, "then gimme a boost so I can get that pear."

I looked up at the fruit, then down to the base of the tree where I'd have to stand. My heart surged and my breath stopped. All I could do was point at the glistening black coil. When I turned to Elton, he was already running. He stopped and yelled.

"Run, Abbie! That's a rattle-headed copper moccasin!"

Back at the house, Uncle El laughed. He was finishing his tea in a deerhide rocking chair on the porch.

"Well, wha'd you see, Hoss? It was either a water moccasin or a rattlesnake or a copperhead, but it couldn't of been all three."

Embarrassed, Elton slunk down the stairs to the comforting shade under the house. The house sat on telephone poles, with latticework on two sides. Uncle El had a workbench by a wood rack, and Elton was convinced that the jangle of pipes and disorderly stacks of lumber hid a treasure chest. I got a splinter in my hand in no time and wandered over to the workbench to open the little drawers. I had found a tray of shiny silver washers and was trying one on for a wedding ring when Elton called out.

When I reached him, he was holding a fat container in his lap. It was a Community Coffee can, rusty orange with white lettering, and it was obviously heavy. Elton wiped at his face and left a swatch of black across one cheek.

Grinning, he popped the lid off in my direction to show me the contents. There were coins of all sizes right up to the brim. My heart swelled like it does when I see the first

Christmas lights of the season.

"It's Deddy's licker money."

Elton slapped the lid back on and hustled the can over to the workbench. He spilled the contents onto the grimy wood.

My eyes widened. "How much you think there is?"

"Oh," he said, "a hundred dollars, easy. Maybe a thousand."

"Let's count it."

He looked at me like I had lost my mind. "That would take forever, you idiot. Besides, it don't matter if it's a million bucks, we can only take enough for some candy and ice cream before Deddy notices."

We ran our fingers through the mountain of coins, then started separating out the quarters.

"That way, we get the most money, and the can don't look like it's been robbed."

We counted out three dollars apiece, then swept the change back into a heap just to admire it. I had a crick in my neck from leaning over, so I twisted it to get some relief. Two inches from my nose, woven all through the latticework, was a long white snake. My legs collapsed beneath me. Elton kept working the coins with his hands as I looked at the snake in frozen horror. I followed the tail until it tapered and disappeared behind a rusty barbecue pit, then traced the other way until the body curved behind a warped calendar blocking its head.

Finally able to move, I reached up and grabbed Elton's arm. Coins spilled all around me onto the concrete.

"Hey," Elton yelled. "What's the big idea?"

I pointed. Elton jerked back, studied the snake for a second, and burst out bragging.

"That ain't nothing but the skin of a chicken snake. Damn longest one I ever seen, though. Let's get Deddy's tape measure and measure it." Elton started rummaging around the cluttered table. "Can you imagine how long that sucker is now that he's shed his skin?"

I stood up. "Well I don't care if it's a fishing worm, I'm not waiting around to see where it pops up next." I started for the stairs.

"Wait! Let's get some plums first."

My stomach had been hurting, but the excitement of the coins covered up the ache. That afternoon, we had eaten blackberries and chewed on honeysuckle. After dinner, I ate the fig.

"Why do you always have to be eating something?"

Elton stared at me. "Because if it's ripe, you gotta eat it right then, that's all."

I held the plums in the lap of my T-shirt as we climbed the stairs. I told Aunt Iota about the snakes while she washed the fruit.

"Elton, honey," she said, "why don't you get those plastic eggs left over from Easter? Y'all could put some treats inside and hide them around the house."

Elton turned so his mother wouldn't see him rolling his eyes. I looked away to keep from laughing. When I looked back, he had flipped his eyelids inside-out. Aunt Iota exiled us to Elton's room to eat the bowl of plums. We filled the purple and yellow eggs with gems from Elton's rock collection and hid them around the house until Uncle El had heard enough squealing.

Sitting still on the porch, I felt my stomachache again.

"I know!" Elton said. "Let's go up in the attic."

From the side porch, Elton looked through the door window. As Aunt Iota would put it, Uncle El was asleep on the couch watching a baseball game. He was real cranky on account of he was starting to stop smoking, so we didn't want to wake him up.

Elton got a chair and put it under the access panel. He pulled the rope real easy so the springs wouldn't squeak. Then he unfolded the ladder. I put the plastic eggs in the belly of my T-shirt, then put the hem in my mouth so I could use both hands sneaking up.

It was dark and hot in the attic. Elton flipped a switch and a bulb sputtered dimly. Old chairs and tables, a baby crib, and some lamps were wrecked against other odds and ends all over the attic. It was the perfect place to hide Easter eggs.

"Step on the joists," Elton said, pointing. "If you step on the insulation, you'll fall through the ceiling into the house. It ain't nothing but sheetrock under there."

We moved around carefully, exploring the junkfield of treasures. Elton got on his hands and knees and crawled to the light seeping from the edge of the house.

"Look at this!" He held up an egg. "There's three of 'em in a nest."

By the time I reached him, Elton was strike-striking a match, trying to catch something on fire.

"Are you crazy?"

"No," he said, holding up a small silver can. "It's Sterno."

I looked at him blankly.

"Canned heat," he said. "For camping out. We'll use it like a candle to look for more eggs."

"Well, be careful. With all this stuff, you tump it over and we'll go up in flames."

Elton shook his head. "What's gonna make me tump it over?"

Elton struck the match again. It lit and he held it over the little can. There was a small explosion and he dropped the can onto the yellow insulation.

I gasped and Elton giggled.

"It's a gel," he said. "It don't spill."

He held the can up like a candle and started crawling along the eaves.

"You reckon they're bat eggs?" I suggested.

"Don't be stupid. Bats don't lay eggs." He kept moving. "They must be owl eggs. Hey, look at this!"

He held the blue flame up to a cluster of hair.

"What is it?"

"Daddy long-legs." He put the flame to the cluster. The spiders scattered. I jerked my head up and hit a bent nail poking through the roof.

"Stop it," I said, rubbing my head. "We're supposed to be hunting for eggs."

We crawled along until we hit some ductwork that veered us toward the single light bulb in the center of the attic. I stood and stretched. Looking down, I saw one egg on the brim of a moldy black cowboy hat. I stooped to pick it up. Elton yanked my arm.

"Watch out!"

A snake peered at me from around the crown of the hat.

My breathing started to stop. "What kind is it?"

We watched the brown snake glide over the yellow insulation.

"I don't know," Elton said. "I ain't never seen one like that, but he's been swallowing them eggs." The snake looked all bumpy, like a long camel with five humps. "His head ain't poisonous, but he might wrap around you like a rabbit and squeeze the death out of you."

As if on cue, the snake turned and glided toward us. A lump of fear filled my throat like I had swallowed an egg. I backed against the ductwork. The snake wanted the last egg. Keeping my eyes on its head, I reached back for something to strike it with. I looked at what my hand grabbed. It was an old fishing rod, broken at the tip.

I lunged forward and swung the rod down. The insulation swallowed my left foot and I broke through the sheetrock. It felt like I had fallen through myself, like a sock turned inside out. I was stuck with one leg in the room below, the other right up beside my face, like a cheerleader doing a high-kick. My face came to rest beside the shabby hat.

"Deddy's gonna kill us," Elton stated like it was a law of nature.

I looked for the snake. My breath was wheezing in and out. I could move my arms but not my legs. I wiggled the foot that was down in my bedroom below. It was like I was in the room, looking up and seeing my leg hanging from the ceiling.

I cried out for Elton to help me, but he was gone. I tried to stop breathing so hard. I heard doors opening and shutting beneath me. Then it was quiet. When I looked back at the hat, the snake was looking at me. It moved toward the hat and unhinged its mouth over the egg. The egg barely moved as it slowly disappeared into the snake.

The egg was almost gone when Elton was suddenly beside me. He was breathing hard, a machete dangling from his hand. He stared at the snake but couldn't move. I reached up and grabbed the machete. I swung at the snake. Detached from its body, the head with the egg inside rolled over and over until it was right beside me. The body kept wiggling. It wrapped around the hat and squeezed. Blood was oozing from the neck.

"Help me outta here, you idiot!"

Elton came unfrozen and started pulling me up. I felt my leg scraping against the sheetrock. When I stood, a thin stream of blood trickled down my leg.

"It cut me when you pulled me through."

"No," Elton said. "You was already bleeding when I saw

your leg dangling in the room. Deddy's gonna kill us. How we gonna fix this hole?"

My head suddenly cleared. "We can worry about that later. Get the snake first. We gotta save those eggs."

Elton looked at me like I was insane, then stepped to block me.

"Get out the way, Elton Jennings." The body of the snake was still twisting, but not much. I used the machete blade to move it over a joist, aimed, then cut that part of the snake in two. I grabbed the segment in my hand and squeezed until the egg came out. Five more times. Then we put them back in their nests, three on the floppy hat brim, three in a hollow spot we found on the insulation by a busted doll cradle.

After Elton's beating and my bath, we were sitting on the porch watching the sun start to stop shining. He didn't say anything about the beating, and I didn't tell him what Aunt Iota had said about the blood when I couldn't find a cut anywhere—she said I was a lady now and the blood coming out of my body was a broken egg and I could have babies now if I wasn't careful.

{9}

Is

Josh was late for the play. The Civic Center lot was full, so he had parked by the funeral home and was walking the half-mile in 90 percent humidity. Midway there, his shirt stuck to his skin. Just two weeks ago, he had driven down from the light Ozark air to this muggy armpit of Louisiana.

"If you want to learn how to write, go to Lake Charles," his teacher told him. "It's produced three Pulitzer Prize winners in ten years. Get there before the mojo wears off."

When the Famous Author dragged in twenty minutes late for his first class, Josh knew he had made a mistake. Plus, the man looked like Jiminy Cricket.

Dr. Cricket missed the next two sessions for autograph parties, then dismissed class after ten minutes. "Attend the play at Rosa Hart Theatre. Drama teaches the power of dialogue. Young writers blather about cochineal sunsets and Ramona's crystalline eyes. Get rid of that crap."

"Great," Josh thought. "Now we gotta watch experimental junk by a dead foreigner."

His shoes slapped the sidewalk with purpose, though not for curtain-rise. It was too late for that. Rushing for the air-conditioned dark of the auditorium, he summarized his dilemma: if I walk slow, I won't sweat as much, but I'll spend more time in the heat; if I walk fast, I'll sweat more, but for less time.

"Josh!" The feminine voice spun him around, and the world went still. "Oh, my gosh, I can't believe this." She rose from the wrought-iron chair and ran towards him, then stopped at an invisible boundary. When he cautiously approached, she reached out and touched his arm. "I can't believe it's you."

"Do I know you?"

The girl looked like she wanted to cry. "It's Rachael."

"Wow," he said. "It *is* you. Where are your glasses? And what—?" He reached up and touched her hair. "—did you do to your hair?"

She laughed. "This is my real hair. I was a death-maiden at Arkansas. You thought coffin-black was natural?"

The world kicked into motion again. Rachael led Josh by the hand to her table, then called to a waiter coming down the steps. An ashtray and two wineglasses covered most of the circular glass. She extracted a lighter from her purse and began twirling it in her hand.

"So you smoke now."

"No, it just gives me something to fidget with."

He nodded, remembering. "What are you doing here?"

"At the café?"

"No, in Lake Charles."

"Oh." She leaned over, excited. "Have you seen the sunsets over the lake? They're magnificent!"

"So there's a—"

"No. At least not a *real* photography school. But the sunsets! You wouldn't believe how beautifully the colors mix with the chemicals spewing from those refineries."

The tables crowded each other, making Josh uneasy. He thought everyone was listening to Rachael's overreaction.

"You seem different," he said.

"I am. I killed the old Rachael to work through all that Arkansas weirdness I was going through."

"Your dad?"

"It wasn't him, it was me. It just took me a while to figure that out."

Josh lifted his drink and gazed into her eyes. All he could think was *crystalline*. Over her shoulder, the Civic Center looked like a stage set propped against a blue wall. *The sky is cerulean*, he thought.

Josh looked back at Rachael. "I'm such an idiot."

She reached over and put her hand on his. "Nooo. Why do you say that?"

"What am I doing here? I couldn't write my way out of a soufflé."

"But you *can*," she said. "You were *so* good at it."

The enthusiasm of her voice made the tables around them go quiet.

"Remember?" she said. "You'd call to say goodnight and I'd make you tell me a bedtime story. After a while, I couldn't stand it so I'd drive to your place and make you act out those scenes. You were *very* creative."

A couple at the next two-top snickered, then turned their heads away.

"Terrific," Josh whispered. "That's just what I want to do, prostitute my talent writing romantic porn."

They talked about Fayetteville, who was still there, what went wrong, then Josh glanced around for a waiter.

"What's the name of this place, Waiting for Godot?"

Rachael giggled. "It's a new place. It's called Is."

"Well, here's a prediction for you. In a month, Is will be *Ain't*. You couldn't buy a waiter with the Hope Diamond."

"They're still getting organized. Have some patience. That's what *you* used to tell *me*."

Josh remembered her manic personality. When Rachael

got overexcited, he'd suggest she pretend to be someone else. He couldn't believe five years had passed.

"Somebody told me you died," he said.

"Died!"

"That's a polite way of saying 'committed suicide.'"

"Why would I commit suicide?" Rachael glanced at her watch.

"It was always something—your father, your car, exams, money. It drove me insane."

Rachael touched his hand, this time letting hers linger there. "That was so long ago I'm not even the same person."

Josh didn't need convincing. He could sense it was true. They talked awhile and he relaxed. When Rachael excused herself to the restroom, waiters swarmed the tables. For the first time, Josh noticed the wooden decks that were cantilevered over the courtyard, exotic plants hanging everywhere, camouflaging dozens of people buzzing like locusts in the heat.

In the fifteen minutes Rachael was gone, Josh ordered and finished a glass of ice water. To stay cool, he sat very still, moving only his eyes to look at the diners—all overdressed for an outdoor café in August, he thought.

Rachael bounded down the brick steps and resumed. "It must be thrilling to study under a Pulitzer Prize winner. You're not fooling me with that false modesty, Joshua Beck. Everyone knows he doesn't take just anybody into his workshop."

Josh shook his head. "He can write, but he sure can't teach. Just spews a bunch of clichés, then turns us loose. *Dialogue is power. Fear adjectives.* He's like a parrot."

Rachael reached over and slapped Josh on the shoulder. "Oh, you're just joshing me."

Several couples on the tier above them laughed.

"What else, what else?" Rachael spoke like a parrot, distracting him from the eavesdroppers.

Josh frowned. He didn't know this Rachael. He spoke like he was testing dangerous waters. "*Friction is the essence of fiction.*" A wounded look appeared on Rachael's face, then she recomposed her muscles into a smile. "But not of relationships," Josh concluded.

"Oh, I don't know. It was kind of fun. Fuss, then kiss and make up." Her eyes went sleepy and she slunk down in the chair. "Don't you remember?"

Josh ran his fingers through his hair. "Please," he said. "It's hot enough out here."

Rachael laughed too loud. When she bent toward him, even her whisper was loud. "That's one thing I was good at. I could melt you like butter on those midwinter nights." She sat back to watch him suffer. After enough time had passed, she leaned over. "I have a studio apartment just around the corner. Let's go." She stood and offered her hand. Josh took it and followed. When they reached the invisible boundary, Rachael stopped and a *maître d'* stepped briskly in front of them.

Josh's heart pounded with lust, fear, embarrassment. "I'm so sorry, sir. We just forgot, honest to God." He reached for his wallet in a panic.

"Well, ladies and gentleman," the stately man said, turning to the crowd of onlookers. "All the world **Is** indeed a stage, wouldn't you say?" His white-gloved hands started clapping soundlessly, followed by thunderous applause.

Josh looked at everyone looking at him. He was horrified. He looked at Rachael.

"What is this? It's a—what do you call it?"

"Improvisational theater," she replied.

Josh saw himself from a distance, as if he were watching

someone else make a fool of himself. On the third deck, a man in a white tuxedo peered around a fern at Josh and raised a glass to toast his performance.

It was Jiminy Cricket.

Josh's mind was racing. "But I love her!" he screamed at the viewers. "My love for her is *real!*"

The patrons stood and applauded louder. Josh turned to Rachael. She was fixing her lipstick in a compact. The cheering subsided into the usual scraping of chairs as the audience prepared to depart.

An elderly man with a bejeweled wife crossed the invisible line and touched Josh's arm. "Yes, but her love for you *wasn't.*"

Josh broke into a sweat. Nausea swept over him. He felt like he was in a play within a play. Rachael grabbed the old man's arm and pulled him back. "How do you know *that?*"

Startled, the white-haired man said, "What?"

"How do you *know* my love for him isn't real?"

As Rachael hooked her arm around Josh and steered him down the sidewalk toward a cochineal sunset, he wondered how he could ever be sure of anything now.

Anything, ever.

{10}

Second Wave

Later that afternoon, at the head of River Road, I was trying to explain the situation to the deputy.

After the first wave of the storm surge, the water on River Road had dropped to three feet, down from eight the day before, when Ike made landfall. In his driveway, Frank and I had loaded his aluminum boat with two Stihl chainsaws and five ice chests of food and water. We were hoisting ourselves into the boat from thigh-deep water.

Frank had just said there was one good thing about the hurricane—the Calcasieu River was quiet. No barge traffic, no jet skis, not even a fishing skiff.

Right then, a bay boat with a 90 Merc came cruising smack down the middle of the road at half speed, shearing off a two-foot wave. If he had planed off, the wake would have been smaller.

Frank had the round, happy face of a Norman Rockwell boy, and he stayed on the alert to help people. "Neighbors first," he always said.

"Hey!" he yelled to the guy. "What are you doing?"

The guy cut the throttle and turned into the driveway like it was a boat stall. Holding a beer and pushing a toothy Hemingway smile at us, he said, "Just looking around to see what I can see."

It wasn't that he was harming anything that hadn't already been water-damaged. The surge had topped out at eight feet on the road, six in our driveways, and five in the houses. For Frank, it was the principle of the thing.

Frank just stared at the guy. This guy was drinking, but not drunk, and he made a quip to bring the heat down a few degrees. When it didn't, he shrugged his shoulders and popped the boat into reverse. The propeller tossed up parts of Frank's lawn like a salad. Just when the boater shifted into forward, Frank took three Paul Bunyan strides and grabbed him by the collar. The guy stopped, but the boat kept going, sliding him over the gunnel into the yard.

Holding the front of the man's shirt with his left hand, Frank hit him three times with his right, pulling him forward each time, like a child working a Bolo paddle.

"Okay," I said, thrusting my arm between them. "That's about fair."

The man staggered back, then pivoted around, looking for his boat. It was passing over the road headed for the river, where he wouldn't be able to retrieve it.

Then the boat took a long, lazy left. "You can tell my account is true because boats always turn left from the propeller's torque." The deputy nodded.

The ghost boat made a sweeping arc and glided between two palm trees on the river side of my lawn. With the evil-seeming intent of a guided missile, it passed over the road, aiming for my house.

A movement in the water drew my eyes down. A school of mullets swam by, working their mouths in a gossipy motion. I don't mean those big mullets. These were finger mullets, just the right size for catching big redfish.

When I saw the boat was going to hit my picture window, I had enough time to expect a sound like a tray of martini glasses breaking in a far room. Instead, the slow-motion impact ended with the sound of a transformer exploding. Right away, I remembered the pane was made of safety glass. It had shattered into thousands of tiny crystals.

The boat's windshield caught on the casing and kept it from entering my house. The boat had been moving so slow its bow wasn't even dented.

The boater's hands clasped the top of his head. "Now look what you've done to my *boat*."

"Your boat?" Frank said. "Your dumb ass has ruined yet another man's property and you're worried about your *boat*?"

Frank hit him again and he sat back in the yellow-brown water, his hands behind his back, bracing himself like a Raggedy Andy doll propped on a pillow, his face looking skyward, barely above water.

When he stood up, watery blood ran from his nose down his chest.

"*Now* look," he complained. "Look what you've done to my *shirt*."

That's when Frank hit him the last time, with the flat part of a paddle.

The deputy frowned at me like he didn't fully comprehend why a man would get so upset over a shirt. My third explanation did the trick.

"It was an Orvis fishing shirt, made of a quick-dry poly/ nylon blend, lined with moisture-wicking fabric, eight front pockets, four interior pockets, two cargo bags on the back, completed by mesh armpits and a vented back for breathability."

"Okay," the deputy nodded, spinning his clipboard around on the hood of his car and tapping. "Sign right here."

{11}

Suburban High Tide

- 1 -

"Wait. Let me get a raincoat."

"Forget the raincoat. You'll get wet anyway."

Halfway down the drive, they launched the canoe in a lake of clear yellow water. Jack guided the canoe into the street and headed south on Ashland. With her paddle, Ami jabbed at debris as the canoe cut a V down the suburban canal.

"Look at that!" she squealed after poking a brown mass that disintegrated into thousands of ants. Later, she touched a big red crawfish with her paddle and watched it scoot to safety. Just as the voyage was growing dull to Ami, a water moccasin dropped from a low branch with a menacing sound and resurfaced as a living S.

Jack touched Ami's hair with his paddle. She screamed and slapped at the imaginary snake, nearly capsizing the canoe. Jack threw his paddle clattering onto the aluminum floor. The moccasin submerged. "Whoa," Jack said, gripping the sides of the canoe and rocking it back and forth until water slipped over the gunnels.

"Stop it, Jack!" Ami cried with a frightened laugh. "You'll tip us over."

In his exaggerated Ami voice, Jack mocked, "You'll tip us

over, Jack. You'll tip us over." Ami swung at him behind her back. Jack laughed. "It's only two feet deep. You wouldn't drown if you fell out, you'd die of a concussion."

Ami twisted around and lunged at her husband with a paddle. With Jack's help, the canoe capsized. Jack managed to keep his head above water. Ami stood up squealing, her dark red hair streaming in her eyes. After a short playfight, they righted the canoe.

"Let's go white-watering," Jack suggested. He ran the stop sign on Ashland, took a left onto Jefferson, and headed for the gully, where the water came to a muddy boil.

"You're not really going to do this," Ami said. She lifted her paddle from the water. Jack dug his in deeper. "Jack-Jack-JACK!" she screamed as the current sucked the canoe forward and propelled it downstream. More confident now in Jack's abilities, Ami laughed with fear and delight.

As they were drawn downstream, Jack reported the sights in his tourism-guide voice. "On the left, ladies and gentlemen, is Old Lady Hawkins's house. To the undisguised pleasure of all her neighbors, the fifty grand she kept buried in the backyard was washed away an hour ago." Occasionally, Jack touched the water with his paddle to steer the canoe right or left. Ami fussed as it began to rain.

"Right," Jack said. "Like you're gonna get wet." Ami giggled, seeing his point. They passed Glover Street and waved at some kids showing off on their bikes for Channel 7's Roving Reporter Newsvan. The cameraman panned towards the canoe and locked on them as they sped downstream. "Coming up, folks, is the McNeese Street rapids." Ami looked up to see foamy water spilling over the street. The canoe bottom struck the cement curb and lodged for a moment before Jack fended off with his paddle and sent the vessel careening across the bridge. The gully curved to the left, parallel with

Sarver Drive. Jack pushed away from a low-hanging limb. Coming out of the turn, the canoe hit a red reflector mounted on a metal pipe and spun around. The gully narrowed and quickened, preventing Jack from straightening the canoe.

"Hold tight," he commanded Ami, who was no longer laughing. A hundred yards later, the gully widened into a peaceful expanse of slow-purling swells. "See," Jack laughed. "No big deal." They relaxed in the canoe and drifted backwards downstream. The gully suddenly narrowed again and Jack felt the canoe lift in the rising water at the bottleneck, then plunge and shoot downstream to meet the bayou. Where Pleasant Drive intersected Sarver, Jack, glancing over his shoulder, saw water splashing against the square maw of a concrete structure built to replace the old creosote bridge.

Facing upstream, Ami was oblivious to the danger behind her. Jack scooped into the current and tried to paddle away from the bridge towards Sarver Drive. Over Ami's head he saw the Channel 7 Newsvan feeling its way down Sarver, its bumper dozing a hump of water before it. The canoe's square stern struck the concrete abutment with a metallic thump. Ami tumbled backwards, hitting her head on a reinforcement strut.

"Don't move!" Jack yelled. "It's all right. Just don't move or you'll tip us over." From the corner of his eye, Jack saw the newsvan ease to a halt. He looked up to see a reporter with a video camera rising out of the sunroof like a periscope. The man focused his camera on the canoe, then panned across the scene for an establishing shot. Jack knew he was covering the area around the canoe so his viewers could see the water rushing from upstream and slapping against the bridge face, forming a backwash of muddy froth, an occasional wave bucking over the curb.

"Hey, can you give us a hand!" Jack hollered at the reporter.

The man waved.

Jack struggled to keep the canoe pointed upstream. With Ami down and towards the stern, the bow cantilevered out of the water. Depending on the shifting current, he paddled on either side of the canoe to maintain its balance. The brief eddies his paddle made reminded him of a flushing toilet.

When the current afforded him relief, he looked up at the newsvan. After several minutes, Jack's arms grew heavy and burned with fatigue. Twice, Jack saw the man set his video-cam on the van's roof and descend into the cab. Once, he opened the driver's door and was about to step into the water towards them when he seemed to recall something and changed his mind.

"Goddammit, give us a break here!" Jack yelled. Then he had to focus on the roiling water. Quickly, he shifted his paddle to the other side. Looking up, he caught a glimpse of the cameraman setting up a tripod on the van's roof.

At that moment, Jack saw himself objectively for the first time, as if through a wide-angle lens. The man was setting up for a once-in-a-lifetime shot. He was going to film their deaths.

- **2** -

Of the many types of love one can be afflicted with, Jack Bell suffered from three: love of photography, love of fame, and love of a woman. And then another woman. And then another.

When he was twenty, Jack wanted to be a photographer. At LSU, he had taken all the available preparatory courses and was planning to matriculate in the fall at Brooks Institute of Photography in Santa Barbara, California. His mother was a broker, his father an optometrist, so life was easy for Jack. He lived in his parents' backyard in a mother-in-law cottage, part of which he had remodeled as a portrait studio. Most of his earnings he spent on film and filters, flash units and backdrops, lenses, chemicals, paper, and the hundred little gizmos of the trade. For a while he thought it was photography he loved. But after the thrill of shutter sounds and flashing strobes diminished, he realized it was the results that intrigued him, not the equipment or procedure.

Slowly, he came to the awareness that his photographs were memorials. To something. Occasionally, hanging the wet, slippery sheets by clothespins in the red dark, he found himself staring trance-like at the ghostly images and would shake his head and wonder how long he had been in that silvery world.

Leafing through a *Modern Photographer* while waiting on a client one rainy afternoon, he discovered what he was trying to capture in silver and black. He flipped from a full-page Kodak ad on page thirty-nine to the most gorgeous woman he had ever seen: her ivory skin bordered by out-of-focus ringlets of black hair, her sensuous lips just parted, as if for a kiss, crystalline eyes smiling and peaceful, her face exuding grace. Next to the portrait was the image of what he thought to call "hag" before reading the caption to find the two subjects were the same woman. At that moment, Jack Bell knew that what he had been trying to do in the darkroom was stop time.

———

When the customer arrived, she apologized for being late while fidgeting with her damp hair. Jack said it was okay; they'd do some shots until it dried and if she didn't like the prints she wasn't obligated to buy them. They'd take some by the window, in natural light, with her gazing out as if disappointed by someone who hadn't arrived.

After the window poses, he suggested swaddling a blanket around her and placing a book in her hand. There was something about being photographed that made certain women develop a quick affection for the man behind the camera directing their movements—complimenting, looking closely up and down, then through the lens, complimenting, then the flash and another compliment, moving cat-like to adjust a lock of hair, careful scrutiny, more directions, a final compliment, the flash.

Often, Jack fantasized about the sessions. The women gone, he spoke to them confidently, unbuttoned their blouses, told them to look down—now, without moving their head, into the camera. Barely able to contain their passion, they complied and suggested other, more daring poses. After the imaginary sittings, the women seduced him on the floor by the fireplace painted on a canvas backdrop.

Jack looked through the viewfinder at the woman looking at him.

"Miss Anderson, right?" he said. "What did you say your first name was?"

"Monique," she said. "And please, not 'Miss.'"

Jack looked up from the camera. "Right." He stared at her. From a foggy distance, he heard his voice say, "Look, why don't you drop the blanket and loosen a couple of those top buttons? You look like a preacher's wife."

Monique laughed and tossed the blanket off. She looked directly at him and laughed again, as if she might think him, not offensive, but ridiculous and would get up and leave without saying a word.

Instead, her face suddenly sobered and she looked down at the buttons. She unclasped the top two.

Jack took a picture.

"One more," he said, and she unbuttoned another.

Jack shot the picture.

"Another," he said with authority. Somehow he knew this woman would do whatever he asked.

The woman looked at him. She was not smiling.

"Do you think I'd look better wearing just the book?"

Jack's eyebrows went up, and a very small part of his mind thought, "People's eyes don't really do that."

He was speechless. After a brief hesitation the woman stood up, faced the wall, and shed her blouse and camisole. When she turned around, she was wearing only the book.

That was the day Jack Bell's interest in photography revived. Each sitting turned into a rehearsal for a scene he had not yet composed. Everything in and outside his studio, not just women, became a photographic event for Jack, something to be stopped once and forever in time.

Over the next few months, he explored the nuances of feminine vanity, became an expert at judging how far certain types of women would go. Three, all married, allowed him to photograph them nude. Jack had refined a line of questions and statements that won their confidence. One seduced him. Jack had dealt the woman a line about capturing her figure while she was still young, and she became instantly deciduous.

This stage of Jack's life came to an end when he showed his collection of proofs to some friends. Big Tony was the older half-brother of a bashful girl who looked a lot more naked than she actually was. From that experience Jack gained a lesson in discretion and a magnificent black eye. He knew it could have cost him much more. He photographed the puffy eye and coded it "Nude Bruise."

At one of the sessions, after his eye had turned from deep to pale purple but hadn't reached the cadaverous yellow phase, a willowy, demure-looking girl walked into the studio and taught him that his personality-reading skills were not as polished as he had supposed.

After peering around the door, the indifferently attractive blonde stepped tentatively in with a puzzled, half-frightened appearance. Dressed in a strapless formal, she looked about as natural as a mannequin. "Welcome," Jack said. "Come in, ah, Anna—right? You look terrific in black." Jack estimated it would take a dozen more compliments than usual to boost this girl's self-esteem enough to give her that confident beauty needed to take the fakery out of formal portraits.

"Are you kidding," she said. "I wouldn't be caught dead in this contraption."

Jack had learned that a question posed with humor in the voice might achieve the desired effect, but if it didn't, the woman could hardly be offended by a harmless joke. This in mind, he asked, "Does that mean you'd like to take it off?"

Anna looked at him unflinchingly. "Not for you, buddy."

This girl was clearly angry at the world for something.

The intriguing subtleties of female vanity had lately begun to flatten into plain conceit for Jack. This specimen was just what he needed to restore his faith in the feminine mystique.

"Okay," Jack said. As they stepped toward the posing seat, he wondered what it would take to figure this one out.

"Sit here," he said. "Now turn your body this way." "Now tilt your head like this." With each statement, he touched her as if testing a hot iron.

Bad vibes, Jack thought. *Acts like she was weaned on a sour pickle.*

Looking into the viewfinder, he said, "Who's your favorite cartoon character?" This usually broke the ice and produced a self-conscious but appealing smile.

"Look," she said. "You could do me a big favor if you'd cut the crap and get on with this. The sooner you finish, the sooner. . . ." That was all Jack heard.

Jesus, he thought, *get a sense of humor.* He stared at her as he would a petulant child.

"Right," he said. He looked through the prism. She was much farther away than any subject he had ever photographed. If she wanted to pretend everything in the world was serious, he would play along and bore her into an early exit.

"What's your take on the presidential race?"

"A peanut farmer and a slapstick clown? Are you kidding me? I'll yank the Pat Paulsen lever."

His usual, clever monologue took a detour into belligerent dialogue. "What's your opinion on the nuclear arms race?" "Population control?" "Are the two related?"

Her replies were like personal insults.

After five minutes, Jack had a difficult time thinking of questions while adjusting his focus and manipulating the light sources. He knew he was onto something. The questions produced an effect on her face he had never captured on film. A kind of beautiful ferocity, or ferocious beauty.

At the end of the session Jack was exhausted.

"Great," he said. "These'll be some really nice shots."

"I'll believe that when I see them," Anna said.

Jack's tolerance switch finally tripped.

"You know," he said, "you really are a very attractive woman, but your attitude makes you look like a witch and frankly I don't give a shit whether you pick up these prints or not, it's your loss."

———

In less than a year, they were married.

Anna was a poet. She had "done time at LSU," as she put

it, before discovering that her idea of poetry did not coincide with that of the professors—any of them.

She quit school and waitressed and wrote poetry. Finally, Anna realized she didn't know what to do with the stuff, even if it was good. That's when she seeped into journalism, writing documentary articles on topics like Huey Long's demogogic legacy in Louisiana and streaking as a psycho-social manifestation of insecurity caused by an eroding value system.

After the wedding, Anna said she was ready to leave for Santa Barbara any time he was. Jack told her he didn't need a degree from Brooks in order to become a good photographer. She said it would be easy for her to land a job in a newsroom and told him to drop the self-sacrificial pose; it disagreed with his character. The discussion ended when he asked her if she had needed a professor to teach her what poetry was.

For two years, Jack and Anna were happy. She wrote; he took pictures. Without intending to, she landed a job at the Baton Rouge *Morning Advocate* through a personal reply to one of the editor's cranky commentaries. Written in a colloquial style, her response began, "You think you change anything with your play editorials?" and closed by calling Mr. Andrew Lofton a heartless bigot. The editor replied, saying she had the true fire, then asked her to join his staff.

During her first year in the newsroom, Anna learned that she had a lot to learn. Occasionally, she noted positive changes in the city resulting directly from Mr. Lofton's cynical essays.

As high school and then college friends dropped away, Jack and Anna made a circle of acquaintances from the newspaper. They ate out and went to parties together. They attended weddings, baby showers, funerals. From the associations, Jack derived a list of loyal clients. In Anna's second year with the *Advocate*, the editor threw a Halloween party at his house.

"Andy's not at all like I imagined he'd be," Anna announced to Jack as she placed the hairy wart on her putty-elongated nose. "He has a great sense of humor and really cares about people."

Jack had wrapped two old, tattered towels around his lower right leg and was strapping them down with leather boot strings.

"Yeah," he grunted while tightening the laces. "Seems like you picked up some of his charm. You sure didn't have any when I met you."

Jack was a big hit at the party, only not in the way he wanted. From an encyclopedia drawing, he had thrown together what he believed was a reasonable facsimile of Genghis Khan. He bought a fake beard from a novelty shop, trimmed it to specification, and topped off the barbaric look with a ferocious pair of horns planted in a Viking skullcap.

"So what if Genghis Khan wasn't a Viking," he explained to Anna while admiring his image in the mirror. "It gives the rig a certain . . . *je ne sais quoi*, no? A kind of chic meanness." Anna laughed.

So did everyone at the party. The first was Mr. Lofton.

"Well," he said, greeting them at the door, "if it ain't the Wicked Witch of the West and Genghis Khan in Drag." The label stuck, much to Jack's chagrin, for he had attempted a vicious look and achieved only impotent silliness.

Jack won first prize for best costume at Lofton's party. It wasn't his fault they thought the getup was a parody of the ruthless Mongol.

Without Jack and Anna's knowing it, the party was the zenith of their relationship and the cause of its decline. Lofton circled back to Jack with regularity, kidding him about the outfit, and got to liking him so much that he asked him aboard the *Advocate* as a full-time staff photographer, promising he could work with Anna whenever possible. Jack said he'd think about it.

For weeks afterward, Anna's colleagues badgered her for a photo of Genghis Khan in Drag.

"Look," they said, "we know Jack took at least five rolls of film at the party. He's bound to have handed you the camera *once*." They were wrong. One of Anna's complaints about the marriage was that Jack was too busy photographing everything and everyone else to live life firsthand.

Jack turned down the job at the *Advocate* in favor of his own, more-flexible hours. Ultimately, however, something productive came of the offer. For months, Lofton had been getting letters from the residents of Roseland Terrace, asking him to write one of his barbed editorials about the City-Parish Council's criminal negligence regarding the most dangerous intersection in Baton Rouge.

"Too easy for me," Lofton said, tossing the batch of letters on Anna's desk. "I'll let you file your teeth on this one."

The most dangerous intersection in Baton Rouge was Park Boulevard at Broussard Drive because people ignored the stop signs on Broussard. Neighbors had long advocated a traffic light, complaining to the Council that their children were endangered at the crossing and their private lives constantly interrupted by accident victims wanting to use their phones to call the police.

Anna took Jack with her to the location on Saturday morning. They parked in the elementary school lot and walked to the intersection. While Jack was setting up the tripod and mounting his camera, Anna observed the drivers and took notes.

Several times before Jack was done she interrupted him.

"Man, would you look at that." Jack glanced up, then went back to fumbling with the knobs and levers. "Did you see that guy? He acted like the stop sign was a mirage that suddenly vanished."

"Will you give me a break," Jack said. "You're making me so nervous I can't get the damn thing secured." When he finished, he looked through the viewfinder and sighted on the intersection.

"Nah," he said. "This'll never do. I need a wide-angle."

He reached into his Halliburton for the lens.

"Talk about a rolling stop," Anna said as an LTD looked both ways and gunned it. She scribbled in her notebook. "I've already noticed a pattern," she said. "It's mostly rich people who run the signs. Figures."

After locking the super-wide in place, Jack focused on the intersection. He lowered the tripod to headlight level and sat on the ground. He was almost settled when a white Impala sailed through the stop sign and intercepted an old Dodge. Jack punched the shutter release button and prayed he had the right f-stop for the ambient light.

Anna dropped her pad and pencil and ran to the wreckage. Jack burned the remaining twenty-three frames in less than a minute.

The Sunday *Advocate* featured the first photograph, taken at mid-impact, on the front page. Two months later, the traffic light was installed. For weeks Jack and Anna argued, not always playfully, over whose contribution was most important.

"The pen is mightier than the sword," Anna would say.

"A picture is worth a thousand words," Jack would counter. Like that, day after day.

———

Jack became obsessed with the photograph, by the violence of the wreck stopped in time. In the picture, the two cars would always be crashing. The incident inaugurated what he called his Motion Phase, during which movement-in-stasis became his dominant theme. At baseball games, he took hundreds of shots to catch the sliding runner just off the ground, the swinging bat at the moment of contact, the ball a millisecond after it left the pitcher's distorted hand.

And his Motion Phase initiated what he could only much later with humor call his First Divorce Phase.

Anna interpreted Jack's photographic relationship with life as a thinly disguised detachment from it based on fear of involvement. Her approach, she felt, was more direct and therefore more honest and therefore better and therefore, by that strange twist of emotional logic often employed by married couples, irreconcilably incompatible with Jack's.

———

Jack felt he needed a change of scenery, a fresh backdrop against which to compose his new life. He moved across the state to Lake Charles, where his brother practiced cardiovascular surgery, and took an apartment on Kirkman Street. The doctor's signature secured him a small lease space in a University Place plaza that contained a pharmacy, a deli, a shoe shop, and a toy store. Business was slow at first, with only drive-by and incidental customers dropping in after their other shopping.

Partly by renewing a close relationship with his older brother Keith, who had just happily ended his second marriage, Jack gradually attracted a sophisticated clientele.

These women radiated more beauty and money than his Baton Rouge patrons. And they didn't wait for him to seduce them. On weekend fishing trips, he and Keith exchanged racy stories of the studio and hospital. Jack dulled the pain of his own failed marriage by referring to his ex-wife as Annabanna-fo-fanna.

Jack was almost happy. A healthy reserve of women kept him physically satisfied, and he entered and occasionally won awards in state or regional photography contests.

What he called his Recovery-by-Overindulgence Phase ended when two women with hair the astonishing color of the copper coiled around an electric-motor armature walked into his studio. They were identical twins named Ami and Jami who taught fourth grade at the same school.

Jack hated the proofs from their first sitting. They looked amateurishly like a Doublemint commercial—clichéd poses facing towards or away from each other. When he called to offer them a free sitting, he discovered they lived in the same apartment.

For Jack the second sitting was torturously long, but the twins kept him entertained by telling him stories of mistaken identity and girlhood mischief. Over the next few months, with their coming into the studio together or alone and his seeing them around town and engaging in small talk, Jack established a casual friendship with the two.

Talking with Ami one day, he teasingly said he'd ask one of them out, but he had no idea which he liked best because he couldn't tell them apart.

"It doesn't matter," she said. "Ask us out twice and we'll either go by our real names or not. Then you can decide which one of us you like best, Bachelorette Number One or Bachelorette Number Two.

"Sounds like y'all have done this before," Jack said.

Ami laughed.

"We'll complicate matters by making sure you never know whether you went out with both of us or only one of us two times."

So Jack went out with either Ami or Jami twice, or Ami and Jami once each, or Jami posing as Ami, or Ami as Jami. The permutations so dizzied Jack that he gave up thinking about it and came to a decision about which one to date by employing the eeny-meeny-miney-mo method.

Jack never found out that his finger finally landed on Jami, who said she was Ami because Ami liked Jack very much, while Jami was infatuated with Bill, the track coach at the junior high across the street from the elementary school where the twins taught. Jack and the real Ami dated for six months, were engaged for a year, and married in a double ceremony with Jami and Bill.

For three years, Jack and Ami were happy. They bought a starter house, fixed it up, and stayed busy trying not to begin a family and duplicate their lives after that of Bill and Jami, who already had two children.

Two years and thousands of senior portraits and cheerleader poses later, Jack, still leasing the studio, was experiencing job burnout and a premature midlife crisis. The second home never materialized because the double-dip recession of '90-91 sent the parents of seniors bargain-hunting at Sears, Olan Mills, or weekend photographers. Jack and Ami began blaming each other for circumstances beyond the control of either.

"You had so much potential, Jack. I can't believe you're still taking pictures of children with baubles."

"*You* can't believe it! Put yourself in my shoes. I'm *me*, and *I* can hardly believe it."

"What happened to our home on the river? What happened to vacations in Alaska?"

The conversation made Jack feel as if the plot of his life had been copied from a soap opera. His dejection intensified almost to despair because he had recently passed the point of indifference in his sex life, so that when he mechanically brought his wife to orgasm, he no longer watched her with wonder as she transformed before his eyes, but instead tried to imagine what she would look like as a skeleton. That is, Jack had just passed forty, a time in his life when he made sure he always had a dark suit dry-cleaned and ready for somebody's unexpected funeral.

Then, as at other depressing moments in his life, Jack experienced a rejuvenation. A week after the soap opera dialogue, he saw a burning house captured on the six o'clock news. The smoke churned from the roof while an old man sat on the curbside and wept. The voice-over identified the owner as a history professor from McNeese State. Jack hated watching interviews of people who had lost their homes to fire or hurricane. Most of them thanked God that everyone made it out alive, or that only one child, and not the whole family had died. Never mind the destruction of the house, Jack thought as he watched the scene, his finger poised to switch the channel. Aloud, he said, "Thanks, God, for chopping off my arms and legs, but leaving me a mouth to thank you for not poking out my eyes."

The professor, it turned out, was childless. Wifeless, too. "We certainly grieve with you over the loss of your home," the interviewer said to him in the unctuous tone Jack despised. The man freely cried. "What is it that you'll miss most from your house, the one thing you would have saved if you could have?"

Jack yelled at the set, "Why don't you rip the guy's heart out!" The man took off his glasses and touched his baggy eyes, first one, then the other, with a soiled handkerchief.

"My books," he said in a quavering voice. He sobbed gently and turned from the camera. As the TV journalist looked mock-dolefully into the camera and was about to segue into a pitch for the station, Jack heard the old man's nearly inaudible voice repeat, "My books."

It was a brilliant moment, Jack thought, and the journalist was too stupid to realize what he had just accidentally accomplished. The next day, Jack upgraded his video system to Super VHS format.

———

By the time Ami said yes, Jack was hoping she'd say no.

What Ami finally said yes to was a video of themselves making love. What made Jack hope she'd say no was the premature detumescence on which so many middle-age jokes turn. But it worked out, and making and watching home movies of themselves revitalized their bedroom life and brought back their old romance: the days of spontaneous sex on the divan, the kitchen table, the lawn.

"Suburban High Tide," Jack said one day, looking out the living room window at the river that used to be Contour Drive while the TV droned, "fifth straight day of record rainfall with no end in sight."

"What, dear?" Ami asked. She was in the kitchen stirring around in a wok. Jack smiled. Ami was pathologically cheerful. On rainy days that made everyone else gloomy, she sounded like Beaver Cleaver's mom. When she was happy, she was obliviously, incurably happy.

"Nothing, Mrs. Cleaver," he said. "Just the name of my next Pulitzer Prize-winning photo."

"You mean your *first* Pulitzer Prize photo?" she quipped.

Boy, Jack thought, she can shred your ego and not even know it.

He stepped into the kitchen.

"Let's go on a canoe trip," he said.

"What? Are you out of your mind?"

"Hey, you're always pestering me about using the canoe or getting rid of it. Come on," he said, grabbing her around the waist and pulling her towards the door.

"Wait-wait-wait," she said. "Let me turn off the burner, for Chri-sake."

"Okay," he said, heading for the den. "I'll get the camera."

"No," she said, making his shoes squeak to a stop on the tile. She was smiling, but tolerantly, as a mother stares down a loved but incorrigible child.

"No. For me, Jack. Just this one time. Live this moment with me, not your camera." Then, trying to readjust the mood, she laughed, "Seize the day."

Jack made some lightning fast calculations, a photograph and his wife on either side of the equation. Then he strode towards her in pretended anger. "Seize your ass is what I'll do," he said, grabbing her. She squealed and they played chase around the table until Jack stubbed his toe on a chair leg and cry-laughed his way out the side door and into the garage where the aluminum canoe lay on its side in lonely neglect.

"Grab that end," he said, pointing.

"Wait. Let me get a raincoat."

"Forget the raincoat. You'll get wet anyway."

- 3 -

At that moment, Jack saw himself objectively for the first time, as if through a camera. The reporter in the newsvan was setting up for a once-in-a-lifetime shot. He was going to film their deaths.

Jack could imagine with clarity what the man was thinking: "I can win a major prize with this shot. It's my ticket to the big time—a national broadcasting system."

Ami turned on her side and looked up at Jack. She had been good, he thought. Not once had she squealed girlishly. In that moment of inattention, the bow sliced into the current, which ripped the canoe sideways and slammed it against the abutment. In the second it took him to think of looking toward the van to call for help, he realized it was too late. The man put a leg down into the sunroof and looked at Jack, then at the camera to make sure it was trained on the canoe.

Jack watched as the water surged into the canoe, weighing it down. He looked for the reporter to emerge from his vehicle, but saw him standing on the van top sighting through the camera.

Jack understood.

The canoe sank another inch and slipped under the abutment. Released, the roll of churning water restrained by the canoe violently shoved it under the bridge, slamming Jack's head against the concrete. Wedged between the canoe and the ceiling of the bridge, he felt his body tumbling in impossible positions. The sound of rushing water and metal scraping cement filled his hearing.

Jack imagined what the footage would look like on the six o'clock news.

Ami. The woman dying with him. She could easily have been her sister. Or anyone. Something was wrong with the composition. His last random thought was that he wanted to do the shoot again.

{12}

Controlled Burn

The game warden glassed the horizon of the marshscape with night-vision binoculars. Two green silhouettes—cattle egrets—rose and flared. She tracked them until they lighted thirty yards downwind, then continued scanning until it occurred to her that the birds would not flush at night unless disturbed.

It was 4:00 a.m., that part of the morning when you can't tell if someone has stayed up late or gotten up early. The officer panned back across the skyline until she caught the poachers in the circular field of her Zeiss binoculars, a faint glow at their feet sharpening their profiles.

Last week, she and Zone Officer Sonnier had cordoned off the sector for a prescribed burn. The area had reached the end of its cycle and needed fire to renew itself.

———

Cecilia Henderson was named after a road sign. It was a name that caused her grief as a child, but it gave her life a sense of direction. Her father, on a celebratory drunk at her birth, ran into the idea on his way to the hospital. It landed on his windshield like a sign from above, Exit 115 CECILIA / HENDERSON. They were villages north and south of the

Atchafalaya Basin Bridge. Odell had descended from the original Hendersons, but named his only daughter Cecilia because he knew the story would stand up under a thousand retellings.

If Cecilia had heard it from her mother once, she had heard it a thousand times: "Your daddy ain't mean-mean, baby. He's just playful-mean."

Like the time he told her to bail the johnboat with a Community Coffee can. The skiff, pulled halfway up the spongy, floating raft of vegetation that served as their backyard, was tied to a tire rim so it wouldn't drift off. Cecilia bailed and bailed, occasionally stopping to sweep a swatch of hair from her eyes. When one arm tired, she switched to the other. Being Odell's only girl, she wanted to please her daddy, prove to him that she was just as good as the boys, Levi and Jervis. When she came crying up to the porch two hours later, her father leaned back in his rocker and laughed. He took a long pull at his beer, thought again of his daughter bailing in the hot sun, and spewed a mouthful on Cecilia. Seeing her dripping with sweat and foam, he laughed again. "Are you ignernt, gal? Didn't you think to put the plug in before bailing?" His laughter bounced off ancient stands of bald cypress and echoed through the dark corridors of the swamp, blending with her crying to form the sound of a wounded animal.

Or the times he told them, "Y'all get out from under us grownups' feet and play under the porch like children's supposed to." Even on the hottest days, Cecilia hated it there in the cool damp. Under the gray, warped planks leaking sunlight, there was often an angry nutria, territorial alligator, or testy water moccasin they had to shoo away to make room for play. When their ball ricocheted into the yard, Cecilia was so caught up in the game that she forgot about her father waiting above them. Sitting near a corner of the rickety porch with a long-handled crab net, he knew where she would emerge based on the course of the ball. When Cecilia bolted from under the house, her father would clap the net over her head and yank her to a stop like a dog reaching the end of its chain.

Crying, Cecilia would run through his laughter to her mother, who held the child against her apron, comforting her. "Now, you know your daddy would never hurt you on purpose, Cecilia. He ain't mean-mean, he's just playful-mean."

When Odell Henderson needed beer-and-cigarette money, he roused his little helper from the deepest part of sleep. Because he called her that, she was glad to follow him into the swamp to collect snakes for LSU's herpetologist, Dr. Herbert Truard. Father and daughter did not actually hunt the snakes. They went about other business—setting traps during the day, at night harvesting catfish from other men's trotlines, then hand-grabbing bullfrogs caught in the beam of a miner's light strapped to Cecilia's forehead—and bagged snakes as they came upon them draped over low limbs or coiled on floating islands. Most of this Cecilia liked, but at sundown, when her daddy smeared her face and arms with levee clay against the swarms of deerflies and mosquitoes, she cried because Odell worked the muck into her skin like it was alligator tough.

As the nasal tenor of mosquitoes danced over the bass-line of football-sized frogs, Cecilia remembered the group of men stranded overnight by a seized-up outboard, welts on top of welts so that she didn't even recognize the young one as her cousin Gene. *Then* Cecilia was grateful for her father's rough tending.

On these trips, Odell Henderson taught his daughter the differences between the flying silhouettes of goose and cormorant, the fighting tugs of bluegill and chinquapin, the cloven prints of deer and wild boar. Two days at a time they'd be gone, with only peanut-butter crackers and warm Coke to get them through.

Then Cecilia would sleep a whole day and awaken to a stench penetrating the sweet, decaying odor of swamp gas. Barefoot and puffy-eyed, she'd wander down the steps and across the yard to the boat and witness the waste of fly-covered catfish and a burlap sack swollen tight with dead bullfrogs.

Before such scenes, Cecilia's mother doled out her wisdom. "Don't take more than you need." "Don't set food where animals ca-ca." "And don't—do you hear me?—don't you *never* marry you no swamp rat like I done."

Suddenly, Odell Henderson was gone. For a week, nobody said anything. He had disappeared before. Days at a time. Then he would show up with a wad of hundreds, huffing about easy money for monkey-work on the offshore rigs. "Come on, Verline," he'd say, and they'd traipse down to Whiskey River Landing to drink and two-step till the money gave out.

On the tenth day, the family started talking.

"He mighta taken one-a them twelve-on, twelve-off shifts."

"And got caught 'tween the chain and the drillpipe."

Some nodded. Others shook their heads. The split-cane rockers creaked doubtfully on the weathered boards.

"Coulda been beat up at The Landing and th'own out in the hyacinths."

"Coulda drown fishing."

"Or been struck by lightning, bit by a snake, or ate by a gator."

Everybody listened. The children were allowed, too. Hiding the truth of the swamp from them could only come to no good.

After a long silence, Cecilia spoke from the steps. "Or he

coulda got beheaded by a low-water trotline." The rocking stopped and the porch-sitters looked down on her like she was a rotten choupique, the only fish not eaten by a people who ate most anything.

After another week, the older folks stopped speculating about Odell. Whatever had happened to him, they knew he was not coming back. The one person who missed the man was Dr. Truard. It took him several months to make it down to Henderson to confirm what he suspected, and when he did, he made a pact with Cecilia.

"I know you, little swamp girl. Your mind's as sharp as cottonmouth fangs. If you supply me with snakes for the next few years, I'll set you up with a fellowship at LSU." Cecilia shaded her eyes against the sun and squinted at him doubtfully, thinking he was trying to hook her up with a boyfriend. "It means you do some lab work for me and get your schooling free. Like the snake gathering, only easier."

For the next five years, Truard filled a vague emptiness in Cecilia. During her sophomore year, when she dated professor of marsh ecology Dr. Raymond Clark, a friend teased her by labeling him a father figure. Cecilia laughed and denied it. Then, that summer while working as an intern on a research ship, it was Dr. Hunter Martin. When the vessel finished trawling, the father of three (one in college) used hand signals to direct the net as it swung like a wrecking ball over the rail and spilled its quivering bounty onto the deck. The movement of his hands made Cecilia's heart hurt. After fighting it for a week, she slipped into his quarters one night and he opened his arms like he had been expecting her. When that was over, she felt like a cliché and came to dread the uncontrollable urge.

The summer before her senior year, she did a stint in the Coast Guard, and it was Captain Bruce Trahan. He taught her to identify water- and aircraft by their distinctive profiles. It all came together then, what her father had tried to show her. Everything had features that gave it away but were not the thing itself. Animal tracks were as distinct from each other as chemical odors or the vocal signatures of songbirds.

Finally, it was Dr. Cullen McBride, professor of lowland game management. It was McBride who recommended Cecilia for the position at Sabine National Wildlife Refuge. She wanted to go back to the swamp that had spawned her, but there were no openings there. And Dr. McBride had known the Sabine refuge manager since their teenage years as fishing guides.

Cecilia drove to the interview almost hoping she wouldn't get the job—until Harold Benoit tried to put her off with the good-old-boy-turned-big-shot role. He conducted the interview on a bench under a moss-bearded chenier oak leaning away from the coastal winds.

"The Bad Lands of South Dakota," he began, pausing dramatically to turn and look her in the eye, "are a carnival funhouse compared to the *Worse* Lands of Louisiana—these Sabine tidal marshes. Takes six-shot to bring down our biggest mosquitoes." He laughed at that. Cecilia had heard it all her life and didn't crack a smile. Benoit was clearly running her through the routine just to tell McBride he had given her a chance. "Why, even the animals look guilty." Benoit took off his white-straw cowboy hat and pointed it at a cormorant atop the welcome sign holding its wings out to dry. "Looks like a city-park pervert opening his raincoat."

Cecilia looked at the tragic bird, its wings devolving back to flippers, and had to admit he was right.

Near the end of the interview, Benoit made a mistake. Standing and reaching for closure, he looked down at Cecilia. "Where you from, Little Bit?"

Cecilia stood and leveled her eyes at the man three times her size. "I grew up on the south side of the Atchafalaya Swamp."

To anyone who knew anything, that said it all.

"Well, then." Benoit put his hat back on and looked at Cecilia like he had stumbled onto a new species. "This oughta be a walk in the park for you."

As they strolled the grounds around Refuge Headquarters, he explained her duties. "You'll check licenses, investigate game and boating violations, do some public education, an occasional search-and-rescue with the Coast Guard, patrol the reserve overtly and covertly, but—and listen to this good, little girl—your number-one priority and the main reason I'm hiring you is to track down and catch the ghost poacher."

Cecilia looked up at the Refuge Manager. She felt like she had been dropped into a *Dukes of Hazzard* episode.

"No offense, Mr. Benoit, but I don't believe in ghosts."

He looked at her while angrily chewing the inside of his cheek. "You will, little girl, you will. He's been haunting me for years. I seen him a dozen times, but never got closer than a hundred yards. And this"—he swept an arm across the marsh—"is where I was raised. Hunted, fished, or patrolled every square inch of it. And I'm tired of him profanin' what's mine."

The man's attitude rankled Cecilia. "I'll have him by year's end," she boasted.

"You better, girl. You better." When he tipped his hat up and looked down at her, the sheriff in *Deliverance* popped into her mind. "You don't, and I'll fire you in the twinkling of a lightning bug's ass."

For the first month, Cecilia fought against liking the place. There were mammals and birds she knew from the Basin— raccoons and nutria, blue herons and osprey—but there were fewer deer and otter, and no owls or bear. The saltwater marsh, though, teemed with pelicans, hawks, ducks, and geese. And the wide sky gave her an expansive feeling far different from the claustrophobic cypress swamp. The Sabine Refuge was a quirky, menacing place of nursery-book clouds frowning into thunderheads and purple-black grackles zootsuiting around for a handout. Finally, Cecilia compromised, writing Dr. Truard that she was trapped in a place she found she liked, like a horse held by gentle reins.

Just when she allowed herself to be happy, she saw him for the first time. Cecilia came to think of him not as a ghost but as a child who challenged others to catch him, setting traps to trip them up and mocking them when they fell.

He never showed himself during the day. She first saw him while patrolling the canals framing Unit 3, the largest freshwater sector in the refuge. Out toward Five Lakes, she saw a light sweeping like an airport beacon and pulled over the rollers at Old North Bayou. He was sliding along in a waterlogged pirogue, snatching frogs off the bank with a Q-Beam. He didn't seem surprised when she idled up to him. He just ground the bow into the mud and stepped off, then turned around like a curious deer and stared at her. She chased him slowly, tumbling over clumps of marsh grass, and was gaining on him after ten minutes when an airboat roared out of nowhere and carried him off.

On a twenty-degree night in January, she saw him castnetting for shrimp off the Hog Island Gully weir. Cecilia pulled the white Wildlife and Fisheries Explorer onto the gray-flint parking lot, trained the searchlight on him, and asked if he knew the refuge regulations about castnetting. He didn't say a word, just kept casting and dropping shrimp into a five-gallon bucket. When she stepped out of the truck and onto the weir, he slid the handline loop off his wrist and turned toward her passively, like he was giving himself up. He looked straight at her, then down at the roiling current, and stepped off into the icy black water. From her training, Cecilia's first impulse was to dive in and rescue him, but his down vest popped him up twenty yards away. She ran off the weir and along the bank to the creosote bridge over Highway 27, where he vanished in the dark.

She did not see him again that winter and smoldered with a quiet fury throughout the spring, pulling nightshifts and logging overtime whenever possible. Benoit taunted her, reminded her, threatened her with dismissal for incompetence. In May and June, when the offshore breezes stagnated, the air was so humid she felt like she was suffocating in warm, soggy cotton.

———

The profile in the night-vision binoculars jolted Cecilia's heart. She had been tracking him for a year that felt like a lifetime. She was the top-producing Refuge Officer—had written more citations, talked to more third-graders, rescued more distressed animals than anyone—but she knew Benoit would fire her if she didn't catch this poacher.

Officer Henderson lowered her binoculars and looked out across the treacherous marsh. The men were near the point of the arrowhead-shaped sector jutting into the ship channel, probably on the water control structure, a weir built at the confluence of a hundred seepings. She stepped toward the pirogue floating by the headquarters wharf. Something crunched under her shoe like a sun-bleached crab shell. Her flashlight illuminated a pack of Lucky Strikes.

Cecilia picked up the crumpled pack and squeezed it tight. "You moron," she said. "You're not even in a boat."

The two poachers were surrounded by water on three sides. Behind them was nothing but marsh. Cecilia's mind raced through the scenarios. If she torched the marsh and caught him, she would lose her job for the unsupervised burn. If she didn't torch the marsh, he would escape, and Benoit would can her anyway.

Cecilia ran to the shed and grabbed a can of Deet and a drip torch, thinking, *If I corner him, he could try for one of the islands across the channel, but I can paddle faster than he can swim.* She imagined herself lassoing him like a rustler in mid-river.

The next thing she remembered, flaming gel was pouring from the nozzle onto the dry grass. In five minutes, she had lined the sector's quarter-mile west boundary with fire. Her uniform soaked through, Cecilia decided not to spray with Deet, which would hold her body heat like liquid cellophane.

The pirogue was a dark darkness against the lighter darkness of the water. She shoved off and paddled hard, then lay on her back to let the outgoing tide sweep her to the weir. As the pirogue spun slowly in the current, she kept her bearings by the stars and the flickering orange of the western horizon. If the men retraced their steps along the levee, she would block the narrow path and apprehend the one she needed.

Fifteen minutes later, she noticed a light in the east and looked over the side of the pirogue. In the golden aura of a Coleman lantern, he was casting a net. Cecilia dipped the paddle in the water and feathered the boat toward the bank. Each time he threw, the light fluoresced the net's monofilament, making it explode like a silent burst of fireworks.

She was close enough now to see the castnetter's familiar pattern: load, cock, release—lifting the leaded hem of the skirt with his left hand and draping it over the hook of his little finger one, two, three times, sweeping the net back and swiveling forward like a discus thrower, flinging the net that blossomed like the bell of a huge jellyfish. Again and again he did this, with no wasted motion—mechanical, relentless, beautiful.

As she drifted closer, each cast left a spectral jellyfish burned on her retina. Knowing he could not see her in the blind spot beyond the lantern's hot glow, she eased the pirogue to the edge of the weir and tethered it to a signpost illumined by amber light.

UNDER PENALTY OF LAW

NO CASTNETTING
without a license
(Free at Visitor's Center)

Five-Foot Nets Only
12 noon to sunset
during shrimp season

From a nail atop the post, a ten-foot cast net was hanging by its horn, the brails splayed out like a bridal train. She surveyed the scene.

Next to the castnetter, a tall Slim-Jim of a man squatted on the weir, fishing tightline. Behind him, two redfish gasping for water bracketed a flounder pattering the mud.

Without looking in her direction, Slim said, "We thought you'd never get here."

The short one ignored her until he pulled his net in and emptied a handful of clicking shrimp into a green ice chest.

When he swiveled toward her, Cecilia was shocked by his horrid face, which had been ruined by fire, or worse. Then she noticed the black mask of mud protecting him from recognition or mosquitoes or both.

She unsnapped her holster and drew her pistol. "You're under arrest for"—she glanced at the sign—"half a dozen violations. You know them as well as I do."

The skinny one said, "Shrimp been running past here for a thousand years. Maybe a million. You can't take away a man's right to 'em just by stickin' a sign in the mud."

She pushed the handgun forward and took a step closer to the one she wanted. That's when she noticed he had lost an eye since their last encounter. He left the wound open for effect, she thought.

"Don't draw down on a man 'less you got the guts to pull the trigger." He picked up a red and white thermos, tilted it back, and sucked on the spout, his Adam's apple bobbing in the light. When he finished, he made a satisfied sound and popped the spout shut for emphasis. "You're just posturin' is what I think."

He turned, loaded the cast net, and threw, then jerked the handline to cinch the net. Slim went back to fishing. When the leader opened the net to drop a dozen thirty-count shrimp into the ice chest, Cecilia stepped forward. During the time she closed her eyes to start her speech, he had taken her gun and knocked her down. He stood over Cecilia, close enough for her to see the gnats crawling around on the raw rim of his empty eye socket.

The men tied her hands and ankles with tarred-nylon cord and returned to their business. Mosquitoes hummed in her ears. When they drilled into her face and arms, she rubbed her skin against mud packed with crushed oyster shell. The controlled burn moved slowly across the dew-dampened marsh. Cecilia imagined the men would weight her body and roll it over the side of the pirogue in the middle of the channel to be eaten by blue crabs.

In an hour, they had filled both ice chests, the follower jabbering the whole time, the half-sighted one mostly silent. At the faintest hint of dawn, the two loaded the pirogue. Then the tall one steadied the boat for the other to step in.

"Thanks for the transportation," he said over his shoulder. "Woulda been hell hauling them ice chests back to Headquarters."

Then she heard it—a faint humming sound, like distant car tires singing on blacktop—and looked up. Ahead of the controlled burn, hordes of mosquitoes were rising out of the marsh like a biblical pestilence.

Desperately, to the one that mattered, she said, "You're a poacher, not a murderer."

The leader laughed. "Now, who said anything about murder?" He looked thoughtfully at his spent cigarette, pinched it between his thumb and middle finger, and flicked it at Officer Henderson. The butt rebounded off her forehead in a small shower of sparks.

"Yeah," the talker said, "we usually just take possum cops and set 'em on a channel island, then let the skeeters gnaw on 'em for a day or two." From her curled position in the mud, Cecilia saw the man's black teeth.

The leader looked at the refuge officer like he was wondering how to dispose of her. "Tell you what." He unhooked the net from the post and held it up. "If you throw a better bloom than I do, you go free."

Cecilia looked at the net, then the man. "And if I don't?"

He looked across the ship channel at the islands, then changed his mind. "Hell, we ain't got time for that." He reached down and picked up the repellent. "You don't, we'll just leave you tied up here and let you inchworm your way back."

The skinny one laughed. "Yeah. Shouldn't take you more'n an hour. Your pretty face might look like skinned nutria meat, but you'll be back to work in no time."

While the tall one untied Cecilia, the quiet one stepped to the edge of the weir, loaded the net, and threw a perfect bloom.

"This oughta be good," the tall one said as the leader handed the net to the game warden. "She ain't five feet tall, and th'owing a ten-foot net. Ha!"

"I'm five-two," Cecilia said. She took the net and coiled the throw line, smoothed and looped the neck of the net twice, reached down and raised the hem to her mouth, clamping her teeth on the line between two lead weights, then grabbed three lengths of the hem in her right hand.

The tall man chuckled as if he were watching a circus animal perform an action not suited to its anatomy. The silent man frowned.

Lifting her lips, Cecilia bared her teeth that were clutching the line and hissed, "You'll have to gimme some room."

The short one stepped back until he bumped his partner.

"You fellows ought to be game wardens."

Slim snorted. "Why's 'at?"

"Because in my job we don't have to worry about going over the limit."

This offended the talker. "You mean they let you catch as many redfish and shrimps as you want?"

"No, I mean there's no limit on poachers."

Cecilia pivoted and threw with an expert sweeping motion, the net blossoming perfectly over their heads. Then she yanked the handline to cinch the lead weights around their ankles. The ensnared men struggled for a moment, tottered, and fell.

"What the hell?" the silent one said. "That ain't nothing but mean."

"Yeah, we give you a chance and this is the thanks we get?"

Cecilia studied the wriggling men for a moment, then nodded. "It's not mean if you're doing what's right."

Cecilia pulled a number of plastic ties from her belt and bound the men's legs, then their wrists. Nearly dehydrated, with inflamed, itchy mosquito bites covering every inch of exposed skin, she picked up the red and white thermos and looked out at the approaching fire.

The quiet one shrugged his shoulder against a mosquito on his cheek, then spoke. "Can I ask you just one thing, little gal?"

"Shoot," she said. Keeping one eye on the men, Cecilia popped open the spout. Not wanting her lips to touch where his had been, she lifted the thermos skyward and let the cool water flow into her mouth like a faucet.

"Who taught you to throw a cast net thataway?"

The question reached her mid-swallow and she almost choked. The water had to go somewhere, so she sprayed it all over the man's mud mask. Seeing how silly he looked dripping marshy gore like a B-movie monster, Cecilia Henderson threw her head back and laughed, then stepped closer and stared the legendary poacher right in his missing eye.

"You did, Daddy."

{13}

Call Forwarding

From the crow's nest of the playground pirate ship, a little Truman Capote of a man looked at his wristwatch, then lifted his eyes toward the eastern horizon. He signaled down to the Civic Center seawall. Mayor Randy Roach raised a hefty pistol, aimed over the lacy steel canopy of the Jean Lafitte Bridge, and pulled the trigger.

The missile corkscrewed skyward, spewing a trail of white smoke. As the flare bloomed like a well-thrown cast net, our boat jumped out of the hole ahead of a hundred others. In sixty seconds we had reached the bridge across the lake, the roaring engines behind us Dopplering down to a feeble drone. We ripped into the ship channel at seventy miles an hour and passed under the colossal legs of the bridge's concrete supports.

Scott screamed, "Can we make it!"

I looked upstream. A rush of adrenalin turned my heart over like a giant piston. The train trestle a hundred yards away was growing toward us in fast motion. The night before, I had calculated low tide at Lake Charles based on a chart for Calcasieu Pass, forty miles downriver.

"Yes," I hollered. "*If* a south wind didn't push the water up!" Then I ducked, just in case the I-beam topped our windshield.

It was Thanksgiving morning. Slowly rising, I held the top of my head like a fragile gift rescued from a high fall. Scott threw his head back and laughed. When his hat flew off, he didn't even look back.

In two minutes *The Double-Dog Dare*—a Pathfinder 22 with twin 250 Mercs squatting obscenely on the transom—had blown by Ripley's Landing and taken the fork into Cripple Bayou, skipping sideways across the light chop like a perfectly thrown clamshell.

Cripple Bayou snaked back toward the city until it was beheaded by the Saltwater Barrier, an ingenious structure the Army Corps of Engineers had designed to prevent saline intrusion from killing the primeval cypress swamp. In thirty-five years the swamp had silted over and heavy machinery moved onto dry land, dozing the majestic trees to make room for another casino.

As the dam's winking red lights came into view, Scott throttled down and I grabbed my favorite rod. When I last saw Scott, he was losing his hair and going to fat. He had lived in Rhode Island for the past fifteen years. I was surprised a state that small could hold his ego for that long. He was a good guy, but you had to take him in small doses.

During those fifteen years Scott had become a major real-estate player and an expert striper fisherman, entering twenty tournaments a year, winning three or four, and placing in the rest. When I jokingly e-mailed him the rules for the First Annual Thanksgiving Day Cripple Bayou Striped Bass Tournament, I was shocked a minute later to hear his brash voice squawking from my cell phone.

Ten years ago come Christmas, the Louisiana Department of Fisheries had released a million striper fingerlings into the Calcasieu River. It was a noble experiment. The doubters predicted instant death for half the stock. Then, they claimed, new diseases would kill most of the remaining fish and summer would finish off the rest.

Yet here we were, a decade later, with a population healthy enough to support a five-fish creel limit. There were no Mid-Atlantic mammoths, but the speed of these southern silver sides was enough to turn a few redfish sports into striper enthusiasts in the late fall and early winter.

Scott used the competition as an excuse to visit his aging parents (not a visit to his parents as an excuse to fish the tourney). He actually hauled *The Double-Dog Dare* over half the country to enter a rinky-dink tournament and beat up the local talent with his fancy gear and veteran techniques.

When Scott cut the engines, *The Double-Dog Dare* glided toward the Saltwater Barrier like an alien spacecraft. He moved to the bow and lowered his 109-pound-thrust trolling motor into the water rushing over the Barrier's lowered cement gates. Above the jabbering turbulence, I heard the sound of a dozen paddles spanking the water—a pod of redfish busting the surface for a school of shad.

I cast and hooked up immediately. Scott laughed and shook his head.

"Hey," I said, defending myself, "just warming up."

In the dawn's early light, I saw for the first time his star-spangled smile of porcelain veneers. I turned my attention back to the redfish. When I lifted, unhooked, and released the six-pounder, I glanced at my old buddy again.

I hadn't seen Scott Cankton in five years, since our thirty-year class reunion, and he looked like a million bucks. His hair implants and neck tuck gave me the eerie feeling that I had been picked up by the wrong person and was fishing with a stranger.

Scott positioned the boat in the slackwater behind one of the dam's columns, then fanned out five rods on the casting deck. After leaning my lone backup against the transom, I draped a duck-call lanyard with a pair of toenail clippers around my neck. I had been wearing the cord for thirty years, and it would last that much longer, even if I did not.

"That reminds me," Scott said. He skipped to the steering console, plucked a dainty silver cell phone from the glove compartment, and slipped it into the chest pocket of his Orvis fishing vest.

It was my turn to laugh, and I made a point of overdoing it.

"What?" he said defensively.

"Man, I've fished with *bass* spoons bigger than *that* little trinket."

"I'm waiting on a call from a major investor," he explained. "About a Martha's Vineyard deal. I gave him my private number, then forwarded the call to my cell."

I cast into the churning water and let the current sweep the jig downstream. "Still Mr. Gadget, huh? Got to have the latest doodad to keep up."

"Not keep up," he said. "Stay ahead. I miss that call, I'm out five million."

Working the jig, I looked behind us. In the distance, our first competitor was rounding the bend. "How far ahead do you have to be?"

Scott set the hook. The striper cut through the water so fast a liquid sheet shaped like a triangular sail fell away from his line. "One fish," he grunted. "Or one property. Sometimes that's all the edge you need."

"What if your phone falls in the water?"

"It's waterproof. Cost me an extra hundred."

"Will it float?"

Scott turned and stared at me blankly. "I hadn't thought of that." He quit reeling, then buttoned his vest pocket and patted it securely.

By the time the boat arrived, Scott had caught and released the twenty-incher. For the tournament, each boat could weigh in two fish. Scott's was a nice striper by local standards, but he threw it back like it was infested with parasites.

After that first boat swung into position, an armada of seven arrived, then a steady queue of slower vessels. At any given moment, a dozen lines were being cast. The mist spinning off the monofilament arches in the sunrise reminded me of sprinklers coming to life on a golf green. I stopped fishing to take a photograph.

"Are you crazy?" Scott said. "Get that rod back in the water. You could cost us the tournament."

Local etiquette requires that anglers fighting a fish drift back to avoid tangling lines. Suddenly, a dozen rods bent double. As the current swept us away from the Barrier into calm water, Scott laughed scornfully. "Combat fishing!" he spat.

Half our group pulled up middling stripers while the others landed reds. Then Scott zipped ahead of the boats struggling against the current with puny trolling motors. We had lost our place to new arrivals cycling into the mix, so Scott pulled up to the sign by the northernmost gate:

!WARNING!
Do Not Tie to Any Part
Of the Lock-and-Dam Structure

I knew Scott was thinking of our old joke: "Don't tie to any part of the damn structure." He cast, then I cast, then we glanced at each other and laughed.

Squinting into the half-risen sun, his eyes looked like Genghis Khan's.

"What the hell did you do to your eyes?"

"Blepharoplasty," he said. "The surgery to correct droop-ing eyelids. Haven't you heard of aging gracefully?"

"Yes," I said, "and I've also heard of aging *naturally.*"

Scott hooked a good striper and we dropped back. While the line was singing off his reel, I connected with a redfish. *The Double-Dog Dare* spun in a slow circle and came into still water. I hustled my fish aboard just in time to grab the net for his. Thirty inches. Scott worked the hook loose and was about to release the fish when I stayed his hand. "That's a keeper," I said.

He shook his head. "Man, off the Outer Banks, they troll with *bait* bigger than this." He popped the lid of the live well and scanned the fish again. "You sure?"

"Around here, another like that'll place us. Bigger, and we'll win. A thousand clams."

Scott dropped the fish into the live well and snapped the lid shut. "Ooo," he said, shaking water from his hands, "big money."

Starting for the trolling motor, Scott stopped dead in his tracks. We had been so focused on the fish that we hadn't heard the boat approaching. Half an hour after our arrival, old man McCourtney, our high-school shop teacher, came puttering by us like something out of a cartoon. He held his wooden bateau steady with a firm grip on the tiller of the 7-horse Evinrude he had been using since before I was born.

Scott called out and McCourtney choked the engine dead. "Is that you, Mr. McCourtney? It's Scott Cankton. Fullback. LaGrange High, 1968."

"I can't make out your face, Scott, but I reco'nize the voice. I don't see so well these days." He jerked a thumb at his part-ner. "That's C. O. Ensminger. Hardware, 1945."

"Hello, Mr. Ensminger. I didn't recognize you."

"No sense talking to him," McCourtney said. "He's as deaf

as an anvil. Both of us together barely make one whole man."
He lifted his beer in salute and took a swallow.

Mr. Ensminger cupped a hand to his ear. "Wha'd you say,
J. D.?"

McCourtney pointed to his beer. "I SAID, 'Both of us together can barely drink one whole can!'"

"Hell yes, I'd like another. Where's the church key?"

While the hearing among us laughed, McCourtney
reached back and yanked the Evinrude to life. After the men
had motored past us, Scott said, "Kev, did you notice? Mc-
Courtney's *exactly* as old as he was thirty years ago."

I nodded. "That's what aging naturally will do for you."

We fished for another hour without boating a striper bigger
than the one in the well. Between every cast, Scott touched
his chest several times to check on the cell phone. It was like
a nervous tic.

McCourtney fished in the slackwater behind the middle
column, sculling his boat with half a paddle. Instead of cycling in after hooking up and drifting back, he would patiently wait for his spot.

I was mesmerized by the movement of the boats elegantly
weaving in and out of position and imagined the beauty of an
aerial time-lapse photograph of the scene.

Scott filled the time between hookups by giving play-by-
play details of real-estate deals as if they were close ballgames.
His fishing exploits interrupted the monologue like annoy-
ing commercials. The art of the deal; the thrill of the kill. He
was Charles Darwin masquerading as Donald Trump.

Still talking, he set one rod down and was picking up another with a different lure when his cell phone slipped between the seam and button of his vest pocket, bounced once
on the deck, and hopped into the water. Scott stopped talking. In disbelief, he dropped to his hands and knees, gazing at

his disturbed reflection in the slackwater.

He looked up at me, his face a sickly white, like he had lost everything.

"No big deal," I said. "If he doesn't get you in person, he'll leave a message."

"No, you don't understand this guy, Kevin. He doesn't work like that. You miss the boat, you miss the trip."

"Oh, well," I said, trying to console him. "What's five mill? You can make it up with two smaller deals."

Scott looked back into the water. "Yeah, but I really wanted to beat this son of a bitch."

"Beat your future partner?"

Scott looked up at me like I was a fool. There was something my old friend didn't understand, but it could not be taught with words, so I held my tongue.

He picked up his rod and stood, staring off in the distance without casting. I hooked up and had to tell Scott to kick the trolling motor and shoot us away from the Barrier. The fish fought for a while, then Scott netted it listlessly.

When Scott recovered as much as he ever would, he returned to fishing with a vengeance. At the Barrier, he picked up his thickest rod. It was rigged with a twelve-inch Sassy Shad. I tried to tell him there were no shad that big in Louisiana but he just kept on casting, touching his chest between each throw, still feeling the pressure of his phone like a wedding band removed after fifty years.

An hour later, Scott was still working the Sassy Shad. Right when I was sure he had completely lost his mind, he hooked up, followed by several other fishermen.

"Man," Scott said. "Now *this* is a fish. *This* is what we been waiting for."

"Well, you gonna reel him in or talk him in?"

McCourtney drifted back, his skiff sliding toward us as if

drawn by a giant magnet in our hold. A striper larger than the one in our live well surfaced with McCourtney's hook in one side of his mouth and Scott's Sassy Shad tacked to the other.

"Christ," Scott said. "Can you believe this! I feel like I'm in the Twilight Zone." He cranked his reel like a wench—hauling in the fish, a skiff, and two men in the late winter of their lives.

"Let him have the fish," I pleaded.

Scott looked at me like I had offered him ten bucks for a million-dollar property.

"If I reel him in, he's mine. I don't care if he's attached to a battleship."

"Scott, look at yourself," I said. "Think of everything you have to be thankful for, then just let it go."

Scott pulled back hard. Midway between the boats, half the fish cleared the water. It was the biggest striped bass I had ever seen.

Scott hollered, "A tagged fish! That's an extra five hundred bucks!" He leaned back and cranked down, pumping like he was muscling in a truck-sized tuna. When I saw that he was dead determined to wrestle the fish from old man McCourtney, something came over me, something like the Spirit taking hold of a preacher, and I proclaimed, "There is none so blind as he who refuses to see."

I stepped forward quickly and snipped his line with my clippers. Scott fell back, the fish went down, and McCourtney's skiff spun away from us downstream.

With Scott sitting utterly dejected in the captain's seat, I manned the trolling motor and tracked McCourtney from a distance until he lipped and lifted the fish from the placid water. Then I pulled alongside to admire his catch. The striper's heavy belly sagged between McCourtney's knees as he worked the hook loose. When he raised the trophy striper to show us, the fish started ringing.

Scott bolted from his seat.

"Hey!" Scott yelled. "That's my cell phone!"

McCourtney called out, "You want I should answer it?"

"No!" Scott shouted. "I'll get it." As our alien craft bumped into the small bateau with a resounding wooden note, Scott went down on his belly to grab the bow. "Quick, cut him open and hand me the phone."

Frowning, McCourtney looked at the ringing fish. "Now let's think about this. Dead, she'll bring first prize for biggest fish. Alive, that's an extra five hundred."

Ensminger chimed in. "What's going on? What's all the commotion about?"

Scott pulled a wad of money from his pocket and started peeling off hundreds. "Five for biggest fish, five for releasing him alive." Scott held out both hands, one to give and one to receive, as if he thought Mr. McCourtney might cheat him. The old timer kept the fish until Scott passed the money over.

Without counting, McCourtney pushed the paper into his shirt pocket. As if on cue, the fish in his lap stopped ringing. "Already got a ten-pounder," McCourtney said. "Add this one to that one and we could win the tournament."

Scott peeled off bills till he ran out at six hundred. Desperate, he skipped to the glove compartment and extracted an emergency credit card from a sleek wallet.

"Here, you can keep this till I get some cash at the landing." Scott thrust the card at the old man. McCourtney turned his body to screen his fish, then took the plastic. Taxed by his poor sight, McCourtney held the card close to his nose.

Squinching one eye closed, he scanned it carefully with his better eye, then handed it back.

"Sorry," he said. "I don't take Discover."

Frantic, Scott kicked the negotiations into high gear. When

he offered up his thousand-dollar GPS unit, McCourtney squinted at it through half-blind eyes.

"Nawp, cain't use that, seeing as how I always know where I am."

Scott finally gave up a telescoping net and a five-hundred-dollar rod.

On his knees, Scott cut the striper's belly open, then slit the stomach and squeezed. Two shad squirted out, then a cell phone, the same size and color as the shad. Flipping the cover open, he seemed hopeful at first. Then his face muscles relaxed more and more until it looked like he had just read his own obituary. Scott clapped the lid shut and fell back on the deck as if he were dead.

"What's the matter?"

With all the blood drained from his face, he looked up at me.

"It's not my cell phone."

———

An hour later, *The Double-Dog Dare* planed off and we headed back to the landing, Scott's blepharoplastic eyes streaming tears at seventy miles an hour.

I lowered my head out of the scouring wind. Thinking of everything I had to be grateful for that Thanksgiving morning as we entered the late fall and early winter of our lives, I didn't have the heart to tell Scott that old man McCourtney would never have entered a fishing tournament.

{14}

The Girl and the Green Gas Can

There is a certain beauty about a troubled woman, even if she is eight years old. Her eyes, hazy with smoke or bloodshot from lack of sleep, look through you as if they see a part of your soul you know nothing about. And when they look away, you know whatever they saw didn't count for much. You feel very foolish because you have never suffered, not like she has, so you get the urge to drive to the hard part of town, pick a fight, and get the crap beat out of you just to feel better.

The green gas can was a government issue my father brought back from World War II and placed on the carport of our two-bedroom house, a house that looked exactly like hundreds of other military bungalows on the east side of Lake Charles, south of Chennault Air Base. Dad kept the eight-gallon rectangular canister, a large X embossed on its front, primed for overnight shrimping trips in Big Lake. I was six and my sister was eight before our combined strength sprung the clamp on the lid.

The first time my sister peered into the can, she didn't come up for nearly a minute. The mouth of the can circled her head completely and I was afraid she had gotten stuck. When I grabbed her ponytail and pulled her out, she had a big smile on her face and a glassy look in her eyes. Or rather in her right eye. Over the left she wore a pink patch that was supposed to exercise her lazy right eye.

"Whoo-wee," she said, "you oughta try this." So we took turns. She stayed down for more than a minute each time. On my turn, I looked and looked into the darkness, trying to figure out what she found that was so interesting. Just when some red and blue splotches appeared, she dragged me away.

"Whoo-boy, that sure smells sweet," she said.

So that's it, I thought. Down I went, intending to do some hard sniffing. This time the colored splotches grew into black-rimmed clouds that burst and expanded again. When she yanked me up by my collar, I was dizzy. Sick, in fact. I walked to the planter on the side of the carport and sat down. Crouching over the can with her pink ruffled panties peeking out from her black-and-white checkered dress, she gripped the rim and deeply inhaled. The white hairs on her tanned legs were brighter than I had ever seen them. Her chest filled up and collapsed like a pillowcase on Mom's clothesline. Little shiny worms swam around in my vision.

"Ahhhh!" she said when she stood up. It was the same sound my father made after taking a long pull at the water jug in the icebox. She stepped back, balanced on one foot like she was playing hopscotch, teetered for a second, and slapped the pavement with her tiny bottom.

"Whee! Don't you look funny, Cotton Top. He-he-he! Ain't that funny? Cotton Top."

Mother always called me Cotton Top, but I had never thought it was funny. It was just my name. Suddenly, it struck me as hilarious.

I bent over to examine my sister's face. It was ragged at the edges. The worms got skinny and died off. I felt a yell coming that I couldn't stop: "Scooby-toots!" I pointed at her lying on the cement and laughed. "Cotton Top!" she yelled back. We laughed and pointed until I felt a lemony squeeze under my ears at the back of my mouth. Then a big ball of sour heat rushed from my stomach and spewed all over my sister. From the way she acted, this was the funniest thing that ever happened. For me, the fun was over. I leaned over the planter and doled another helping onto the marigolds.

When Mom came home from work and discovered our crime with her exquisitely fine-tuned, trouble-sniffing nose, she was as mad as a hornet. Scooby and I had hosed each other off and splashed on some of Dad's Aqua Velva but couldn't mask the distinctive aroma of gasoline and puke. In an atmosphere of guilt and doom, we ate supper, twirling nervously on the yellow Naugahyde barstools.

"Wait'll your father wakes up and hears about this."

As I understood it, Dad usually worked on a train called the KCS. Sometimes, though, he worked an extra job in the graveyard at night. "Your father's working graveyard this week," Mother would announce, "so y'all stay outside and play." Lying in bed, I tried to imagine him digging in the dark by the light of the silver railroad lantern he kept in his mildew-smelly work satchel.

When Mother turned around, Scooby twisted toward me and sniggered. Dad was always on our side. He was easygoing because everybody liked him, and everybody liked him because he had been an All-Star southpaw for Harry Chozen's Lake Charles Lakers before TV squeezed the life out of the minor leagues in the early '50s. On Saturday nights, Dad took us to Joseph's Drive-In for burgers wrapped in wax paper, then to the American Legion hall on Third Avenue where black men in white tuxedos greeted him at the door as Mr. Bobby and even twenty years later admirers still called him one of the Chozen Few. Scooby and I reaped the benefits of his lingering fame. From the gambling room we were forbidden to enter, loud, cigar-smoking men kept a steady supply of orange Nesbitt's coming our way.

As soon as Dad woke up, Mom launched her tirade. A woman of great beauty, with jet-black hair and full, red lips—the type who marry famous athletes—she could generate a fury that only disappointed women can muster and only beautiful women get away with. She had expected to be wafted into a glamorous life of ease on the tailwind of my father's blazing fastball, but the Gulf Coast League collapsed and now he was a railroad brakeman and she was a very unglamorous switchboard operator.

Dad listened, faintly smiling, as if, despite Mother's scowl, he couldn't wait to hear what we had gotten into this time. Wearing the same tolerant grin, he would usually tell us what Mother had told him to tell us. He stepped onto the carport to inspect the can. We all looked at it together: mother, father, and children—only the father smiling. When he snapped the lid shut, though, he said, "Y'all stay away from this can. It's dangerous, you hear?"

These were the harshest words he had ever spoken to us. It seemed to us that he was always working or sleeping, and when he sat on the couch in his underwear, waking up with Lucky Strikes and a pot of Seaport coffee, he would silently entertain us by pulling dollar bills out of cigarettes or making quarters disappear up his nose, so I knew he meant business when he spent that many words telling us the can was dangerous.

———

There's something about childhood that makes us all accomplices. Even while disapproving, we enjoy watching the delinquencies of our friends and brothers and sisters. So when Scooby got bored after school one day the next week and asked me to help her pry the lid off, I said "No way, José" and sat on the edge of the planter waiting to see what would happen. She finally popped the lid with a butter knife. Down she went, surfacing now and then to say, "Ahhhhh!"

The sweet, mellow odor of gasoline reached my nostrils, but I was not tempted. The sickness I recalled overpowered the allure of the pleasing fragrance. I was awakened from my meditation on pleasure and pain by the sound of my sister's head hitting concrete. I thought, *That's it, she's dead.* I shook her and shook her, begging her to wake up. "Please don't be dead," I repeated many times, already imagining the scene: I would be standing over the pale, lifeless form of my sister while looking way, way up at my parents, trying to explain how I had sat right there and watched my own sister kill herself. My face was itchy hot from crying when Scooby sleepily lifted her unpatched eyelid, her left cheek smudged with oily grit.

She spread her arms out to keep from sliding off the carport, then sat up. "Whoo, that was really something. The last thing you see is a big blue spring that turns round and round."

Mom was out of the question, but I did want to tell Dad what had happened. He listened to everything we said, serious or not, and always with a smile. Winners are like that. Somehow, though, what Scooby was doing kept me quiet.

For endless days, she and I caught honeybees in Blue Plate mayonnaise jars in the frontyard clover patch or competed to see who could toss the most clothespins into the rotund, silver-bladed air vent spinning over the bomb shelter in our backyard. On sunny afternoons, wearing Chiquita banana stickers on our faces, we spread out her painted-tin tea set in the shade of the front porch. There were four settings: one for me, one for Scooby, one for a large, unkempt wooden doll she called Philodendron, and one for Pheety, her imaginary friend she held long conversations with. I looked hard where Pheety was supposed to be sitting. Although Scooby thanked her for saying she liked the tea and poured some more, which was also imaginary, I never saw Pheety lift a cup.

This, my first grade year, was a puzzling time for me. Everyone seemed to take as common knowledge things I hadn't the faintest clue about. Like "Pease porridge hot, pease porridge cold, pease porridge in the pot, nine days old." *What the heck does that mean*, I wondered. Since everybody else seemed to know, I was embarrassed to ask. So it didn't surprise me that I could neither see nor hear Pheety.

In those, my ignorant days, I spent most of my time thinking of ways to keep Scooby's mind off the green gas can. I did whatever she wanted. I even began to talk with Pheety, who day by day grew more real to me. She had three children and her husband was away for months at a time hunting in Africa. She had terrible headaches and often talked about wanting to go to the moon with the first astronauts. She liked cats, but not dogs. She occasionally cursed.

On Friday nights, we folded the couch down and stayed up with Dad eating popcorn and watching Alfred Hitchcock in the dark. At the scary parts, Scooby buried her head in a blanket, crying, "Save me, Daddy, save me!" On her knees, she covered her head with her arms and thrust her butt in the air. From the time she was a baby, we were told, she had done this. By a long series of mutations, the name Scooby-toots had evolved from the original Doodlebug. Dad said she had looked like a little doodlebug balled up in her crib. Mostly, Dad called her Scooby-toots, but now and then he switched to Scootle-toots, Tootle-bug, Buggy-scoots, Tooty-boots, and dozens of other variations whose bafflingly similar differences ran through my head at night.

Long days passed, the green can a tiny fear in the back of

my mind like an ominous hole covered by weeds deep in center field. Then, without warning, Scooby would be draped over the can, and my heart would surge with Hitchcock fear.

Soon, I noticed a pattern. Every time she had a bout with the gas can, she was wearing the black-and-white checkered dress. So whenever I saw her put on the dress, I tried to engage her in one of the pressing duties of post-war childhood: picking up the long metal bristles behind the streetsweeper, or catching mosquito hawks by their drooping wings as they perched on rosebush thorns, or riding our bikes into the eye-stinging fumigation and cumulus exhaust that billowed from the weekly mosquito truck.

Or I tried other distractions.

"Pheety wants to come over for tea this afternoon," I attempted one day when I found her embracing the can. She looked up at me with a murky, nearly-closed eye.

"You dope, Pheety ain't even real."

This was my sister. This was my dad's Scooby-toots, her cruel words forced by the evil in the green can.

I whimpered, "Why do you do it, Scooby?"

A lazy, heavy smile spread slowly over her face. "When you reasha certain point, smells like wallamelon."

The episodes grew progressively worse. This time, she passed out and peed in her pants and went around all day smelling like a rest-stop potty.

It was to be a bad year for Scooby-toots. At recess one day, she tried to skip two bars on the horizontal ladder. She was doing fine until halfway, when she lost her rhythm and fell, breaking her arm in three places. At home, she usually washed the dishes standing on a wooden footstool while I dried them from a dinette chair. For the next couple of months, I had to wash to keep her cast from getting wet. One day we were going through our paces, talking and laughing.

I handed her a plate, and when it wasn't taken from my hand, I almost dropped it. Scooby was looking out the window, far away.

"Oh, Lord, life is so hard," she said. "I could really use some gaz-o-line about now." Hitchcock horror gripped my throat. Then she sang. "Born to lose, I've lived my life in the sink. Bor-horn to lose, and now I'm loozin . . . you-hoooo." She sighed, her eyes still far away out the window. A long tear trailed from her good right eye down to her chin, where it gathered in a fat, quivering globe and dangled for a while before dropping into the sink.

Then she looked at me with a big smile. "That was good, wasn't it? I just learned how to do that. All you have to do is keep your eyes open, no matter what, even if they burn, and the tears start falling like rain."

So she was acting. I felt like laughing and crying at the same time. A few more days of relief.

Friday after school, I was beating banana leaves with an old fishing rod when from around the corner I smelled gasoline. *Oh God, please, no*, I thought. When I reached her, she was already drunk.

"Scooby, please stop it! You'll get hooked like a dope fiend."

She looked up, said, "Oh, thassa bunsha bool-shit!" and bowed her head once again in strange devotion to the green can.

"I'm gonna tell Mom!"

"I dare you," she said with a metallic echo, her head still engulfed by the can. "You do and I'll crack your skull with this cast." She waved the L-shaped weapon above her head like a fiddler crab's mutant claw.

"I will tell. And I double-dog dare you to hit me."

"Triple-dog dare *you*," she said, lifting her face from the rim.

"Four-dog dare!"

"Five-dog!"

"Six-seven-eight!" we yelled in unison. Then she let out that high-pitched scream only little girls can produce. She was going to kill me.

I ran alongside the house and cut into the banana trees at the corner. I heard her slapping the leaves behind me. I jumped over an azalea bush and dove through the space under Dad's oil-drum barbecue pit. "Whung-*klang*!" I heard behind me. It was the sickening sound of a human body hitting metal, followed by plaster on metal.

Dazed, Scooby sat with her legs splayed out like a Raggedy Ann doll propped on a bed. Blood was spattered all over her dress and cast.

"Don't just stand there, stupid, get Dad!" Dad had worked in the graveyard the night before and was asleep in the back bedroom. While running to get him, I marveled at how calm and adult-sounding Scooby was, like she wasn't drunk or hurt or anything.

Whenever we injured ourselves, as soon as Mother found out we were all right, she got mad. "What were y'all doing? You were into that gas can again, weren't you?" We never even had to reply. Mom knew the answers to her own questions. When she started yelling at Dad, he said, "Lighten up, Honey, it's just a phase."

———

I'm looking at a black-and-white photo propped on my desk. It's Easter. I'm wearing black shorts, a white shirt with a dotted bow tie, and a toothless smile. Scooby is wearing a frilly dress and the pink eyepatch. Her upper lip is bruised and distended. The spider beneath her nose is made of stitches poking from a black scab. Her Easter basket is hooked on the blood-stained cast. She is not smiling. Our feet are cut off and we're way over on the right edge of the picture.

———

Every five seconds for the next couple of weeks, Scooby made a nasty sucking noise to clear her mouth of the continuously flowing saliva. These were her lowest days. After school, at the kitchen sink, I washed and rinsed while she dried and stacked. Thoughtfully, she expounded her views of life, pausing every few seconds to vacuum the spit down her throat.

She would talk awhile and then, as if to give a musical demonstration of her pain, sing songs we heard in Dad's big black Plymouth at night on our way to the American Legion hall. The glowing green numbers and red lines that lit up the dash evoked in me a sad anticipation for the sharp taste of orange and the raucous sounds of men chanting those mysterious phrases—earned run average, knuckler, low and inside, grand salami, tailing fastball, ground rule double, no-hitter, Triple-A. The Bigs. I remembered the songs well enough to know Scooby wasn't getting all the words right and often mixed several songs into one, but somehow her words seemed better than the original.

"I'm crazy for crying and I'm crazy for crying and I'm crazy for crying . . . ah-hall day." Patsy Cline.

"Oh, baby, why'd you leave? I'm waltzing the floor over you, I'm so hurt what can I doo-hoo? Oh, come back and walk across Texas with me." Ernest Tubb.

"I've loved and lost again, oh, what a crazy world we're li-hivving in. Oh, if you'll come back, I'll shine your shoes again." Patsy Cline. I don't know where the shoes came from.

"Moon river, wider than a smile. I'm crossing you in style, too-daaay. And that lucky ole sun just keeps rolling a-huh-waaay." Andy Williams and Ray Charles.

Her short versions of the songs made me very sad. Such pain coming from the voice of a little girl.

In late April, her stitches were removed. Soon, she took to striking matches, blowing them out and, after they had cooled, eating the black residue. "Mmmm, tastes like Sal-tine crackers," she said. Whether her new habit was related to the gasoline compulsion or not, I never knew, but I prayed she wouldn't strike the matches around the green can. I had heard of people sitting in recliners or just walking along and suddenly bursting into flames. This, Scooby told me, was called spontaneous combustion, and I feared one day find-ing by the gas can a small pile of cinders that would be the charred remains of my daring sister, who had finally pushed her luck too far.

A week later, I came upon Scooby flirting with disaster. She would sniff from the green can, then light a match, blow it out, and suck on the black, crusty ashes. I yelled at her from a safe distance. "Please don't do that, Scooby, you might 'spaneously combust!" Unmoved by my pleas, she went right on striking matches and sniffing until she got woozy and crawled off the carport onto the lawn and fell asleep in the grass. Don't ask me how, but Mom found out and spanked us both with a fly swatter, like I was responsible, too.

Dad was barely out of the car when Mom started a tirade that carried into the house and dragged on through supper and after. Most of it we'd heard before, but there were some new things: "If you hadn't got drunk every damn time you won *or* lost, you'd have signed a Big League contract and we'd be in Boston now instead of this piss-ant little town. And about that damn hussy down at Pete's Bar, don't think

I'm blind or stupid. You keep that up and I'll divorce your ass right quick." On and on it went, right up to bedtime.

In our room, standing with her hand on the light switch, Scooby looked at me, frowning hard. "Something's cooking between Mom and Dad. We best make ourselves invisible for a while." Then she turned off the light.

In the dark, I wondered what she meant. Could we, like Pheety, really make ourselves invisible? As I was fading into sleep, Scooby, imitating Mom's argument voice, said, "It's that damn Philodendron causing all this trouble. I'm gonna fix his ass, and I mean the next chance I get."

I was awakened that night by Scooby crying in her sleep. I got in bed with her and woke her up and held her, because she had done the same thing for me plenty of times.

The next morning, I found an invitation, scrawled in green crayon, tucked inside one of my shoes.

Tea Party With Pheety
Saterday Noon
Please Come

Two days later, after spending the morning netting craw-fish at the ditch, I went to the front porch where Scooby held the tea parties, but she was nowhere in sight and the dishes weren't set. An odor of something burning charged me with Hitchcock fear and I ran for the gas can. I reached the side of the house too late. Scooby was draped over the green can, black smoke billowing from her slack form.

Then someone with a water hose pushed me out of the way and started aiming a feeble spray of water at my dead sister.

"Scooby!" I yelled.

She glared at me. "Well, don't just stand there, stupid! Go get the kink out the hose!"

Laughing and crying, I ran until I traced where the hose was crimped and opened the flow. Returning to the gas can, I saw a soggy mass of clothing over the remains of Philodendron.

"Scooby," I said. "I thought you was dead! But that's just Philodendron."

She scornfully looked at me with her one good eye. "You stupid, that's Pheety!" She stared at me until her eyes filled with tears and her bottom lip quivered. "Philodendron killed her because Pheety wouldn't let him have a turn sniffing the gas."

Scooby ordered me to get a shovel from the storeroom, then led the way to the field behind our house, carrying Pheety's remains in a cardboard box from a case of Jax beer.

We took turns digging with the unwieldy shovel and when Scooby placed Pheety in the hole, she picked up some dirt and sifted it through her fingers. "Ashes to ashes and dust to dust," she said, "if the smoke don't get you, the fire must."

After Scooby packed the dirt with the shovel, I asked, "If these are Pheety's ashes, where's Philodendron?"

For what seemed like an hour, she stared right through me with one eye.

"You really are ignorant, aren't you? Philodendron excaped across the border to Mexico. We'll have to send a posse after him and bring him to justice."

As confused as I was, I got more confused half an hour later when Scooby set three places for our tea party and asked Pheety if she wanted one or two sugar lumps in her tea.

"Scooby, I thought Pheety died."

Exasperated, she said, "You really don't know anything, do you? How many times have I told you that Pheety was my imaginary friend? This," she pointed, "is Pheety's evil twin. She just goes by the same name to fool everybody, but I know the difference. This Pheety is my imaginary *enemy*."

This truly amazed me, my sister's inexhaustible capacity for making up total nonsense.

Scooby molted her cast in May and was again able to wash dishes. I thought there would be more pain, more singing the blues, more gas sniffing. Instead, she was distracted by her new interest in hunting down Philodendron in Mexico, which was located in a stand of pine trees just beyond the ditch where I crawfished.

Then I feared the end of school, which would give the can more time to lure Scooby into its evil snare, but she started dividing her time between excursions to Mexico and tormenting her imaginary enemy for clues about the location of Philodendron's hideout.

In just the first week after school ended, Scooby flushed the evil-twin Pheety down the toilet, scalped her with an oyster shell, made her eat mustard on a banana, put sand down the front of her bathing suit, and made her walk barefoot on fresh, hot blacktop. Then we gave her a cold so we could put Vick's salve up her nose just like Mom did to us.

I thought there would be no end to this sort of fun.

But then at the end of July, Scooby was talking about the beginning of school as if she'd be sent to jail. She started sneaking Lucky Strike butts from Dad's ashtray and smoking them till her eyes turned red.

I thought her next move was going to be for the green gas can.

A week before school started, Scooby sat the evil Pheety at the kitchen table with a discarded math book missing its cover and made her do long division for a whole afternoon. By September, Scooby no longer wore the pink eyepatch. Without the stitches, cast, and patch, she could have passed for anyone's little girl.

Her life as a childhood derelict was over.

And the rest of her life was just beginning. Things got better for a long time. Then worse. Then much better. And so on, until a month ago, when her life would never get better or worse again.

{15}

The Arrow That Never Came Down

"RUN!" Smitty says. We scatter and my heart feels like an eye that needs to cry. When all of us are safe—Smitty, Jello, Napalm, Snake Eyes, and me, Worm—when we are all safe from the plummeting arrows, backed against the yellow brick under the eaves of my house, I look to the center of the field and see my brother, twelve years old, standing with a mocking grin on his face as arrows strafe the ground around his feet. Fear rips my heart, for though I think he will surely grow up to be a Class-A son-of-a-bitch, at the moment, the summer before my fifth-grade year, he's all I've got to guide me into the unknown world. He doesn't see the last arrow, shot the highest and falling like a dream. He is laughing and pointing at us and I can see the arrow aiming for his life and know it will not miss. I hear my heart screaming up through my throat.

"Hunh!" I awaken. My heart hurts. I'm sweating. I am a middle-aged man somewhere in Kansas, if you call forty middle-aged. The pain is not angina. It's the vestigial pain of a childhood full of good and bad memories. My eyes filled with blackness, I think of my brother, who did not turn into a son-of-a-bitch, Class-A or otherwise.

When he was a child, he lived completely as a child, and you could tell by watching him that he knew he would never die, not as a child. Years later, I saw George C. Scott as Patton standing in the middle of a dusty road shooting enemy airplanes with his pearl-handled revolvers, and I thought of my brother. At ten, on a dollar bet, he swam across Lake Charles in choppy water. At eleven, *because* it was dangerous, he shallow-dived off the I-210 overpass into Contraband Bayou, among the twisted cypress knees. When he was twelve, he swallowed a marble, a lady dime, and a .22 bullet just to see if they'd come out in the same order he swallowed them. These are the actions of people who know they can't die until their number is called.

By far what my brother loved most as a child was dodging arrows.

So his name was Dodger, but to me he was just plain Brother. He and I grew up in Lake Charles with a tribe of baby boomers, at a time when everyone went by nicknames or mutations of their last names, yet no one took offense. Blackman became Blackhead, Snatic Snatch-it, Lambert Lambchop, Victor Little Bickty and so on, except for Snake Eyes, who got his name from having one eye crossed. Even Harry Roach, a funny name in its own right, became Roachbreath. I lost touch with most of these guys, but from what I hear no one turned out really weird, though Blackman was one of maybe five people in the United States who later bought a yellow Volkswagen Thing, one of those armored jobs that looked like a sissified Nazi panzer.

———

One Christmas around 1960, Brother and his friend Napalm got identical cream-colored fiberglass bows and plastic quivers stuffed with twenty-six-inch wooden arrows. How do you suppose such coincidences happen? My guess is that our mothers ran into each other at the TG&Y: "What does little Nathan want for Christmas?" "Ooo, that sounds like a dandy idea." Probably like that.

Shooting at the blue, yellow, and red target against a burlap bag crammed with other burlap bags soon became a bore, so we started going for distance. After adjusting the trajectory, we could fling those pigmy javelins beyond the ditch between our backyard and Lake Street—then a white shell road, now a two-lane blacktop. That didn't last long, either. Napalm (who grew up to be an engineer; it figures) decided we could reach the shell with longer arrows. So we swiped as much change from our fathers' pockets as we thought we could get away with and biked up to TG&Y.

The thirty-two-inch lances had a deadly beauty about them. When Brother launched the first one toward the road and it cleared the highlines over the ditch, I thought it would never come down. But it did, just shy of the shell, about a hundred and fifty yards from our house. Back and forth we ran, taking turns shooting the arrows. Rooster, Napalm's little brother, finally got one to catch a rising gust. We knew it would hit the road and hauled across the field to get as close as possible before it landed. When it splashed white shells and ricocheted, we somersaulted to the ground laughing like madmen. I don't know what it was we found so funny, but I came to love the laughter that burst from my lungs whenever I saw something demolished.

After a short hunt, we carefully extracted the arrow from a blackberry bush, its tin point bent into a little pignose. This went on for a few hours until Snatch-it got the wise idea of lying on his back, bracing the bow against his feet, and drawing the string with both hands. Right through Mom's kitchen window. Had she been washing dishes, she would have been a living valentine for sure. We had fouled baseballs through nearly every window on the backside of the neighborhood, so a few well-placed lies took care of that problem.

So, distance was out and altitude suddenly in. I think my first aesthetic experience was watching those long arrows whip from the bow and diminish to a dot at the apex of the arc, where they seemed to pause and daydream awhile before coming down. Jello was the one who started it. He was a smart-ass, square-headed fat kid constantly doing stupid, dangerous things to the rest of us, I suppose to make himself feel better about his weight. Once, he almost broke my neck by loosening the nuts on the front wheel of my Spyder bike. The tire popped off after I wheelied from a plywood ramp, the fork ground into the pavement, and I flipped over the butterfly handlebars and kissed the gritty cement, sanding half the freckles from the right side of my face.

One day, about ten of us were in the field. When Jello's turn came, he shot straight up and yelled, "Kamikaze!" We flushed like quail and ran for cover. When the arrow landed, we gathered around it and had a good laugh. Jello was rolling on the ground about to bust a bladder. Brother, though, seemed more impressed than amused.

"Satisfactory, man! Wow, was that satisfactory!" Brother and Napalm shot the next pair up together and everybody ran again. The third time, we didn't run as far. The fourth time, Brother stood right where he was and traced the arrow until it fell ten yards away. Pulling it from the ground, he announced Rule Number One: An arrow never lands where you shoot it from. Rooster and I fired the next set. Throughout the afternoon, rules were formulated, some of them logical, some not. Rule Number Two: If you lose an arrow in the sun, your chances of getting shish-kabobbed are reduced if you stay put. Rule Three: If you get hit, it probably won't kill you. Four: If Jello gets hit, nobody call an ambulance. And so on.

During the summer, more birthdays added more bows and arrows, and the field came to look like Custer's worst nightmare. What were the odds of two arrows colliding in midair, we wondered, and went right to the task of finding out. We'd shoot ten or twenty volleys and take a break to try other experiments. We discovered that plastic containers filled with water, like Clorox jugs, explode along the seam when an arrow strikes them. Coke bottles don't break under any circumstances, but if you hit one solid, your arrow shivers into a dozen wicked splinters. My favorite episode involved a Cornsucker, a hard-sugar candy shaped like an ear of corn stuck on a popsicle stick. They cost a nickel, and about every tenth one had a coin in it, sometimes a quarter, but usually a nickel or dime. If you were fool enough, you could suck on one all day to find out if you got a dime to buy two more with.

My aching jaws convinced me one day that these things weren't called suckers for nothing. We rubberbanded a purple one to a bundle of *Life* magazines and started firing. Ten or twenty shots later, I hit it dead center and it simply disappeared, pulverized into a million glassy slivers. We all fell backwards on the ground and kicked our feet in the air, each laughing his customized, signature laugh perfected over the past few years. "Satisfactory, man. That was just too much," we said, slapping each other's palms. Afterwards, we tested everything pulverizable. The next best thing to Cornsuckers were those blue washing-powder tablets shaped like giant Sweet Tarts that were popular for about two years until some kid ate one and his mom sued the company.

Between these shenanigans, we kept after the mid-air collision. If we shot enough times, it was bound to happen. Other times, we went "exploring" and tried to shoot deer or bears. We really believed we'd run across a bear maybe down by the bayou washing off a salmon that hadn't thought of Louisiana since the Ice Age. Then we saw the movie *Robin Hood*. For some reason Robin Hood had to split an arrow in order to beat the bad guy, for Maid Marian's hand or something. And I'll be dog if he didn't do it. So we figured we could, too. Attempts at arrow-splitting and mid-air collisions kept us busy for weeks. After our paper target got shot to pieces, we made a more durable one by stuffing newspapers in a cardboard Canadian Club whiskey box. When it was new, I ran to fetch my arrow, grabbed hold, and yanked. Gripped by the newspapers, the arrow stayed put, an intriguing rectangular flap of my palm draped over it like a clock in a Salvador Dalí painting. The raw flesh burned like acid for a week.

Sometime the next summer it happened. Only, the arrow doesn't peel into halves like on *Robin Hood*. It shatters. Roachbreath, Snatch-it, and Lambchop were with me when I scored. First, we jumped up and down, whooping and swinging our arms in big circles. When we arrived at the target to inspect the fragments, we flopped to the ground and rolled around. "Saaa-*tis*!" Lambchop said in the hoarse voice he got from a baseball crushing his Adam's apple. "Was that satis, or what?" To liven up his silent laugh, Snatch-it slammed his palms on the grass while I hooted away.

Our confidence in The Colliding Arrow Theory restored, often as many as fifteen of us gathered in a knot shooting flights of arrows. We even tried to launch a second series before the first came down. If the arrow's nock slipped off the string on the first try, we threw down the bows and ran in panic-stricken laughter for the eaves of my house. Everyone except Brother, who got braver and braver. He'd casually walk outside the barrage of arrows and trace a loner with his index finger until it thumped the ground closer and closer to his toes. Ten feet, eight, five, one, until he could almost touch the blurry dart before it hit.

He became an expert, admired for his heart-stopping daring, better than anything we saw at the Shriners' Circus. He'd pick an arrow, call to the chickenlivers on the outskirts of the field to "watch this," and as the arrow hurtled earthward—sixty, eighty, a hundred miles an hour?—he'd give a theatrical bow, his head and the arrow touching the ground simultaneously within inches of each other. He worked variations on this act, catching arrows with a slat of Styrofoam or making a circle with his arms and spitting at the death needle as it threaded the hoop.

One gust. I knew that's all it would take. I wanted to grab his shoulders and shake him. I needed to say, "Brother, please don't do this! Please!" But you can't say these things to your brother in 1960. That comes in the late '60s, when tongues loosen and you call anyone your brother.

I was glad it happened on a cloudy day. Cloudy days are best for seeing arrows high in the air. Snake Eyes had a twenty-pound bow while most of us had fifteens. This was just before school started. For some reason Snake Eyes released a bit late. I saw his arrow catching up with the others, then, "*teek*," a tiny sound that didn't match the deranged cavorting of the arrow veering towards my house. "Cool!" Snatch-it hollered. We took a quick sighting and sprinted for the arrow's estimated landing spot. Our hearts sank as the arrow dropped behind old man Arnold's basket-weave wooden fence, constructed for the sole purpose of keeping our basketballs from turning his garden into a salad. Once, I saw the old fart knock the Blackwells' grey Persian off the fence with a twelve-ounce can of Del Monte apricots.

We hit the deck, motionless until Brother chanced a peek over the fence. Still hugging the grass, we watched his dusty flat feet curl around the boards. At the top of the fence, his head scanned back and forth like a radar. Then it stopped and seemed to be thinking. He jumped back, fell to the ground, and slapped both palms over his eyes. "HO-ly shit," he said.

Jello tested the rain-rotted boards with his weight. Carefully, he shambled down and rolled on his back, smacking his forehead. "HO-ly shit is right," he said.

One after another we scaled the fence and fell back. I climbed the boards to a chorus of holy-shits behind me. An icicle pierced my stomach when I saw the arrow. "Holy shit," I whispered. It had harpooned a prize watermelon. We were in trouble, big time. We flipped quarters to see who'd fetch. I won. Bracing against the melon with a bare foot, I extracted the arrow. When the rind closed on its wound as if nothing had happened, I said, "Thank you, Jesus," and I meant it, though I rolled the melon over anyway, for good measure.

———

The next year Brother and Napalm got thirty-pound recurve bows. I admired their terrible beauty in reverential silence. With the bows came six light-green aluminum arrows. Even though I had a fifteen-pounder, Brother occasionally let me shoot his recurve. I could barely pull the string to my shoulder and couldn't hit a rhinoceros at five paces. Napalm made the first kill, a robin. The secret, we discovered, was to aim high and let them jump up into the arrow. A direct hit sounded like *Flut!* A milk carton sounded like *Blat!* Napalm wondered what kind of sound a tree would make. He picked a tallow, figuring he could dig the arrow from the soft pulp with his Barlow knife. It sounded like su-*KUNK!* when it hit, but the impact bent it beyond rehabilitation.

From movies like *Fort Apache*, we got the idea to wind a strip of old sheet around an arrow tip and douse it with lighter fluid. Brother held the loaded arrow out for Napalm to light.

"*Kuhwooosh*!" went the flames. Brother tilted the flambeau skyward, pulled and released. The arrow went *thwick*, right through the cloth. The fireball dropped onto Brother's chest and in a fit of screaming laughter, he and the rest of us beat it into a hundred smoking pieces. Napalm, the future engineer, figured we hadn't tied the cloth on tight enough.

Around the Fourth of July, Napalm rigged up an arrow with a fifty-cent skyrocket. He broke the pink stem off and Scotch-taped the missile to the end of the arrow. We waited for dark, but only made it till twilight. The itch was just too great. I remember the metallic sound as Napalm flicked the top of his dad's Zippo. "Wait till the fuse disappears before letting go," he instructed. The fuse sizzled. Right before it disappeared, Brother drew and we backed away. "*Foomp*," the arrow said heavily. In a split second it was fifty yards high and decelerating quickly. "It's a dud," Little Bickty said. We kept watching and hoping as the arrow dragged to a halt and dipped its heavy nose. Then red sparks and a faint *shhhhh* and Snatch-it shrill in my ear: "Run for your life!" The arrow, in a crazed corkscrew flight of showering sparks, headed straight for us.

"Your life ain't worth running for," Brother said to our footsoles and elbows and stood right there, tempting fate and chance. He dashed for the arrow and after it hit the ground, the rocket still spewing fire, grabbed it by the feathers and slung it at us. It died midway to us and plopped smoking on the grass.

Fifty cents a shot was too expensive, no matter what the thrill, so we tried penny rockets, but their effect was so puny compared with skyrocket fear that we set about devising other ways to scare the daylights out of ourselves and live to tell about it. We taped smoke bombs to the shafts, then sparklers, then Black Cats. All too boring. We stood around thinking, looking down and shuffling our feet in the dry grass, as if the idea might be lost where the blades met the roots. Napalm thoughtfully rasped his Zippo's toothy wheel against the flint. When I looked away, I saw little spark-flashes burned on my retina. Suddenly, Brother said, "I know!—NIGHT SHOTS!" I was puzzled until, drawing his bow, he recited Rule Number One: "They never land exactly where you shoot from." I couldn't believe it. He let go. The arrow went upward into blackness. With fear-laughter, everyone scrambled for house-safety or tree-safety.

Everyone except Brother. With my cheek pressed against the rough, cool bricks under the eaves by our bedroom window, I could hear him laughing in the night. I was terrified. I prayed for him and cursed him at the same time.

Then his laughing stopped. I've heard you don't immediately know whether you've been hit by a bullet. It numbs the tissue and you have to actually see the blood to believe you've been shot. His laughing stopped, as if he were mulling something over. Then a chilling scream made my stomach clinch. I reached him first. He lay flat on his back, the silhouette of an arrow stuck in his chest. I couldn't move, I couldn't force myself closer. I see now that I should have known. He started to scream, but the shriek changed to convulsive laughter, and when I realized he was faking us out, I fell to my knees and cry-laughed with him. But I was glad it was dark because my tears were real. I should have known the arrow couldn't have been sticking from his chest at that angle.

We speculated for a while about death by arrow. What would it *really* be like? We all agreed you should leave the arrow in, as a plug against the flow of blood. Our trauma finally smoothing into a philosophical afterglow, Brother said, "Let's do it again." Five or six arrows were swallowed by the night. Eight or ten boys scattered in the dark. Minus one. Against the eaves again, I thought, *My brother's insane, he must be insane, there's no other explanation.* But he made it. He is a walking, talking miracle because he survived his life as a child. Now he has a wife, his second, and five children, two by his first marriage, and he doesn't have time to reflect on his boyhood. He works at a branch of NASA in Slidell, Louisiana, and I see him and his children once a year at Christmas.

If you think back a moment, I'll bet you a thousand dollars you can't remember when you ceased being a child and reached adolescence, that never-never land between the sleepy eternity of childhood and the steady dying of adulthood. I remember the day and hour, the exact moment I was catapulted like an arrow into mine. Before then, time passed, but I had no fixed mark to log its passage. I was twelve and by myself at dusk in the dying November field, my feet pinpricked with cold on the last barefoot day of the year. By some quirk of fate, I had a single arrow left, its green aluminum shaft shading to silver towards the tip, from being pulled through targets and buffed by dust innumerable times. Brother was a freshman at the high school and I still thought he'd turn into a son of a bitch, though by one of the contradictions of brotherhood I also admired him.

Out by the ditch I aimed the arrow as close to perpendicular as I could and released it. I watched the arrow vanish in the twilight. I stood still, refusing to run or cover my head. "They never hit exactly where you shoot from," I repeated over and over. My nerves couldn't stand it. How could *he* be so damn sure? I waited. The tears rose from my heart to my throat, squeezed out of my tightly shut eyes, and rolled down my cheeks. I never heard it hit. I walked around in widening circles, sweeping my bow in the weeds to locate the arrow. I didn't find it that night, nor the next day, nor the next. Sometime after Thanksgiving it occurred to me to look again.

I must have been a sight, wandering around the field with my head down like an old man. After I'd kicked at the tall weeds for an hour, I got a crick in my neck and rolled it back and forth with my face skyward. What was it about the arrow sticking in the top of the telephone pole that stunned my heart with wonder?

I can't get it off my mind. It might as well have struck me in the head. All through junior high, the arrow stayed.

It took three years for the feathers to drop off. At least once a week during my high school days, I walked to the middle of the field to check on the arrow. My interest transformed into obsession. In college, I learned new words for the curious spell the arrow held me under. Fixation. Neurotic attachment. Fetish. Monomania. *Idée fixe*. While others scrawled things like "Kappa Sig Sucks," I carefully printed in my anthropology notebook, "The arrow is to me a totemic emblem of eternity." In a junior composition class, I concluded an essay on memory, "Einstein believed that all the events of our life are taking place somewhere simultaneously. When I think of the arrow, I think of Duchamp's *Nude Descending a Staircase*. The universe grows in time like a flower exploding through its bud in a fast-motion film. We cannot see all the frames, but they have a unified, uninterrupted existence in a spatio-temporal continuum."

Now I am a middle-aged man living in Kansas. Our father is dead. Our mother is old. (Or are they somewhere getting married, having children, living and dying?) The arrow is still atop the telephone pole in the field behind my childhood home in Lake Charles, Louisiana. It has endured heat and cold, hail, hurricanes, and lightning storms. I have seen birds, large and small, even once a crow, attempt to land on the arrow, but none has succeeded. Occasionally, I see a mosquito hawk test the air around the nock and finally alight. After a brief vigilance, its wings relax and droop and the arrow looks as if it could stay there forever. On visits to my mother, one of the first things I do is check the arrow. I step out the back, the screen door slamming with a sound from the past, and walk across the field. I shade my eyes with a hand and build suspense by slowly climbing the pole with my eyes. Then I see the arrow and grin. "Satisfactory," I whisper. "Very satisfactory."

{16}

Always On My Mind

Dr. Esther Bukoski led me to the shadowbox where five X-rays were spread out like the worst poker hand you've ever seen.

"You see this," she said, pointing with a reflex hammer.

My heart pulsed fear. "This" was the size of an egg, and it was nestled between the lobes of my brain just under my forehead. Not a chicken egg, but not a hummingbird egg, either.

"It's called a cavernous meningioma. Very common in adults."

I waited for her to say, "And very deadly." Instead, she wrote something on her clipboard. When I leaned over, she read it to me. "Pressing on sixth nerve, causing monocular diplopia." She looked up. "That's the double vision in your right eye."

My first thought was, Great, just when my new life with Regina is starting, this has to happen. How can I possibly tell her?

I hadn't heard from Regina in fifteen years. We had a short but intense relationship at the University of Texas—"lived a lifetime in two months" is how she put it before disappearing into the Colorado mountains.

Down through the years—single, married, or divorced—I thought about her, remembering our relationship with mixed emotions. She was just another girl I dated in college.

In the past year, though, I had been thinking of Regina more and more. I had dated the other ones longer—six months, a year, Belinda for two. Why couldn't I get Regina off my mind? We had what I called a relationship in a vacuum. I never ran around with her friends and she didn't know any of mine.

Willie Nelson's Fourth of July Picnic was our first date. Sweat pouring down his face, The Red-Headed Stranger closed the concert by crooning "You Were Always on My Mind." I had no idea what the song would come to mean to me. Every time I heard it for the next fifteen years, I thought of Regina. In the past year, I started missing her, then longing for her, then needing her. Why?

Finding her was easier than I imagined. Five Google moves, and there she was, living in Houston, a quick slide down I-45 from Dallas.

Our e-mails were tentative at first. No, she wasn't married. Anymore. Yes, she still thought about me. On occasion. She had a son, Tyler, named after his hometown. She was a business woman. Several dozen more exchanges. Yes, she would meet me. But not in Houston. She didn't want to alarm Tyler. We decided to meet—where else?—in Midway.

After a decade and a half, she still wore the same luscious side ponytail draped over her shoulder. Right there in the parking lot, I held her and held her and held her. Partly, I didn't know what to say or how to start. Partly, I didn't want to let her go, ever again.

She didn't seem at all surprised when I finally stepped back, looked into her sea-green eyes, and spoke my first words to her in fifteen years. "I would rather die than lose you again."

Her reply was to pull me closer and squeeze me tight. Next, I asked her ear a question. "Do you still have that watercolor of the horse?"

"Which one?"

"There was more than one?"

"Hundreds," she laughed.

I had to think. "A chestnut horse running in a wheat field at first light."

"Liquid Reality," she said immediately.

She did not bother to hide the gray at her temples— seemed, in fact, proud of it, sweeping her hair back to accentuate the streaks. And the crinkles at the corners of her eyes made me want to cry. They were promises that one day she would die, and I couldn't imagine anything as beautiful as Regina ever ending.

We talked for three hours straight, nursing margaritas at the Casa Mañana. I didn't want to jinx our beginning, so I waited that long before asking.

"Regina, you seem so peaceful. At UT you had lots of— what do they call them now?—issues. How did you work through all that?"

"I had Tyler."

"Tyler?"

"It's amazing how having a child will take your mind off yourself."

Back then, it was like she had two tightly wound springs, one driving her mind, the other her body. She was into everything, and none of it seemed to go together: student government, a sorority, opera, line-dancing, insect collecting, lacrosse, yoga, poetry, pottery, pot. I don't know where she found time for art classes.

But when she painted, she went still, and I wasn't sure if she was escaping from or to something. Covering her apartment walls, the watercolors were never about what you thought they were about.

A seascape hung over the stove. Barely recognizable objects appeared through the image, like a canvas Chagall might have painted in an opium trance.

Tacked beside the toilet was a chambered nautilus done in cool, opalescent colors. And the title underneath? "Self Portrait." What did that mean?

Taped cattywampus over the head of her bed (a garage-sale mattress thrown on the floor) was an oil painting in twenty gradations of white. It made you stare until the image came clear—a man brutally knifing a woman. "Achromatic Study."

A work titled "Untitled" was painted right on her television screen. I couldn't make heads or tails of it, but didn't want to offend Regina by asking. Finally, my curiosity got the best of me.

"That?" she said, cocking her head as if she, too, were looking at it for the first time. "That's an exact replica of a vague thought."

Regina was as beautiful and elusive as her watercolors—and ultimately as frustrating. For a month, I spent every spare moment with her. Then I saw her holding hands on campus with some sparsely goateed goof. Two days later I ran into her on Sixth Street, hanging all over a professor type in a tweed jacket. When I asked her about these guys, she gazed at me with stunned innocence.

"You thought we were dating steady?" She asked the question like I was the dumbest toad on the evolutionary ladder.

In my favorite painting, two slender cats, diaphanously gray, spiraled around themselves: "Double Felix." Why would she undercut such a brilliantly executed piece with a bad pun?

Now she was a distributor for Honeywell air-conditioner parts. But her mind was bright and lively, her spirit as joyful as the day I first met her feeding squirrels in the shade of The Tower. Air-conditioner parts.

What did we do after fifteen years? Almost nothing. Stayed in hotels for days at a time, sneaking food, watching movies like obligatory chores—because that's what dating people are supposed to do. But we didn't need anything on the outside. We had each other, again. It was the old self-contained relationship in a vacuum.

———

Dr. Bukoski said glasses would fix my double vision while we watched the egg to see if it would grow. It did. But most meningiomas are benign. The operation, she said, was simple. Get in, take out, close up, go home the next day. Unless the tumor was enshrouding a nerve. Get in, leave alone, close up, treat with other options.

I finally decided to have the procedure without telling Regina. Go in, get cut, see her the next weekend. "That? Oh, I slipped and hit my head on a doorjamb." Continue with our wonderful life. In a year, Tyler would graduate, and we would be together forever.

Lying on the gurney, being wheeled to surgery, I was thinking of Regina. That led to the chambered nautilus, and from there my brain went to mother-of-pearl. My heart surged with fear as the thought struck me. It takes a sandy irritant to grow a pearl, beauty quarantining danger.

"Dr. Bukoski."

"Yes?"

"Is it possible that my obsession with Regina was caused

by this tumor?"

"What do you mean?"

"Is it possible that I love Regina because of this egg on my brain?—that it's pressing on the cells holding my memories of her?"

She looked at me as if she were diagnosing my mental health.

"Anything's possible, Roman. With the brain. But I don't think it's likely."

"But it is possible. And that means if you relieve the pressure, I could lose my desire for her, right?"

We had reached the double doors to Surgery. The gurney stopped.

"Roman, the brain is very delicate. So, yes, anything's possible."

I remembered what I had told Regina—that I would rather die than lose her love again. So I sat up, like Lazarus rising from the dead.

I popped the sheet off and stepped down from the gurney. As my feet hit the cold floor, the hospital started spinning. I steadied myself against the wall and waited a few seconds until everything cleared.

With my first step, I was not sure if I was hastening my death or heading for more life. But with my second step, I knew I was moving in the direction of more love.

Bibliography

"Dead Dog Lying." *The Virginia Quarterly Review* 78.4 (Autumn 2002): 710-27.

"Merger Talks." *Shenandoah* 56.1 (Spring 2006): 108-119.

"Deerboy." *Aethlon* 13.2 (Spring 1996): 23-29.

"Ditchboy." *Kaleidoscope* (United Disability Services, Akron, OH). (January 2009): 14-20.

"Dogboy" was originally published as "Olympian." *Aethlon* 21.1 (Fall 2003): 11-24.

"Sportfishing with Cameron" (short version). *Salt Water Sportsman* (October 2003): 140, 122-3, 126, 128. The longer, "literary" version was published in *Wide Awake in the Pelican State*. Ed. Ann Brewster Dobie. Baton Rouge: LSU Press, 2006.

"The Threshold of Plenty." *Sou'wester* 18.2 (Winter 1990-91): 63-77. Nominated for a Pushcart Prize, which recognizes "the best of small press literary work" in the country in a given year.

"Snake Summer." *The Louisiana Review* 13 (Spring 2015): forthcoming.

"Is." *The Louisiana Review* 5 (2007): 26-30.

"Second Wave." *Fiction Southeast*: forthcoming, Summer 2015.

"Suburban High Tide." *Sou'wester* 23.1 (Fall 1994): 37-54.

"Controlled Burn." *Sport Fishing* 21.7 (July/August 2006): 48, 50, 52.

"Call Forwarding." *Salt Water Sportsman* (June 2004): 152, 148-150.

"The Girl and the Green Gas Can." *The Connecticut Review* 23.2 (Fall 2001): 163-73.

"The Arrow That Never Came Down." *Louisiana Life* (March/April 1991): 89-95.

"Always on My Mind." *Country Roads* (June 2005): 36-37.

About the Author

Lake Charles native Dr. Norman German is an English professor at Southeastern Louisiana University, where he has taught for twenty-seven years. His novel *A Savage Wisdom* imaginatively reconstructs the life of Toni Jo Henry, the only woman executed in Louisiana's electric chair. His prize-winning *No Other World* novelizes the life of Marie Thérèze, known as Coincoin, the ex-slave slaveholder who founded Melrose Plantation. By special request from the Major League Baseball Hall of Fame, copies of his novel *Switch-Pitchers* reside in their library and museum in Cooperstown, New York.

German's award-winning stories about baseball, football, track and field, and fishing have appeared in major literary and commercial venues in the U.S., Canada, and England, including *Gray's Sporting Journal*, *Shenandoah*, *The Virginia Quarterly Review*, *Salt Water Sportsman*, and *Sport Fishing Magazine*.

German earned degrees in history, philosophy, and English from McNeese State, the University of Texas, and the University of Southwestern Louisiana and has published scholarship on major American writers such as Ernest Hemingway, Nathaniel Hawthorne, Zora Neale Hurston, and Ralph Ellison. With artist Raejean Clark-German, he makes his permanent home on the Calcasieu River in Lake Charles.

The stories of *Dead Dog Lying* shine a hard light on society's misfits: the misshapen in mind and body, children mystified by the adult world, and grownups trying—but never quite managing—to get it right. A man receives a message from a cell phone swallowed by a fish he's caught. A boy grows antlers that give him athletic prowess. A fiction writer learns about reality by walking into an improv play. Long after these allegorical stories are ingested, they will haunt the reader's troubled sleep.

UNIVERSITY OF LOUISIANA AT LAFAYETTE PRESS

LOUISIANA WRITERS SERIES

The Louisiana Writers Series is dedicated to publishing works that present Louisiana's diverse creative and cultural heritage. The series includes poetry, short stories, essays, creative nonfiction, and novels.

BOOKS IN THE LOUISIANA WRITERS SERIES:

The Blue Boat by Darrell Bourque (out of print)
Amid the Swirling Ghosts by William Caverlee
Local Hope by Jack Heflin
New Orleans: What Can't Be Lost edited by Lee Barclay
In Ordinary Light by Darrell Bourque
Higher Ground by James Nolan
Dirty Rice: A Season in the Evangeline League by Gerald Duff
Megan's Guitar and Other Poems from Acadie by Darrell Bourque
The Land Baron's Sun by Genaro Smith
You Don't Know Me: New and Selected Stories by James Nolan
Duck Thief and Other Stories by David Langlinais
Dead Dog Lying and Other Stories by Norman German

FOR MORE INFORMATION VISIT:
WWW.ULPRESS.ORG

THE NEWLY OPENED LINE 14: MÉTÉOR

reception all contribute to the charm of the place. Rooms from 680F with a rooftop view of Paris and the Sacré Cœur. Breakfast is served in what used to be the dressing rooms of 'Dom Juan', a former 1930s cabaret.

Hôtel des Grands Hommes (A D3)
→ *pl. du Panthéon (5th)* Tel. 01 46 34 19 60
This elegant 18th-century hotel has 32 spacious rooms with exposed beams and wrought-iron bedheads. Views of the Pantheon dome from the 6th-floor balconies. Reserve well in adavance. From 750F.

OVER 800F

Hôtel des Jardins du Luxembourg (A C3)
→ *5, Impasse Royer-Collar (5th)* Tel. 01 40 60 08 88
In 1883 Freud stayed here.

This splendid hotel has now been completely renovated in a Provençal style: kilims, wood-paneling, small balconies, flowers and tiling give the rooms an unforgettable charm. The extremely spacious Room 1 even has its own entrance. Sauna, elevator, patio and air-conditioning. From 810F.

Hôtel des Marronniers (A B1)
→ *21, rue Jacob (6th)* Tel. 01 43 25 30 60
A good address. Views of the clocktower of Saint-Germain or the garden from some of the rooms. Breakfast is served on the veranda. From 825F.

PALACES

Hôtel Raphaël (D A1)
→ *17, ave Kléber (16th)* Tel. 01 53 64 32 00
www.raphael-hotel.com
A minute's walk from the

Champs-Élysées, this is probably the smallest but most charming of Parisian palaces. Ninety rooms and suites whose antique furniture is cared for daily by the in-house cabinet-maker. Aubusson tapestries, 18th-century inspired mural paintings, Louis-XV wood paneling, and magnificent views of the Arc de Triomphe from the 7th floor. There, on the biggest and most romantic terrace in Paris, have lunch or just a drink. From 2,700F.
And if a night at the Ritz (tel. 01 43 16 30 30), the Crillon (tel. 01 44 71 15 00), the Plaza-Athénée (tel. 01 53 67 66 65) or the Hôtel Costes (tel. 01 42 44 50 00) is just a dream, why not treat yourself to breakfast there (expect to pay between 200 and 350F). Smart dress required. Book in advance.

PUBLIC TRANSPORT

Métro
16 lines (numbered from 1–14) within Paris and the nearby suburbs (zones 1–2).
→ *Daily 5.30am–12.30am*
RER
5 fast trains (A, B, C, D, E) across Paris and the Île-de-France (zones 1–8).
→ *Daily 5.30am–12.30am*
RATP trains
The regional network is divided into 5 zones: 1–2 (city center – single fare) and 3–5 (suburbs).
Buses
58 lines. Reduced service Sun and public holidays.
→ *Mon–Fri 5.30am–8.30pm*
Nightbuses
Run from 1am to 5am.
RATP information
→ *Tel. 01 36 68 77 14*
Fares
Tickets for the métro, the RER and buses are available from métro stations (ticket offices and ticket machines) and tobacconists.
→ *8F single ticket, 55F book of 10 (carnet)*
Travel passes
Paris Visite
→ *55–350F depending on the number of days (1, 2, 3 or 5 days) and the zones covered)*
Applies to all modes of transport.
Reduced prices to the monuments of Paris and the surrounding area.
Mobilis
→ *40–110F depending on the zones covered*
Valid for one day only in the relevant zone(s).

Index des stations de métro et de RER (Paris intra-muros) :

E3 Abbesses
D7 Alésia
G5 Alexandre Dumas
C5 Alma – Marceau
B4 Anvers
B4 Argentine
E7 Arts et Métiers
D5 Assemblée Nationale
D2 Auber
C6 Avenue Émile Zola
B5 Avenue Foch
B5 Avenue Henri Martin
G5 Avron
B7 Balard
F5 Barbès-Rochechouart
F5 Bastille
F5 Bel-Air
G4 Belleville
G6 Bercy
F7 Bibliothèque François Mitterrand
C6 Bir-Hakeim
D3 Blanche
B5 Boissière
G3 Bolivar
E4 Bonne Nouvelle
G3 Botzaris
B5 Boucicaut
B5 Boulainvilliers
B7 Boulevard Masséna
B7 Boulevard Victor
E4 Bourse
F5 Bréguet – Sabin
D3 Brochant
G3 Buttes Chaumont
E4 Cadet
C6 Cambronne
C6 Campo-Formio
E7 Cardinal Lemoine
E7 Censier – Daubenton
C6 Champ de Mars Tour Eiffel
D5 Champs-Élysées Clemenceau
B6 Chardon-Lagache
C6 Ch. de Gaulle – Étoile
B6 Charles Michels
C5 Charonne
F4 Château d'Eau
E4 Château-Landon
F3 Château Rouge
E6 Châtelet
E6 Châtelet – Les Halles
D4 Chaussée d'Antin La Fayette
E7 Chemin Vert
F7 Chevaleret
E6 Cité
C7 Cité Universitaire
E5 Cluny – La Sorbonne
F4 Colonel Fabien
C6 Commerce
D5 Concorde
C7 Convention
E7 Corentin Cariou
E7 Corvisart
G4 Courcelles
G4 Couronnes
F4 Cour St-Émilion
F2 Crimée
D3 Danube
G6 Daumesnil
D6 Denfert-Rochereau
G6 Dugommier
C6 Dupleix
D6 Duroc
D6 École Militaire
D6 Edgar Quinet
B6 Église d'Auteuil
E5 Étienne Marcel
D4 Europe
B6 Exelmans
F6 Faidherbe – Chaligny
D6 Falguière
C6 Félix Faure
F5 Filles du Calvaire
C4 Franklin D. Roosevelt
D7 Galté

G4 Gambetta
F6 Gare d'Austerlitz
F4 Gare de l'Est
G6 Gare de Lyon
D5 Gare Montparnasse
E3 Gare du Nord
C5 Gare St-Lazare
C4 George V
E7 Glacière
E4 Goncourt
G3 Grands Boulevards
D2 Guy Môquet
D2 Haussmann – St-Lazare
D4 Havre – Caumartin
E6 Hôtel de Ville
C5 Iéna
D5 Invalides
B6 Jacques Bonsergent
B6 Jasmin
B6 Jaurès
B6 Javel – André Citroën
B5 Jourdain
B6 Jules Joffrin
B6 Jussieu
B6 Kennedy – Radio France
B5 Kléber
F3 La Chapelle
D3 La Fourche
F2 Lamarck – Caulaincourt
C6 La Motte-Picquet Grenelle
B5 La Muette
C5 La Tour-Maubourg
G3 Laumière
F5 Ledru-Rollin
E5 Le Peletier
E7 Les Gobelins
E5 Les Halles
D3 Liège ◆
F3 Louis Blanc
E5 Lourmel
E6 Louvre – Rivoli
C6 Luxembourg
D5 Mabillon
D4 Madeleine
F3 Magenta
C4 Maison Blanche¼
G3 Maraîchers
G4 Marcadet – Poissonniers
F2 Marx Dormoy
D6 Maubert – Mutualité
G4 Ménilmontant
D6 Michel Ange – Auteuil
B6 Michel Ange – Molitor
B6 Michel Bizot
B6 Mirabeau
C4 Miromesnil
C4 Monceau
G6 Montgallet
D6 Montparnasse Bienvenüe
D7 Mouton-Duvernet
D5 Musée d'Orsay
G6 Nation
E7 Nationale
D3 N.-Dame-de-Lorette
D6 N.-Dame-des-Champs
E6 Oberkampf
E6 Odéon
G3 Opéra
G3 Ourcq
F3 Palais Royal Musée du Louvre
B5 Parmentier
B5 Passy
G5 Pasteur
H4 Pelleport
C6 Pereire
G5 Père Lachaise
D7 Pernety
G5 Philippe Auguste
G6 Picpus
E3 Pigalle
D3 Place de Clichy
G4 Place des Fêtes
E6 Place d'Italie
E6 Place Monge
D7 Plaisance
E4 Poissonnière
C4 Pont de l'Alma
E5 Pont Marie

E5 Pont Neuf
B4 Pte Dauphine
A6 Pte d'Auteuil
H4 Pte de Bagnolet
C3 Pte de Champerret
G7 Pte de Charenton
F7 Pte de Choisy
D2 Pte de Clichy
C2 Pte de Clignancourt
F2 Pte de la Chapelle
G2 Pte de la Villette
H5 Pte de Montreuil
G3 Pte de Pantin
A7 Pte de St-Cloud
D2 Pte de St-Ouen
H4 Pte des Lilas
D7 Pte de Vanves
C7 Pte de Versailles
H6 Pte de Vincennes
F7 Pte d'Italie
G7 Pte d'Ivry
G7 Pte Dorée
D7 Pte d'Orléans
B4 Pte Maillot
E6 Port-Royal
G3 Pré-St-Gervais
D5 Pyramides
G4 Pyrénées
F7 Quai de la Gare
F6 Quai de la Rapée
E4 Quatre Septembre
F5 Rambuteau
B5 Ranelagh
D7 Raspail
E4 Réaumur – Sébastopol
D6 Rennes ◆
E4 République
G6 Reuilly – Diderot
F5 Richard-Lenoir
E4 Richelieu – Drouot
F3 Riquet
D3 Rome
B5 Rue de la Pompe
G5 Rue des Boulets
C5 Rue du Bac
G4 Rue St-Maur
D4 St-Augustin
H4 St-Fargeau
D5 St-François-Xavier
E3 St-Georges
D6 St-Germain-des-Prés
E7 St-Jacques
D4 St-Lazare
F6 St-Marcel
E6 St-Michel
E6 St-Michel Notre-Dame
F5 St-Paul
D5 St-Philippe-du-Roule
D6 St-Placide
F5 St-Sébastien Froissart
D6 St-Sulpice
C6 Ségur
E4 Sentier
B6 Sèvres – Babylone
B6 Sèvres – Lecourbe
E2 Simplon
D5 Solférino
F3 Stalingrad
E4 Strasbourg St-Denis
F6 Sully – Morland
F4 Télégraphe
F4 Temple
C3 Ternes
F7 Tolbiac
D5 Trinité d'Estienne d'Orves
B5 Trocadéro
D6 Tuileries
D6 Vaneau
D5 Varenne
G4 Vaugirard
D6 Vavin
C4 Victor Hugo
C3 Villiers
C5 Volontaires
C3 Voltaire
G5 Wagram